ALSO BY A. S. BYATT

Fiction

The Shadow of the Sun

The Game

The Virgin in the Garden

Still Life

Sugar and Other Stories

Possession: A Romance

Angels and Insects

The Matisse Stories

The Djinn in the Nightingale's Eye

Babel Tower

Elementals

Criticism

Degrees of Freedom: The Novels of Iris Murdoch

Unruly Times: Wordsworth and Coleridge

Passions of the Mind: Selected Writings

Imagining Characters (*with Ignês Sodré*)

The Biographer's Tale

The Biographer's Tale

A. S. BYATT

Alfred A. Knopf   New York   2001

THIS IS A BORZOI BOOK
PUBLISHED BY ALFRED A. KNOPF

www.aaknopf.com

Originally published in the United Kingdom by Chatto & Windus, an imprint of Random House UK Limited, London, in 2000.

Knopf, Borzoi Books and the colophon are registered trademarks of Random House, Inc.

Grateful acknowledgment is made to the following for permission to reprint previously published material: *Curtis Brown Group Ltd.:* Excerpted text from *The Compleat Naturalist* by Wilfrid Blunt, copyright © 1971 by Wilfrid Blunt. Reprinted by permission of Curtis Brown Group Ltd., London, on behalf of the Estate of Wilfrid Blunt. *David Higham Associates:* Excerpted text and poetry from *Ibsen* by Michael Meyer (London: Chatto & Windus). Reprinted by permission of David Higham Associates. *Linnean Society of London:* Illustrations on pages 63, 66, and 133. Reprinted by permission of the Linnean Society of London. *Methuen Publishing Limited:* Excerpted text from *Peer Gynt* by Henrik Ibsen, translated by Michael Meyer (1963). Reprinted by permission of Methuen Publishing Limited. *Penguin UK:* Excerpted text from *Ghosts and Other Plays* by Henrik Ibsen, translated by Peter Watts (Penguin Classics, 1964), copyright © 1964 by Peter Watts. Reprinted by permission of Penguin UK.

Library of Congress Cataloging-in-Publication Data
Byatt, A. S. (Antonia Susan), [date]
The biographer's tale / A. S. Byatt — 1st American ed.
p. cm.
ISBN 0-375-41114-3 (alk. paper)
1. Biography as a literary form—Fiction. 2. Biographers—Fiction.
3. Young men—Fiction. I. Title.
PR6052.Y2B56 2001
823'.914—dc21 00-062012

Manufactured in the United States of America
First American Edition

For Tibor Fischer and Lawrence Norfolk
who insisted

Diese Gleichnisreden sind artig und unterhaltend, und wer spielt nicht gern mit Ähnlichkeiten?

These similitudes are charming and entertaining, and who does not enjoy playing with analogies?

Goethe, *Wahlverwandtschaften*

The Biographer's Tale

I made my decision, abruptly, in the middle of one of Gareth Butcher's famous theoretical seminars. He was quoting Empedocles, in his plangent, airy voice. "Here sprang up many faces without necks, arms wandered without shoulders, unattached, and eyes strayed alone, in need of foreheads." He frequently quoted Empedocles, usually this passage. We were discussing, not for the first time, Lacan's theory of *morcellement*, the dismemberment of the imagined body. There were twelve postgraduates, including myself, and Professor Ormerod Goode. It was a sunny day and the windows were very dirty. I was looking at the windows, and I thought, I'm not going to go on with this anymore. Just like that. It was May 8th 1994. I know that, because my mother had been buried the week before, and I'd missed the seminar on *Frankenstein*.

I don't think my mother's death had anything to do with my decision, though as I set it down, I see it might be construed that way. It's odd that I can't remember what text we were supposed to be studying on that last day. We'd been doing a lot of not-too-long texts written by women. And also quite a lot of Freud—we'd deconstructed the Wolf Man, and

Dora. The fact that I can't remember, though a little humiliating, is symptomatic of the "reasons" for my abrupt decision. All the seminars, in fact, had a fatal family likeness. They were repetitive in the extreme. We found the same clefts and crevices, transgressions and disintegrations, lures and deceptions beneath, no matter what surface we were scrying. I thought, next we will go on to the phantasmagoria of Bosch, and, in his incantatory way, Butcher obliged. I went on looking at the filthy window above his head, and I thought, I must have *things*. I know a dirty window is an ancient, well-worn trope for intellectual dissatisfaction and scholarly blindness. The thing is, that the thing was also there. A real, very dirty window, shutting out the sun. A *thing*.

I was sitting next to Ormerod Goode. Ormerod Goode and Gareth Butcher were joint Heads of Department that year, and Goode, for reasons never made explicit, made it his business to be present at Butcher's seminars. This attention was not reciprocated, possibly because Goode was an Anglo-Saxon and Ancient Norse expert, specialising in place-names. Gareth Butcher did not like dead languages, and was not proficient in living ones. He read his Foucault and Lacan in translation, like his Heraclitus and his Empedocles. Ormerod Goode contributed little to the seminars, beyond corrections of factual inaccuracies, which he noticed even when he appeared to be asleep. No one cared much for these interventions. Inaccuracies can be subsumed as an inevitable part of postmodern uncertainty, or play, one or the other or both.

I liked sitting next to Goode—most of the other students didn't—because he made inscrutable notes in ancient runes. Also he drew elaborate patterns of carved, interlaced plants and creatures—Celtic, Viking, I didn't know—occasionally improper or obscene, always intricate. I liked the runes because I have always liked codes and secret languages, and more simply, because I grew up on Tolkien. I suppose, if the truth were told, I should have to confess that I ended up as a postgraduate student of literature because of an infantile obsession with Gandalf's Middle Earth. I did like poetry too, and I did—in self-defence—always know Tolkien's poems weren't the real thing. I remember discovering T. S. Eliot. And then Donne and Marvell. Long ago and far away. I don't know, to this day, if Ormerod Goode loved or despised Tolkien. Tolkien's people are sexless and Goode's precisely shadowed graffiti were anything but. *Plaisir, consommation, jouissance.* Glee. He was—no doubt still is—a monumentally *larger* man. He has a round bald cranium, round gold glasses round round, darkly brown eyes, a round, soft mouth, several chins, a round belly carried comfortably on pillars of legs between columnar arms. I think of him, always, as orotund Ormerod Goode, adding more *O*s to his plethora, and a nice complex synaesthetic metaphor—an accurate one—to my idea of him. Anyway, there I was, next to him, when I made my decision, and when I took my eyes away from the dirty glass there was his BB pencil, hovering lazily, tracing a figleaf, a vine, a thigh, hair, fingers, round shiny fruit.

I found myself walking away beside him, down the corridor, when it was over. I felt a need to confirm my decision by telling someone about it. He walked with a rapid sailing motion, lightly for such a big man. I had almost to run to keep up with him. I should perhaps say, now, that I am a very small man. "Small but perfectly formed" my father would say, several times a day, before his disappearance. He himself was not much bigger. The family name is Nanson; my full name is Phineas Gilbert Nanson—I sign myself always Phineas G. Nanson. When I discovered—in a Latin class when I was thirteen—that *nanus* was the Latin for dwarf, cognate with the French *nain,* I felt a *frisson* of excited recognition. I was a little person, the child of a little person, I had a name in a system, *Nanson.* I have never felt anything other than pleasure in my small, delicate frame. Its only disadvantage is the number of cushions I need to see over the dashboard when driving. I am adept and nimble on ladders. But keeping up with Ormerod Goode's lazy pace was a problem. I said, into his wake, "I have just made an important decision."

He stopped. His moon-face considered mine, thoughtfully.

"I have decided to give it all up. I've decided I don't want to be a postmodern literary theorist."

"We should drink to that," said Ormerod Goode. "Come into my office."

His office, like the rest of our run-down department, had dirty windows, and a dusty, no-coloured carpet. It also had two high green leather wing-chairs, a mahogany desk and a tray of spotless glasses which he must have washed himself. He produced a bottle of malt whisky from a bookcase. He poured us each a generous glass, and enquired what had led to this decision, and was it as sudden as it appeared. I replied that it had seemed sudden, at least had surprised me, but that it appeared to be quite firm. "You may be wise," said Ormerod Goode. "Since it was a bolt from the blue, I take it you

6

have no ideas about what you will do with the open life that now lies before you?"

I wondered whether to tell him about the dirty window. I said, "I felt an urgent need for a life full of *things*." I was pleased with the safe, solid Anglo-Saxon word. I had avoided the trap of talking about "reality" and "unreality" for I knew very well that postmodernist literary theory could be described as a reality. People lived in it. I did, however, fatally, add the Latin-derived word, less exact, redundant even, to my precise one. "I need a life full of *things*," I said. "Full of facts."

"Facts," said Ormerod Goode. "Facts." He meditated. "The richness," he said, "the surprise, the shining *solidity* of a world full of facts. Every established fact—taking its place in a constellation of glittering facts like planets in an empty heaven, declaring *here* is matter, and *there* is vacancy—every established fact illuminates the world. True scholarship once aspired to add its modest light to that illumination. To clear a few cobwebs. No more."

His round eyes glowed behind his round lenses. I found myself counting the *O*s in his pronouncements, as though they were coded clues to a new amplitude. The Glenmorangie slid like smooth flame down my throat. I said that a long time ago I had been in love with poetry, but that now I needed things, facts. *"Verbum caro factum est,"* said Ormerod Goode opaquely. "The art of biography is a despised art because it is an art of things, of facts, of arranged facts. By far the greatest work of scholarship in my time, to my knowledge, is Scholes Destry-Scholes's biographical study of Sir Elmer Bole. But nobody knows it. It is not considered. And yet, the ingenuity, the passion."

I remarked, perhaps brashly, that I had always considered

biography a bastard form, a dilettante pursuit. Tales told by those incapable of true invention, simple stories for those incapable of true critical insight. Distractions constructed by amateurs for lady readers who would never grapple with *The Waves* or *The Years* but liked to feel they had an intimate acquaintance with the Woolfs and with Bloomsbury, from daring talk of semen on skirts to sordid sexual interference with nervous girls. A gossipy form, I said to Ormerod Goode, encouraged by Glenmorangie and nervous emptiness of spirit. There was some truth in that view, he conceded, rising smoothly from his wing-chair and strolling over to his book-case. But I should consider, said Ormerod Goode, two things.

Gossip, on the one hand, is an essential part of human communication, not to be ignored. And on the other, a great biography is a noble thing. Consider, he said, the fact that no human individual resembles another. We are not clones, we are not haplodiploid beings. From egg to eventual decay, each of us is unique. What can be nobler, he reiterated, or more exacting, than to explore, to constitute, to open, a whole man, a whole opus, to us? What resources—scientific, intellectual, psychological, historical, linguistic and geographic—does a man—or a woman—not need, who would hope to do justice to such a task? I know, I know, he said, that most biographies are arid or sugary parodies of what is wanted. And the true masterpiece—such as Destry-Scholes's magnum opus—is not always recognised when it is made, for biographical readers have taste corrupted both by gossip and by too much literary or political ideology. Now you are about to reconstitute your-self, he said, to move off towards a *vita nuova* you could do worse than devote a day or two to these volumes.

I was somewhat distracted by counting the *O*s—which included the *oo* sounds represented by *U*s—in Ormerod Goode's words. In the late afternoon gloom he was like some demonic owl hooting *de profundis*. The sonorous *O*s were a code, somehow, for something truly portentous. I shook myself. I was more than a little slewed.

So I nodded solemnly, and accepted the loan of the three volumes, still in their original paper wrappers, protected by transparent film. They filled the next two or three giddy days when, having decided what I was *not* going to do and be, I had to make a new life.

Volume I, *A Singular Youth*, had a frequently reproduced print of a view of King's College, Cambridge, on the cover.

Volume II, *The Voyager*, had a rather faded old photograph of the Bosphorus.

Volume III, *Vicarage and Harem*, had a brown picture of some stiff little children throwing and catching a ball under some gnarled old apple trees.

It was all very uninspiring. It was like a publishing version of the neighbour who insists on showing you his holiday snaps, splashes of water long smoothed out, ice-creams long digested and excreted. I flicked through the pages of old photographs reproduced in little clutches in the middle of each book. Scholes Destry-Scholes had been sparing with visual aids, or maybe they had not been considered important in the late 1950s and early '60s. There was a photograph of Sir Prosper Bole, MP, looking like God the Father, and one of the three buttoned-up and staring Beeching sisters with scraped-back hair—"Fanny is on the right." I assumed Fanny was Bole's mother. There was a very bad drawing of a youth at

Cambridge, resting his head on his hand. "Elmer (Em) drawn by Johnny Hawthorne during their Lakeland jaunt." There was a map of Somaliland and a map of the Silk Road, and a picture of a ship ("The trusty *Hippolyta*") listing dangerously. Volume II had a lot more maps—Turkey, Russia, the Crimea—a *cliché* of the Charge of the Light Brigade, another of the Covered Bazaar in Constantinople, a photograph of a bust of Florence Nightingale, a ridiculous picture of Lord and Lady Stratford de Redcliffe in fancy dress as Queen Anne grandees receiving Sultan Abdulmecid, and what I took to be Sir Elmer's wedding photographs. He appeared, in a grainy way, to have been darkly handsome, very whiskered, tall and unbending. His wife, who also appeared in a miniature silhouette, in an oval frame ("Miss Evangeline Solway at seventeen years of age"), appeared to have a sweet small face and a diminutive frame. Volume III was even less rewarding. There were a lot of photographs of frontispieces of Victorian books, of poetry and fairy stories. A lot more maps, vicarage snapshots and more conventional views of the Bosphorus. They all had that brownish, faded look. I looked on the back flap, then, for information about the author himself. I think most readers do this, get their bearings visually before starting on the real work. I know a man who wrote a dissertation on authors' photos on the back of novels, literary and popular. There was no photograph of Scholes Destry-Scholes. The biographical note was minimal.

Scholes Destry-Scholes was born in Pontefract, Yorkshire, in 1925. He is working on further volumes of this *Life*.

Volumes II and III added critical encomia for the previous volumes to this meagre description.

And so I began reading, in a mood at once a grey-brown smoky penumbra, induced by the illustrations, and full of jagged shafts of bright lightning on purplish vacancy, induced by my own uncertain future. Odd lines of Scholes's description of Bole's life have become for me needle-like mnemonics, recalling alternate pure elation and pure panic, purely *my own*, as Bole prepares to fail his Little Go, or sneaks out to stow away on a vessel bound for the Horn of Africa. Most of these mnemonics are associated with Volume I. For it has to be said that as I progressed, the reading became compulsive, the mental dominance of both Bole and Destry-Scholes more and more complete. I do not pretend to have discovered even a quarter of the riches of that great book on that first gulping and greedy reading. Destry-Scholes had, among all the others, the primitive virtue of telling a rattling good yarn, and I was hooked. And he had that other primitive virtue, the capacity to make up a world in every corner of which his reader would wish to linger, to look, to learn.

"There were giants in those days." Bole used that phrase frequently—in his speculative work on the Hittites, in his history of the Ottomans, in his work on Cromwell. Bole himself crammed more action into one life than would be available to three or four puny moderns—and I include, amongst action, periods of boredom in a consular office in Khartoum, periods of studious seclusion in Pommeroy Vicarage in Suffolk, working on his translations, romances, and poems. He travelled long distances on sea and land—and along rivers, exploring the Danube as a student and the Nile as a middle-aged grandee. He went to Madagascar and wrote on lemurs. He travelled the Silk Road from Samarkand. He spent years in Constantinople, the city which, perhaps more than any human being, was the love of his life. He conducted secret negotiations in Moscow and St. Petersburg, in Cairo and Isfahan. He was—and this is soberly attested—a master of disguise, could pass himself off as an Arab, a Turk or a Russian, not to mention his command of Prussian *moeurs* and Viennese dialect. He fought in the Crimea, and gave moral and practical support to Florence Nightingale, whom he had known as a young woman, frustrated by family expectations in the days when his great friend Richard Monckton Milnes (Lord Houghton) had wanted to marry her. He was part of Monckton Milnes's dubious circle of Parisian sexual sensationalists, as Destry-Scholes proved conclusively with some fine work in the archives of Fred Hankey and the Goncourts in Paris. He had known everyone—Carlyle, Clough, Palmerston, George Henry Lewes and George Eliot, Richard Watson Dixon, Swinburne, Richard Burton . . . And yet, beside this incessant journeying, political activity, soldiering and dining out he had found time to write enough books to fill a library. Nowhere had been visited without a record of his travels, which would include an account of the geography and climate, the flora and fauna, the history, political and military, the government, the beliefs, the art and architecture, the oddities and distractions of places as diverse as the Sudan and Austria-Hungary, Finland and Madagascar, Venice, Provence and, always returning, Byzantium, Constantinople, Istanbul,

Stamboul. He wrote histories—one of the great days of Byzantium, one of its fall, one of the Ottoman rulers, one of the reign of William the Silent, as well as his more technical works on Cromwell's New Model Army and military organisation under Louis XIV. If he had done nothing else—as Destry-Scholes points out—he would be remembered as a great translator. His collections of Hungarian, Finnish and Turkish fairy tales are still current in reprinted forms. His loose translation of the early eighteenth-century divan poetry of the great Tulip Period "boon companion," Nedim, once rivalled Fitzgerald's *Omar Khayyám* in popularity, with its haunting rhythms and hedonist chants. He translated the Arab chivalric romance, *The History of Antar,* all thirty-three volumes, as well as several erotic oriental works for the furtive presses of Fred Hankey and Monckton Milnes.

The most exciting of these translations—Destry-Scholes certainly thought so, and conveys the excitement—was his version of the travels of the seventeenth-century Turkish traveller, Evliya Chelebi. Elmer Bole's translation included those passages expurgated by the Ritter Joseph von Hammer, the first Western translator, who had felt it proper to omit, for instance, Evliya's initiation into "all the profligacies of the royal pages, the relation of which, in more than one place, leaves a stain upon his writings." Bole had also followed Evliya through bath-houses where the Ritter had stopped at the door. Evliya Chelebi had, it appears, had a vision of the Prophet, in his twenty-first year, in which, stammering as he was, blinded by glory, he had asked, not as he meant to, for the intercession of the Prophet *(shifaá't)* but for travelling *(siya'hat)*. Travelling had been granted, in abundance. Elmer

Bole, undertaking his dangerous journeys disguised as a Turkish bookseller, had used Evliya's other name, Siyyah, the Traveller, and Evliya's dream-stammering, written in Arabic, transliterated according to William Jones's system, appeared on the front pages both of Bole's account of his Syrian escapade, and of Destry-Scholes's second volume, *The Voyager*. I was delighted, as humans are delighted when facts slot together, when I saw the significance of these lines.

Bole wrote many romances of his own, all popular in their day, all now forgotten. *A Humble Maid at Acre, Rose of Sharon, The Scimitar, The Golden Cage of Princes, A Princess Among Slaves* are a few of the titles. He also wrote verse, also now forgotten. A verse-novel, *Bajazeth,* collections of lyrics— *Shulamith, How Beautiful Are Thy Feet, A Spring Shut Up, The Orchard Walls.* The lyrics are conventional, and the novels are wooden, melodramatic and stilted. This judgement has its importance, beyond the unmournable disappearance of the romances, because it has a bearing on what is generally (in this, as in everything I say, of course, I follow Destry-Scholes) acknowledged to be Elmer Bole's literary masterpiece.

This was his translation, if it was a translation, of Evliya's account of his travels through Europe, his exploration of "the seven climates," setting off from Vienna, where he had been secretary to Kara Muhammad Pasha's embassy in 1664, travelling through Germany and the Netherlands, as far as Dunkirk, through Holland, Denmark and Sweden, returning through Poland, via Cracow and Danzig, to the Crimea, after a journey of three and a half years. This European exploration was well attested, and constantly referred to by Evliya in his accounts of his Middle Eastern travels. The problem was that no manuscript existed, and experts, including the Ritter von Hammer who had searched salerooms and bazaars, had come to believe that he never wrote the European volume being, as the Ritter puts it, "probably prevented by death when he had completed his fourth volume."

Elmer Bole, however, claimed to have found the manuscript of Evliya's fifth volume, wrapped as packing round a seventeenth-century Dutch painting of tulips, in an obscure curiosity shop deep in the Bazaar. He had compared it to that manuscript of Eusebius which was in use as a cover for a milk-pitcher. Scholars, including, especially, Scholes Destry-Scholes, had made exhaustive attempts to rediscover this lost manuscript, in Istanbul, in London, in the libraries to which Bole's papers had been bit by bit dispersed, in the attics and dusty ottomans of Pommeroy Vicarage. It had never come to light, and many scholars, both Anglophone and Turkish, had concluded that it had never existed, that the *Journey Through Seven Climates* was an historical novel, a pastiche, by Bole himself.

Destry-Scholes came down, cautiously, arguing every inch of his conclusions, on the other side. His argument, a delicious example of 1950s pre-theoretical intuitive criticism, derives in part from the extraordinary deadness and badness of Bole's acknowledged fictions. They are vague, verbose and grandiose. Bole's Evliya, like the earlier Evliya, is precise, enumerative, recording buildings, customs, climates with scrupulous (and occasionally tedious) exactness. He notices things about the personal cleanliness (or lack of it) in Germany, about the concealed ostentation of rich Dutch burghers, the behaviour of women servants in Stockholm and Krakow—

things which, as Destry-Scholes points out with effortless comparative cultural knowledge, would have been those things a Turk in those days, far from home, would have noticed. The account is full of lively action, dangers from pirates and footpads, amorous encounters with mysterious strangers, conversations with connoisseurs and savants, discussions of the price of tulips and the marketing of new strains from the Orient, comparisons of Turkish and Dutch tastes in these precious bulbs (the Dutch prefer closed cups, the Turks pointed petals like daggers). How, asks Destry-Scholes, could Bole have known all this well enough to *inhabit it imaginatively* with such concrete detail, such delightfully provocative *lacunae*. He remarks on the fact that Bole's translation is written, not in high Victorian English but in a good approximation of seventeenth-century prose, the prose of Aubrey and Burton, Walton and Bunyan. When I have one of my frequent fits of wishing to disagree with Destry-Scholes, I tell myself that his "voice," this put-on vocabulary, this imaginative identification, were perhaps in themselves enough to transmute Bole the banal follower of Scott and Lytton into Bole the inventor of Evliya Chelebi. But it is hard to disagree with Destry-Scholes for long. He knows what he is talking about. It was his belief that Evliya's manuscript was given to the young Nedim, who may have taken it on his own travels. I am getting ahead of myself. I have not got to Nedim.

Another possible argument for Bole's authorship—also, it has to be said, carefully considered by Destry-Scholes—is his capacity to soak up knowledge, to make himself an expert on matters of historical or linguistic or aesthetic scholarship. His

knowledge of Ottoman court ceremonies, of religious tolerance and intolerance under successive rulers of the Sublime
Porte, his study of the weaponry of Cromwell's forces, his
investigations into British military hygiene, are remarkable—
as of course, in another vein, is his study of pornographic
Roman jars, or his famous collection of *phalloi,* from many
cultures. He read, and wrote, as the great Victorian scholars
did, as though a year could contain a hundred years of reading, thought and investigation. I have often wondered what
has happened to my own generation, that we seem to absorb
so pitifully little. I have strange dreams of waking to find that
the television and the telephone have been uninvented—
would those things, in themselves, make the difference?
Would it be desirable?

Like Destry-Scholes, I was most drawn to Bole's mono-
graphs on Byzantine mosaics and on Turkish ceramic tiles,
especially those elegant and brilliant tiles from Iznik, with the
dark flame-red (tulips, carnations) whose secret has been lost.
Where did he find time to travel to Ravenna and Bulgaria, to
spend so long staring, I ask myself (and Scholes asked himself,
before me). Scholes permits himself to express surprise that
Bole did not rediscover, or claim to rediscover, the chemistry
of the Iznik red. He certainly haunted potteries, in Iznik and
in Staffordshire, discussing glazes with the Wedgwoods. One
of the most beautiful things I have ever read is Bole's account
of the creation of light in the mosaics of Hadrian's Villa,
Ravenna and Sancta Sophia, the rippling fields of splendour
created by the loose setting of blue glass tesserae at various
angles to catch the light, the introduction into these fields of
light of metallic tesserae (first gold, then silver), the effect of

candlelight and polished marble to make soft, fluid, liquid light . . .

I say, the most beautiful thing I have read is Bole's account, and so it is, I stand by that. But it is displayed and completed by Destry-Scholes's account both of Bole's research (into the colour and composition of the beds of red glass on which the gold was set, into vessels of layered glass, with leaves of gold foil sandwiched between them) and of Christ in the church of the Chora in Istanbul, covered in plaster and unknown in the days of Bole's study. Destry-Scholes writes as though he were looking with Bole's eyes, describing in Bole's measured yet urgent paragraphs. Yet he introduces, tactfully, integrally, modern knowledge, modern debates, about perspective, about movement and stasis, which do not supersede or nullify Bole's thought, but carry it on.

Destry-Scholes believed that Bole's life was shaped by the ease with which he learned languages. He had the usual British schooling, for his time, in Latin and Greek, and could compose poems in either, with facility. Destry-Scholes says that these classical poems are better than his English effusions. My own Latin, I regret to say, although good enough to make a rough translation of the sense of his poem on Galla Placidia's mausoleum, is nowhere near good enough to assess its aesthetic qualities. I have taught myself to read the Greek alphabet, and therefore to recognise certain recurrent key Greek concepts from Plato and Aristotle. But I have to rely entirely on Destry-Scholes for his judgements of these works. (I do speak and write good French, and reasonable German, and have always made a point of studying critical theory written in those languages in the words in which it was written and, indeed, *thought*. This linguistic interest of my own, this delight in linguistic parallels and differences, encouraged me to accept the justice of Destry-Scholes's interpretation of Bole's very different intellectual "set." I know, in my small way, the pleasures of grammatical exploration, the seductions of different articulations and rhythms.) Bole went on in a purely scholarly way to acquire classical Arabic, which led him to Turkish, and to the Finno-Ugric language complex.

Destry-Scholes believed Bole's travels were to a certain extent dictated by romantic visions opened up by the acquisition of these tongues. Even Russian he appears to have learned as an exercise in a new alphabet, although he travelled several times to St. Petersburg and out towards Mongolia. He is on record as saying that his time spent disguised as a Russian student of religious history was undertaken initially out of pleasure in keeping up the rhythms of the speech. Destry-Scholes appears to have learned Bole's languages. He is able to comment knowledgeably—to quote—in Russian, Hungarian, Turkish, Arabic—as well as the usual Romance languages and German. It is part of the complex pleasure of his text that he is able to convey the complex pleasure of linguistic fluency from insider knowledge, so to speak. And if he had not been able to read Turkish manuscripts, he would never have made his most dramatic discoveries.

It occurs to me that I have just written a summary—one of many possible summaries—of Destry-Scholes's three volumes from the point of view of my own initial interest in them, which was that of a man in need of facts—of things—of facts.

I have listed facts, and facts about Bole's interest in other facts. That was the richness and strangeness I found in the text, and I am being true to my first excited understanding. Destry-Scholes found his bright idea in his understanding of the fundamental importance of linguistic forms in Bole's life. I found mine, I could say, provisionally, in Destry-Scholes's resourceful marshalling and arranging of *facts*. Nevertheless the facts I have listed are hardly of the kind which attract the British chattering classes to the endless consumption of biographies. I have hardly mentioned Bole's personal life. His loves, hatreds, rivalries and friendships are what these readers would look for, skipping his (and Destry-Scholes's) speculations about Byzantine *ekphrasis* or Lord Raglan's inadequacies in the field.

The wooden hagiography, written at his widow's behest by Thomas Pittifield, observes the Victorian conventions of respecting privacy and not speaking ill of the dead. Destry-Scholes wrote at the beginning of what I would call the first wave of Freudian biography. By the first wave, I mean those biographies which made the assumption, explicit or implicit, that the direction of a subject's libido (more particularly the unconscious and unacknowledged directions) is the single most important thing about his, or her, life. The second wave of psychoanalytic biography entails elaborate unmaskings of contrary and hidden senses and motivations, so that often the "real" story appears to be the exact opposite of the "apparent" story, a loving father must be an abusive rapist, an object of detestation and contempt must be a secret object of desire, and so on. Two tales for one. If Destry-Scholes considered a Freudian life of Bole, he rejected the idea quite deliberately—

I am sure of this, because of the tact with which he introduces a Freudian reading where it *is* appropriate, in Bole's aversion to self-mortifying clergymen, for instance, or in his failure ever to mention, anywhere, his maiden (unmarried, at least) aunt Theodora, who lived with the family from his birth until his final rupture with them at the time of his marriage—which Pittifield ascribes to a quarrel over financial settlements.

No, Destry-Scholes recounts Elmer Bole's personal life exactly as far as it can be known, and no further. His own magnificent coup in this area was provoked, rather beautifully, by a coded metaphor in Bole's field journals from the Crimea, a metaphor which he later discovered, in abundance, to abound in the lyrical poems. This metaphor is one of apples. Bole was peculiarly fond of the contrast between red apples and green apples. Destry-Scholes has an elegant statistical table showing the incidence, in Bole's published and unpublished works, of references to green apples, red apples, and the two together (the most frequent). In his account of his deciphering of this riddle Destry-Scholes permits himself to depart from his usual detached narrative tone (he was fortunate enough to live before the idea of "objectivity" was deconstructed) and take on the note of personal involvement and excitement of Symonds's *Quest for Corvo* (the analogy is Destry-Scholes's own).

The "red apple" was, of course, the Ottoman image for the Other, the Kingdom to be conquered—Rome, or later Vienna. High Byzantine Christian officials were also represented with red apples in their hands as a sign of office. So for some time, Destry-Scholes believed that the red apple represented some desired promotion for Bole, and the green the bitterness of disappointment. It was only when ferreting through the Turkish correspondence of a pasha who was a friend of Bole, in whose *yali* on the Bosphorus he was believed to have stayed, that Destry-Scholes found the clue to the riddle.

The red apple was a Turkish lady, Yildiz, the sister of a pasha, who had a dashing reputation. The green apple was Bole's childhood sweetheart, Evangeline Solway, daughter of an impoverished evangelical clergyman. Destry-Scholes established that Bole had married both, in the same year, and had in the same year established two households, one in an old red-painted wooden house on the shore of the Bosphorus, and one in the little Old Vicarage at Pommeroy. Yildiz, the red apple, had borne three sons, called after Turkish poets, Nedim, Fuzûlî and Bâkû, and Evangeline had borne three daughters, Rose, Lily and Violet, who became the Principal of an Oxford women's college. Destry-Scholes points out that although Bole's associations with the red apple are of rich sweetness, warmth, fullness and ripeness, his associations with the green apple are not negative, but speak of tartness that makes the mouth water, of unexpected sharpness that makes sweetness sweeter, of firmness which is better than softness, and so on. He also quotes letters (found by himself) from Evangeline to her intimate friend, Polly Fisher, describing the advantages of her husband's long absences, in terms of a lessening of the terror of pregnancy, and an increase in delight on his return. "For we have tales to tell each other, whose mysteries would fade with daily intimacy, and to him returning from the sordid and teeming East, my little life of green grass and clean sheets has freshness, a paradisal quality, he says, which is constantly renewed by absence."

Destry-Scholes invokes *The Quest for Corvo* again, when, after his meticulous description of Bole's disappearance and the British reaction to it, he discusses Nedim's hypothetical arrival at the vicarage three years later, as a young man of about twenty-five years. As Destry-Scholes rightly says, decorum forbids any account of an event of which there is absolutely no record. You cannot, he says, introduce phrases like "What must the sorrowful widow have thought, seeing the handsome dark stranger carrying his small valise through the apple trees?" We know neither that Nedim forewarned her, nor that he did not. We do not know for certain that Nedim revealed his parentage to his stepmother and half-sisters, though, Destry-Scholes says cautiously, we must suppose that he did, or why did he come? We know, from Rose's letters, that he stayed in the vicarage for a year, and we know, from the Goncourts' journal (another brilliant *trouvaille* by Destry-Scholes) that when Nedim took up his post at the Sorbonne, as Professor of Finno-Ugric languages, Rose went with him, as we know that she was with him during his travels in Finland, which are described in the French account of his journey found in an antiquarian bookshop in Oslo by Destry-Scholes.

It is difficult to recall the state of febrile excitement I was in over my own release from a life of theoretical pedagogy. I *did* nothing about my new future. I sat in my little flat, or walked about in bare feet, and occasionally completely naked, to mark my new state, but this brought me no nearer any sort of future. Perhaps because my own life was a fluid vacuum, I became obsessed with the glittery fullness of the life of Elmer Bole. Compared to the busy systems, the cross-referred abstractions, of the life I had renounced, the three volumes loomed in my mind as an almost impossible achievement of contact with the concrete world (always eschew the word "real" is an imperative I *have* carried over from my past) of arrangement of things and events for delight and instruction.

On each re-reading I transferred more of my attention from the myriad-minded Bole to his discreet historian. It was a surprise that Bole knew the morphology of Mediterranean solitary bees, the recurring motifs of Turkish fairy tales, the deficiencies of the supply-lines of the British army. It was, on reflection, even more of a surprise that Scholes Destry-Scholes knew all that Bole knew, had tracked down his sources and corrected his errors, where necessary (they were frequent). Not only that, Scholes Destry-Scholes was able to satisfy the reader's (that is, *my*) curiosity in that he knew more of Bole's subjects than Bole did, or could. He had the benefit of Paul Underwood's exemplary revelations at the Church of the Chora. He had read the secret military telegrams— including those about Bole's activities—which Bole had no access to.

It is true that the force, the energy, the first fierce gaze of desire, the first triumphant uncovering or acquisition were Bole's. He was a free agent, Destry-Scholes followed in his footsteps. (I found myself in my wilder moments of naked abandon chanting "King Wenceslas" to myself on hot summer evenings, a can of beer in one hand, *The Voyager* in the other. ("Mark my footsteps, good my Page, Tread thou in them boldly. Thou shalt find the winter's rage, Freeze thy blood less coldly.") Destry-Scholes's work was a miracle of metamorphosis. Bole was always Bole. Even his Burtonian versions of seventeenth-century Turkish had a Bolean ring, so to speak. But Destry-Scholes was subtle. He could write like a connoisseur of faience, like a brisk strategic analyst, like John Addington Symonds or even like George Eliot, where it was appropriate—some of his accounts of Evangeline's attitudes to Bole's curious mystical beliefs could have come out of *Daniel Deronda.*

He could write, as I have suggested, like a good literary critic, pointing out salient words and echoes of other texts. He could describe alien cultures in a supremely tactful and intriguing paragraph—his own account of the Turkish *hamam,* the bathhouse, is not, as far as I can ascertain, derived from Bole, but from other sources, or from personal knowledge.

Or from personal knowledge. This faceless writer constructed this edifice of styles, of facts, and even wrote in the first person where it seemed to him appropriate to do so. Sometimes it seemed as though he thought he was doing journeyman-work, making a record, simply. Sometimes there appeared to be a glimpse of pride in his own mastery, his art, you might even say. I had a vision of him sitting over a desk in lamplight, deftly twisting a Rubik's Cube into shape. Or, in a more complex vision, selecting the tesserae—blue, green, ivory, white glass, gold and silver, laying them at different angles on their bed of colour to reflect the light in different ways.

The project may have come to me in a dream. I am not being fanciful, simply precise. I woke one morning and thought, "It would be interesting to find out about Scholes Destry-Scholes." I had a vague memory of a dream of pursuit through dappled green and gold underwater caverns. Of rising to the surface and of seeing a pattern of glass balls, fishermen's floats, on the surface of the sea, blue, green, transparent.

"I could write a biography," I said to myself, possibly even aloud, "of Scholes Destry-Scholes." Only a biography seemed an appropriate form for the great biographer. I never had any doubt about that. I had discovered the superiority of the form. I would write one myself.

I made an appointment to discuss this idea with Ormerod Goode. He gave me dark, syrupy sherry on this occasion, Oloroso. I was offered no choice, though the half-full bottle of the spirituous Glenmorangie stood amongst the clean glasses. I had brought the three volumes to return to him, and explained my project. He smiled mildly, and said I could keep them until I had contrived to procure copies of my own, which could easily be done from good secondhand book-shops. He said that it might be possible to continue to hold my postgraduate scholarship, if I were to change subjects and transfer to Goode himself as supervisor. This—although it lacked the drama of renunciation—seemed a prudent course of action. He asked about the dissertation I was about to aban-don—had abandoned. Its title was "Personae of female desire in the novels of Ronald Firbank, E. M. Forster and Somerset

Maugham." I sometimes thought it should have been "Female personae of desire in the novels of Firbank, Forster and Maugham" and could not make up my mind as to whether this changed the whole meaning completely, or made no difference at all. I did not discuss it with Goode, who simply nodded solemnly when I told him, and remarked that there was certainly no one else in the department who would be interested in a biographical study of Scholes Destry-Scholes.

"You must understand," he said, "that I have no particular competence in the field either. I am a philologist, a taxonomist of place-names. I met the man, but it cannot be said I knew him."

"You met him?" I said, swallowing my excitement. "What was he like?"

"I hardly remember. Blondish. Medium-sized. I have a bad memory for faces. He came to give a lecture in 1959 on the Art of Biography. Only about half a dozen students attended, and myself. I was deputed to manage the slide projector. I invited him to a drink, but he wouldn't stay. Of course, when I heard the lecture I hadn't read the biography, didn't realise it was out of the ordinary, or I'd have pressed him harder, perhaps. I had a problem I wanted to get back to, I remember. I was waiting for him to go away. He probably noticed that."

We looked at each other. I sipped the unctuous sherry. He said, "Come to think of it, I can give you your first research document. He left his notes. Well, a carbon copy of the notes of his lecture. I put it in a drawer, meaning to send it to him, and didn't. It was only a carbon, I expect he had the top copy. I'll hunt it out."

His filing-cabinet was orderly. He handed me the desiccated yellow paper, with the faint blue carbon traces of typing. Three foolscap sheets. "The Art of Biography." The full-stops had made little holes, like pinpricks. I put it in my bag, with the returned biography. I said,

"How do you suggest I set about finding out about his life?"

"Oh, the usual ways, I suppose. Go to Somerset House, look up his birth and death. Advertise in the *TLS* and other places for information. Contact his publishers. Publishers change every three or four months these days, but you may find someone who remembered him, or some letters in an archive. That's the way to begin. I've no idea if he was married or anything. That's for you to discover. All I know for certain is how he died. Or probably died."

He poured more sherry.

"Probably died?"

"He drowned. He drowned off the coast of the Lofoten Islands. Or at least an empty boat was found, floating."

I didn't know where the Lofoten Islands were. I vaguely assumed they must be not far from the Dardanelles, the Bosphorus, the haunts of Bole.

"The Lofoten Islands, you know, off the north-west coast of Norway. He may have had an idea of taking a look at the Maelstrøm. There was a small item in the press—I remembered, because I had read the book, I had an interest. The Norwegians said they had warned him, when he set out, about the dangerous currents. He was on a solitary walking holiday, the press said. I was a bit surprised. It's my stamping-ground, I thought, not his, full of nice linguistic titbits and old legends. He was never found, but then, he wouldn't have been."

28

My imagination wouldn't form an image of the Lofoten Islands.

"You'll have to find out what he was doing there, too," said Goode, cheerfully. "Detective work. What fun."

I went home, quite excited. It seemed to me I was about to embark on new ways of working, new kinds of thought. I would talk to people who, like Goode, remembered the man, remembered facts and events, and with any luck, remembered more, and better. I would hunt down Destry-Scholes, I told myself, I would ferret out his secrets, I would penetrate his surface compartments and lay bare his true motives. I then thought, how very nasty all these metaphors were, and one at least of them contained another word ("penetrate") I had vowed for ever to eschew.

Moreover, the clichéd metaphors weren't accurate. I didn't want to hunt or penetrate Destry-Scholes. I wanted, more simply, to get to know him, to meet him, maybe to make a kind of a friend of him. A collaborator, a colleague. I saw immediately that "getting to know" Destry-Scholes was a much harder, more anxious task than hunting or penetrating him would have been. It required another skill, which carried with it yet another word I most vehemently avoided—"identify." I hate marking essays by female students who say plaintively that they can't identify with Mrs. Dalloway or Gwendolen Harleth. It is even worse when they claim that they *do* "identify with" Sue Bridehead, or Tess (it is almost always Hardy). What on earth does "identify" mean? See imaginatively, out of the eyes of? It is a disgusting *skinned* phrase.

Destry-Scholes certainly never "identified with" Elmer Bole, though I think it is clear from his writings that most of the time he liked him, or liked him well enough. Bole didn't annoy him, morally or intellectually, even when he betrayed friends, even when he wrote badly. Or else he was a supremely tolerant man (Destry-Scholes, I mean). It occurred to me that it was a delicious, delicate tact, being, so to speak, the third in line, organising my own attention to the attention of a man intent on discovering the whole truth about yet a third man.

I was brashly confident in those early days. I wrote off to the publisher of the biography, Holme & Holly, which had been subsumed in an American conglomerate, which had been bought by a German conglomerate. I addressed my letter "To Whom It May Concern." I wrote, and paid for, an advertisement in the *TLS*—"letters, information, manuscripts, anything helpful for a biographical study of Scholes Destry-Scholes, biographer of Sir Elmer Bole." I went to Somerset House and made my own first discovery. Scholes had indeed been born in Pontefract, on July 4th 1925; but his given name had been not Scholes Destry-Scholes, but Percival Scholes Destry. His parents were Robert Walter and Julia Ann Destry née Scholes. It had to be the same man. Two men cannot be born in the same small town on the same day with Destry and Scholes in their name. He must have given up the Percival for reasons of his own, and doubled the Scholes for other reasons—did he love that side of his family better? I know about not liking one's given name. My mother must have thought Phineas was an inspiration—I remember her saying, when I was a little boy and cried because I was bullied for being odd, that I would grow up to be glad to be unusual, to have something remarkable about me, if only a name. I think Percival—or any diminutive—Percy, Perce—would have been worse than Phineas for a little boy in a provincial Yorkshire town. I wondered, in a moment of random inspiration, if he had chosen his name because its rhythm matched that of Ford Madox Ford, who had remade himself as an Englishman after the First World War.

Of course, I immediately read, and re-read, and annotated Destry-Scholes's notes on "The Art of Biography." A large part of these three pages was, unfortunately, simply typed-out quotations from Elmer Bole, including the famous references to the red and green apples, with the terse instruction "explain and discuss." He appeared to have conceived his lecture as a primer—and to a certain extent a theoretical enquiry—for aspiring biographers. This in a sense included me, although, of course, the lecture was delivered many years before my birth. I found it hard to put aside my ingrained habits of suspicion and contentiousness, even before the simple reasonable tone of the document, which said many things I had already thought might indeed have been written by the friend and colleague I was looking for. I could not throw off a 1990s need to think a 1950s critic both naïve and disingenuous. He wrote:

About Facts

First find your facts.
Select your facts. (What to include, what to omit.)
Arrange your facts.

31

Consider missing facts.

Explain your facts. How much, and what, will you explain, and why?

This leads to the vexed question of speculation. Does it have any place, and if it does, on what basis?

He had also written:

A Hypothetical Situation

We may say, "He travelled by train from Edinburgh to London." We know that, because we have the ticket, let us say, as well as knowing where he dined in London and whom he visited in Edinburgh. We do not have to adduce the railway ticket. A biography is not an examination script.

We may also say, "He would have seen, from the train, Durham Cathedral where he was married." But we do not know. He might have been looking the other way. He might have been asleep. He might have been reading The Times—*or* War and Peace, *or the* Inferno, *or the* Beano. *He might have looked out of the window on the other side of the train and witnessed a murder he was not sure was a murder, and never reported.*

If he were a character in a novel, the novelist would have a right to choose between The Times, War and Peace, *the* Inferno *and the* Beano, *and would choose for his own reasons, and would inevitably be right. Though if he did not explain the* Beano, *he might lose a little credibility, unless he were a surrealist.*

A biographer must never claim knowledge of that which he does not know. Whereof we cannot know, thereof must we be silent. You will find that this requirement gives both form and beauty to a good biography. Perhaps contrary to your expectations.

On another page, he had written:

Values

A life assumes the value of an individual. Whether you see that individual as unique *or as a* type *depends on your view of the world and of biography; you will do well to consider this before setting pen to paper. (There are many possible positions to take up.)*

You may believe in objectivity and neutrality. You may ask, "Why not just publish a dossier with explanatory footnotes?" Why not indeed? It is not a bad idea. But you are probably bitten by the urge [change this silly metaphor, SD-S] to construct a complete narrative. You may be an historian or a novelist manqué, *or that* rara avis, *a true biographer. An artist-biographer, we may nervously and tentatively claim.*

An artistic narrative in our time might analyse the leitmotifs *of a life, as a music critic analyses the underlying form of a Wagnerian opus. A good biographer will do well to be lucidly aware of the theoretical presuppositions he is making use of in such an analysis. In our time, the prevailing sets are Freudian, or Marxist, or vaguely liberal-humane. The Freudian belief in the repetition-*

compulsion, for example, can lead to some elegant discoveries of leitmotifs. *The Marxist belief that ideology constructs the self has other seductions. We are not now likely to adopt mental "sets" of national pride, or hero-worship, though both of these are ancient propensities, like ancestor-worship, from which none of us are free. We cannot predict, of course, future sets of beliefs which will make our own—so natural to us—look naïve or old-fashioned.*

I was particularly moved by Destry-Scholes's note to himself about the metaphor. I was delighted by his choice of adjective—"silly," the straightforward, *right* adjective for that metaphor, as I was delighted by his preoccupation with silly metaphors. There was an affinity between us. It would reveal itself in other ways, I was sure.

Whilst I was waiting for answers to my letter and advertisement, I thought I would walk in Destry-Scholes's traces, at least in the place where I myself was most at home, the British Library. I asked, jokingly, at the issue desk if it was known where he had sat, or when he had come, but such records are not kept. It is known where Karl Marx sat, because he never moved away from his singular place. I had the silly idea that if I were to move round the whole reading room, from Row A to Row Z, and to sit once in every seat, I would necessarily have sat where Destry-Scholes had sat. I had no idea of the shape of his bottom (I imagined it thin) or of the cut of his trousers (I imagined them speckled tweed). I found it necessary to have *some* image, however provisional.

I proceeded in an orderly way, ordering all the books in the extensive bibliographies of Destry-Scholes's three volumes. I read the three volumes themselves again and again, mostly at home in bed, noting new riches and felicities of interpretation at each reading. I also embarked on a course of scholarly study of my own, giving myself a competence in Byzantine art, Ottoman history, folklore motifs, nineteenth-century pornography, the history of the small-arm, and the study of Middle Eastern Hymenoptera—this turned out to be the area of Bole's gentleman-amateur expertise which excited me the most. I was a keen bug-collector and bird-watcher as a boy. I knew the names and species of most British butterflies. I spent a pleasant few days sitting along rows EE and FF in the library, studying bee books, ancient and modern.

During a lunch-time stroll in the little Bloomsbury streets surrounding the library, my eye was caught by the image of the Bosphorus I knew so well, in a tray of bargain books. I acquired, that day, both *A Singular Youth* and *The Voyager* in copies which had belonged to someone called Yasmin Solomons ("Yasmin from Woody, with love on your birthday, May 23rd 1968"). The shopkeeper rummaged for a long time in boxes and shelves but could not come up with *Vicarage and Harem.* This meant that, at least in the case of the first two parts, I could now interleave and annotate Destry-Scholes's record of Bole with my own record of Destry-Scholes.

I wanted both to read everything Destry-Scholes had read, and to go beyond him, to know more, not only those things I could know simply because I came later, when more work had been done; I wanted to notice things he had missed. I was full of pointless pride when I was able to insert in *The Voyager,* next to Destry-Scholes's reproduction of Bole's drawing of the reproductive organs of *Bombus lucorum,* a neat copy of my own of the expert Chris O'Toole's recent drawings of the huge penis, knobbed and hairy, concealed inside the modest folds of the male organ, its presence unsuspected by Bole, and not indicated by Destry-Scholes.

But this pleasurable pride was, to use Destry-Scholes's word, silly, because he could not have known Chris O'Toole. The true delight was to track him through the maze of his and Bole's reading, and come unexpectedly on a trace of his presence, or even of a mistake he had made. Correcting his errors (unlike Bole's, they were *rarissimae,* shining little jewels hardly observable in moss—the analogy is from beetle-hunting)—correcting his errors gave me a peculiar thrill of achievement, of doing something solidly scholarly, adding to the sum of facts. But the thrill was just as great when, three-quarters of the way through a book I believed Destry-Scholes should have read, and had not, I would come upon his tracks—a quotation he had used from a critic or a soldier, or, often enough, a sentence he had included in his own work, lifted whole, or loosely rewritten.

Postmodernist ideas about intertextuality and quotation of quotation have complicated the simplistic ideas about plagiarism which were in force in Destry-Scholes's day. I myself think that these lifted sentences, in their new contexts, are almost the purest and most beautiful parts of the transmission of scholarship. I began a collection of them, intending, when my time came, to redeploy them with a difference, catching different light at a different angle. That metaphor is from mosaic-making. One of the things I learned in these weeks of research was that the great makers constantly raided previous works—whether in pebble, or marble, or glass, or silver and gold—for tesserae which they rewrought into new images. I learned also that Byzantium was a primary source for the blue glass which is the glory of Chartres and Saint-Denis. The French, according to Theophilus, were skilled at making panes of blue glass from ancient vessels, such as Roman scent-bottles. They also recycled ancient mosaic cubes, making transparent what had been a brilliant reflective surface.

At this time I had a recurrent dream of a man trapped in a glass bottle, itself roughly formed in the shape of a man. Sometimes it was blue, sometimes green, sometimes clear with a yellowish cast and flaws in the glass. This man was and was not myself. I was also the observer of the events of the dream. Sometimes he was cramped by the bottle, sometimes a small creature scurrying at the base of a sheer glass cylinder. I mention this, because it seems to fit, but I do not offer any interpretation of it. I have done with psychoanalytic criticism.

It took me longer than it should have done, moving along D and G and even H as I found vacancies where I had not sat before, to realise that I was acquiring only second- or third-hand facts. I was not discovering Destry-Scholes, beyond his own discoveries. No answer came to my letter or to my advertisement. I realised I did not have much idea about how to look for any more facts. I decided that I would do something Destry-Scholes himself claimed often to have done in his own research. I would visit the house where he was born. It was, after all, the only place where I knew he had been—apart, of course, from Bole's birthplace, London home, Pommeroy Vicarage, Bosphorus *yali* and other brief resting-places. Pontefract was the place to start. It was the place where Destry-Scholes was Destry-Scholes, as opposed to the biographer of Bole.

I would have liked to go to the Bosphorus, but it was financially out of the question.

Pontefract is a small town in Yorkshire with nothing much to recommend it, except a very large, largely ruined castle, where Richard II died. It must once have commanded a confluence of important roads and rivers, but now is famous only for a kind of liquorice coin called a Pontefract cake. I do not like liquorice, and wondered whether Destry-Scholes did. He might have felt a local pride in the local product. Or not. I went there on a coach, changing at York to a local bus.

I had the address of the house from which his birth had been registered; it was on the way out of the town, in the direction of a village called East Hardwick. I walked there, looking at shopfronts, bus stops, pubs, supposing I might feel his presence, and registering, accurately and honourably, that I felt nothing. His parents' names were what I thought of as "posh." Robert Walter and Julia Ann—especially Julia—were not working-class names. I had expected number 8 Askham Way to be a substantial house, a house with an orchard, or anyway a big garden, where an imaginative boy might play, a house with gables and dormer windows. When I found 8 Askham Way, it was a red box in a row of red brick boxes, all attached to each other.

They had little strips of front garden, and, for the most part, little wrought-iron garden gates with latches. They had tiled roofs and identical fronts—a thin door, with a high knob and a dull metal letterbox, beside a cramped bay window with leaded lights. Above the door were little porthole windows, and two square upper-storey windows, also leaded, with catches, not sashes. There was a laburnum tree in flower next to the gate of number 8, which had a well-kept lawn, and a border of Californian poppies. I do not know how long-lived laburnum trees are. I stood there, trying to think what to think. Askham Way is simply this row of red brick boxes set back from a main road. There is a new and shiny Texaco garage on the other side, which certainly does not date back to 1925. Nor do the street lamps, which are concrete and ugly. The house resembles, quite a lot, the square red brick box in which I was born in a suburb of Nottingham. I tried not to think of this. I don't like the place where I was born, and don't go there. Destry-Scholes's childhood is nothing at all to do with mine. The sky was blue with a few aeroplane exhaust trails, also things not to be seen in 1925. A woman came past me, carrying a brown imitation-leather bag of shopping (bread and bananas sticking out) and wearing a bright green beret. She asked if I needed help.

I said I was looking for a man who used to live there. Who was born there in the late twenties, I said, trying to make it less remote. She said she had only been there five months and couldn't help, and the people she had bought it from hadn't been there long, either. She smiled, and went down the path, and into the house, and shut the door.

I went on looking at the red box, trying to think what to think. I felt a feeling I used to have going into our own red box—that such boxes are the only *real* homes *real* people live in—everything else is just images and fantasies. I also felt that they were traps, with their narrow doors, and boxy stairs, and busily divided-up little windows. Or like beehives, repeating similar cells.

I noticed that the woman was looking at me out of an upstairs window. She drew the curtains with a swish. After a moment, she appeared at the other upstairs window, looked at me again, and swished those curtains, too. She may have done that every evening. Or not.

I felt like a voyeur. I also felt like a failure. I could have said something different and she might have asked me to tea and told me about the Pontefract of the past. (It was quite improbable that she knew anything about the Pontefract of the past.) I could have knocked at the meagre door of every house in that meagre row, asking if there was anyone there old enough to remember. . . . But I wasn't going to. I was beginning to feel trapped by this ordinary place. I set off back to Pontefract, and the bus station. I could have walked round the Castle, but I didn't. It was just a castle. He had been born into that box, that was certain, but anything he might have felt as a boy, patrolling moats and dungeons, came under his own heading of Speculation, and was a little disgusting.

Thinking about the impossibility of the Castle made me see that I had, in some sense, registered the red box. I knew it. I had been there, even if I had not gone in.

Action of some kind was becoming necessary. I began to wonder if it had been foolish to address my letter "To Whom It May Concern." I decided to use the telephone. One amongst my many disadvantages as a biographical researcher is a horror of initiating phone calls. The switchboard lady at the mega-publishers was kind but unhelpful. Holme & Holly had been subsumed into Deodar Books, which had been swallowed by Hachs & Shaw. At Hachs & Shaw I was passed from voice-mail to voice-mail, forced to listen to the Rolling Stones and Ella Fitzgerald and a mournful snippet of plainsong. Finally I got an elderly female voice who said, as though I was a silly boy, "But you want the *archivist*." I said I didn't know there was one, and what was the extension? The archive had been sold to the University of Lincoln, said the voice. You want *their* archivist. She had a moment's kindness. "Her name is Betty Middleton."

I wrote to Betty Middleton, and continued my progress round the Reading Room. Rows L, M, N. Persian and Turkish ghazals, prayer book revisions, the siege of Vienna. Lady Mary Wortley Montagu, on a whim. Destry-Scholes had taken several of her *minor* sentences, and reset them. Betty Middleton answered. All that could be found were a few typed letters. Did I want copies? She was afraid they were not very exciting, she added, sounding like a human being.

When they came, I experienced a moment of pure discouragement. There were only about a dozen. Of these, three said, "I return the proofs herewith, as requested. I have not made any substantial changes. Yours sincerely, S. Destry-Scholes." Two more pointed out minor errors in the accounting of royalties, and one asked, baldly, whether the royalties were overdue, or whether there were none and the publishers had not seen fit to inform the author, as the contract required them to. One said, "I shall be very happy to meet you for lunch, on Thursday next, at the time and in the place you suggest." One—the only one of any conceivable interest—asked if Mr. Holly knew any source of finance for authors wishing to undertake journeys for research purposes. "I have, as you know, already had a British Academy grant for my Istanbul trip. I should like to be able to take a look at the Maelstrøm. I wonder if you can help?"

There was no copy of any responses to these letters. They were all written on the same typewriter, and headed Jolly Corner Hotel, Gower Street. I went, of course, to look at this hotel, which was still there, another version of the blank façade in a repeating series, this time grey and, to my untutored eye, Georgian. I summoned up my courage, went in and asked if anyone would know anything about an author who appeared to have lived there in the early 1950s. The owners were Pakistani and friendly. They had been there five months. They didn't have any of the records of the previous owners. "It was a little dingy, you know, quite a bit of a sad sort of a place. We are modernising, and cleaning it up. We are trying to make it jolly, though we are seriously considering changing the name."

I wrote to the archivist and asked if any of the answers to these messages had been preserved. She wrote back, still amiably, saying no, and that there was a note saying Aloysius Holly always replied in his own hand, on carefully selected postcards. I could see the royalty statements if I liked.

There was one more thing, she said. A packet that had been nagging her because it had been lying loose *under* the hanging folders in the cabinet. It did appear to contain a bundle of sheets (thirty-seven to be precise) typed on what she was convinced was the same typewriter, on foolscap sheets of blue carbon. The material appeared to be biographical. There was even a mention of the Maelstrøm. She would be quite glad, she said, if I were able to identify the fragments positively as belonging to the Destry-Scholes archive, since she had no idea where else to put them. It would, she said, give the archive a little more body, so to speak. Would I like photocopies? She was afraid she would have to charge 5p per page.

I was excited by the idea of foolscap sheets of blue carbon, for I knew, as she did not, that the "Art of Biography" notes had been made in that form. I wrote back, saying I would like to have the thirty-seven pages, and enclosing a cheque.

They arrived a few days later. The numbering, Betty Middleton wrote, was her own, the archivist's numbering. The pages had been, so to speak, pushed in a crumpled way into the packet. She would confirm that they were all carbons, not top copies. As I would see, the typing stopped and started. Some pages were full and consecutive, others scrappy. Some were more worn than others. "He, or his typist, was not very good at page-endings or line-endings. He runs off, words are lost. I think you may be interested in the reference to the Maelstrøm. Odd," wrote Betty Middleton. I did not know if she knew that Destry-Scholes had putatively disappeared in its maw. She added, "I am afraid these are very foul papers. My own opinion is that they form part of several works, not just one. I shall be interested to know what you think."

It was true that the foul papers were even shuffled as to order; pages 10–13 seemed to belong between pages 26 and 27. The reference to the Maelstrøm followed, naturally it seemed, some references to fjords, but after some thought, and consultation of syntax and common sense, I became convinced that it too had become misplaced, and should have been attached to what appeared to be a quite different narrative. I decided that what I had before me was three sections of three different biographical accounts. It was possible, of course, that they were meant to form parts of one book. Ms. Middleton confirmed, what I knew, really, that there had been no label or title on the package. The heroes, or central figures, of the passages were referred to with initials only, CL, FG and HI. This may have been a device to assist a poor typist, but I read it, involuntarily, as part of a teasing reticence, not to say wilful concealment that I was beginning to ascribe to my fictive Destry-Scholes, with his thin buttocks, speckled tweed trousers and cramped, identity-less dwellings. So we piece things together. I shall transcribe the narratives as I found them. The subjects were reasonably easy to identify, and I do not propose to mystify anyone. Anyone? Who is going to read this? I give them baldly, out of their original crumpled chaos. There were no headings. The Roman numerals are mine, as Miss Middleton's (not transcribed) were Arabic.

The Three Documents

[The first document, to which I gave the provisional title "L . . ."]

As HE STRUCK OUT of the country of the Lapps, he noted a horse's jawbone hanging by the roadside.

"By the road hung a *maxilla inferiori equi,* which had *6 incisores sat obtusos et detritos 2 caninos et distincto spatio, 12 molares utrinque.* If I knew how many *dentes et quales,* and how many dugs each animal had, and *ubi,* I think I could devise a *methodum naturalissimum omnium quadripedum.*"

THE MENTION of dugs and teeth suggests he was thinking of clarifications beyond the simple quadruped, though he had not, at this early point, conceived of the mammal. He noted it in his little notebook and continued on his way north. He was wearing, he tells us, "a little unpleated coat of West Gothland cloth with facings and a collar of worsted shag, neat leather breeches—purchased secondhand at an auction—a pig-tailed wig, a cap of green fustian, a pair of top boots and a small leather bag, nearly two feet long and not quite so wide, with hooks on one side so it can be shut and hung up." In this bag he carried a shirt, two pairs of half-sleeves, two nightcaps, an inkhorn, a pen-case, a magnifying glass and a small spy-glass, a gauze veil as protection from midges, his journal and a stock of sheets of paper stitched together, to press plants between (both in folio), a comb, and his manuscripts on ornithology, his *Flora Uplandica*, his *Characteres Generici*. He had a short sword, and a small fowling-piece between his thigh and the saddle. It was Friday, 12 May 1732. He was twenty-five years old, all but about half a day.

He travelled north round the Gulf of Bothnia on the coastal route to Umeå (about 400 miles), dismounting frequently to study a flower or a stone, or to snatch a young horned owl from its nest. Then he turned inland, travelling now due west into the country inhabited by the Lycksele Lapps. He set off up the River Umeå by boat, in perfect weather, noting:

"It was an immense joy to observe at sunrise the tranquil stream, disturbed neither by the Naiads with their floods and torrents, nor by the soughing of Aeolus, and to see how the woods on either side of it were reflected to provide for the traveller a subterranean kingdom below the surface . . . Such of the giant firs as still defied Neptune smiled in the waters, deceptive in their reflection; but he and his brother Aeolus had taken revenge on many of them, Neptune devouring their roots and Aeolus casting down their summits."

He was disposed at times to think of the Lapps as innocent inhabitants of a primitive paradise, or of the late pastoral simplicity of Ovid's Silver Age. "Their soil is unwounded by the plough, their lives by the clash of arms. They have not found their way into the bowels of the earth; they do not wage wars to establish territorial boundaries. They wander from place to place, live in tents, lead the patriarchal life of the shepherds of old." He took note, when he managed to reach the Lapp people, of their relations with the reindeer, "their estate, their cow, their companion and their friend." He solved the problem of the clacking sound their hooves made on snow (their hooves were hollow) and correctly ascribed the pattern of small holes on most reindeer skins to the amorous activities of the gadfly, *Oestrus tarandi*, who deposits her eggs under their skins, and causes their frequent shifting flights across the snow. He observed that the gadfly was completely covered with hairs—a providence of the Creator, so that she could survive in the icy mountains.

He was himself a genuinely devout Christian, and made considerable efforts to reach the scattered churches in these remote lands, where, he remarked, churchgoers often had to "wade up to the armpits through icy water, arriving half dead from cold and exhaustion." The parish priests at Umeå punished their parishioners, who had to travel two whole days, if they missed major festivals. He arrived at Granön church to find it empty, as the pike had chosen that day to rise. At Jokkmokk he took against the ignorant priest and schoolmaster, who assured him that clouds in Lapland sweep over mountains, bearing away stones, trees and animals. CL tried to explain that it was the violent winds that moved the objects, and that clouds were composed of mist, of water bubbles. The two men sneered at the savant's ignorance, and assured him that the clouds were solid, leaving solid and slimy traces of their passage on the mountains. These, CL replied, were vegetable, known as *nostoc*. The two men continued to mock.

NEVERTHELESS, the scientist himself cherished unfounded beliefs, which we may call credulous, or mythical, or magical. These cross his scientific course in strange and beautiful ways, inspiring his curiosity, opening new roads, conducing also to new errors. Here was a man who not only adopted the prevailing scientific view of the time, that Man was an animal, but included the creature in his *Systema naturae* first under anthropomorphs, and later, when it was objected that anthropomorphs simply meant "man-like," under a new category, *primates*, which included monkeys and apes, and also the sloth, and the bat. *Primates* were a subsection of *Mammalia* (hence his interest in the dugs of the dead horse and its fellows); *Mammalia* included whales, which his great friend and fellow-taxonomer, Artedi, had included in his *Ichthyologia*. CL was not inclined to the view that Man alone had a soul, and that other living things were simply machines, *bruta, bestiae*. He wrote in his *Diaetia Naturalis*, "One should not vent one's wrath on animals. Theology decrees that man has a soul and that the animals are mere *automata mechanica*, but I believe they would better advise that animals have a soul, and the difference is in its nobility . . ." We feel, he said, greater compassion for a dog than an insect, and more still for an ape. Indeed, he applied the adjective *sapiens*, first of all, not to

Homo sapiens but to a species of monkey, *Simia sapiens,* which was said to be able to learn to play backgammon excellently well, and to keep watchmen posted on the lookout for tigers, so that the rest of the group could sleep safely. He kept monkeys and mourned the death of his own tamed friend, the raccoon Sjupp, in 1747; he subsequently dissected Sjupp, paying particular attention to his sexual organs.

During his lifetime the boundaries between *Homo sapiens* and his fellow anthropomorphs were drawn and redrawn. At varying stages the *Systema naturae* contained creatures such as the tailed man, *Homo caudatus,* the pygmy, and the satyr, which is also the orang-outan and *Homo sylvestris,* which walks bolt upright in the forest, has hands for feet, has arboreal claws, and is full of lust, so that women of our species dare not walk alone in its vicinity. It also has good table manners, and sleeps at night on a pillow under a quilt "like a respectable old lady." CL sometimes referred to *Homo sapiens* as *Homo diurnus,* and gives a detailed description of his strange double and opposite, *Homo troglodytes* or *Homo nocturnus,* "the child of darkness which turns day into night and night into day and appears to be our closest relative."

The troglodytes are short (the height of a nine-year-old boy) and white as snow, since they are active only at night; they have white fuzzy hair, round eyes with orange pupils and irises and a transparent micturating membrane, like those of bears and owls. They live in caves and holes, and are quite blind by day, stumbling, if they are dug out, as though their eyes have been put out. They have a language, guttural and impenetrable, but never learn more than "yes" or "no" in the speech of *Homo sapiens* or *diurnus.* At night they see well, and make thieving raids; populations of men, where they see them, exterminate them as vermin and refer to them as *blafards*, cockroaches. CL as always, was interested for classificatory reasons in their genitalia (they were said to have a fold of skin which fell forwards over the sexual organs of the female, as in the Hottentot). He begged for details, particularly of the *nymphae* (labia) and clitoris of a ten-year-old female troglodyte on show in London in 1758, but could not be satisfied, for the sake of the child's modesty.

He believed also, as did Artedi, in sirens and mermaids, and in the sea-cows, the cattle of the undines—he examined a calf found on the seashore, and concluded that it must have been born prematurely, since it had not developed suitable lungs for underwater breathing. He believed to the end of his life that swallows spent the winter on the bottom of lakes, beneath the ice.

He also believed in, and indeed, claimed emphatically that he had been attacked by, a pestilential creature called *Furia infernalis*, the Fury from Hell, or "the shot." The Fury was wingless, and fell from the skies in Lapland, where one had once been observed when it landed in the plate of a vicar. CL, in the days of his fame, offered a gold medal for a preserved Fury, and despatched his students into the Lapp wastes in search of the creature. CL gave each of his students a farmyard beast to shadow, one a cow, one a pig, one a goose, one an ass, requiring each student to count and describe the hundreds of species of plants consumed as they vanished down their familiars' throats (the students had nicknames derived from "their" beasts, the Oxman, Lord Swine, Rooster, Balaam [from the speaking Ass] and so on). Such a teacher was a true scientist; but the same teacher despatched the same students to hunt the Furies among the Sami witches, or as we would now say, shamans.

CL was an inhabitant of that borderland between magic and science, religion and philosophy, observation and belief, where most of our fellow men still wander, questing and amazed. It is true that he had his necessary armour of scepticism. The tone of his observations in the court building at Jönköping is robust. He saw there,

"a large collection of witches' paraphernalia, such as treatises on black magic which we read and found to be full of deceit and vanities, antiquated and false receipts, idolatry, superstitious prayers and invocation of devils . . . We blew the sacred horn without conjuring up the devil, and milked the milking-sticks without drawing milk. Here were to be seen sorceries, made neither by witches nor by devils but from the triple stomach of a ruminant animal. Here were eagles' feet with outstretched claws, with which wizards tore the stomachs of those who had colic; I should think that they no more deserved to be burned than do the Chinese who pierce a hole right in the belly . . . And here also we were able to see the genuine instruments of wizards; knives, hammers, cudgels and iron bullets by the use of which men have been killed by their enemies."

But the same man saved his eight-year-old sister, Emerentia, from death by smallpox, by killing and flaying a sheep, and laying the child in the skin, to "draw her from death." The inspiration, he claimed, was biblical, drawn from King David, who "when old took two young girls into his bed so that by their healthy transpiration they might revive him."

Later, in his medical notes, *Lachesis Naturalis,* CL endorsed David's advice, prescribing a bed-rest between two young people as a quick cure for a cold.

In 1935, workmen repairing the house in the Botanic Garden at Uppsala found under the floorboards, buried in a pile of rubbish, a little notebook which proved to be the notebook he had carried on that memorable journey, noting distances, phrases, descriptions of people. They found also a kind of writing-tablet on which jottings could be made in pencil and erased. CL records, in his public account, how he showed a Lapp some of his drawings. The man "was alarmed at the sight, took off his cap, bowed, and remained with his head down and his hand on his breast as if in veneration, muttering to himself and trembling as if he were just going to faint . . ." Scholars have generally supposed that the Lapp thought that the drawings were magical, like the drawings on the Lapp drums which are used in the *sejdhr,* or shamanic ritual. CL, a poor draughtsman, drew reindeer, anatomised, horned, pulling sledges. He drew also owls, naked women and female *pudenda,* intent on his classification. There are some pages, in a private collection, which I have been able to see, apparently detached from the notebook, which are written in an agitated hand, with fragmentary disjointed sentences, and hastily sketched drawings, which suggest that CL had experiences of Samic magic, of the *sejdhr* itself, which had affected him profoundly, although he was too cautious, or too shaken, to record them for the general public. He was, and remained, a respectable, God-fearing bourgeois, however great his international reputation. His ideas on the sexual life of plants aroused opprobrium amongst the respectable—a hostile spiritual atmosphere not so distant from one of the forms of northern magic, *nídh,* a series of magical acts designed to ruin a man's life and reputation by destroying him with sexual taunts and humiliations. Magic is closely entwined with science; alchemy, the occult sciences, astrology, however strange or to modern men unacceptable their systems of belief or projects, resemble the true sciences in their preoccupation with techniques of studying, and changing, the physical world. Magic, like science, is concerned with *matter,* with the world of *things,* of rocks, stones, trees, creatures, also clouds, rain, wind and water vapour.

The world of magic is double, natural and supernatural. Magic is impossible in a purely materialist world, a purely sceptical world, a world of pure reason. Magic depends on, it makes use of, the body, the body of desire, the libido or life-force which Sigmund Freud said stirred the primitive cells as the sun heated the stony surface of the earth-cells which, according to him, always had the lazy, deep desire to give up striving, to return to the quiescent state from which they were roused. Our savant might mock the divination of cow-stomachs and milking-sticks, but he was the author of *Nemesis Divina,* a collection of tales of divine retribution, including that of the Pastor of Kvikjokk, encountered on this journey—"The pastor's wife whores with the regimental quartermaster Kock. The pastor in despair takes to the bottle; his daughter becomes a strumpet and is tumbled by a Lapp." There are several scatological and raucously erotic anecdotes in this work. There is also the tale of Yeoman Slickert, who loved the widow von Bysen and gave her a manor house. This upset his son-in-law, who fired three bullets through the window one night; the shots entered the Yeoman's stomach, and killed him. The son-in-law in due course developed cancer of the stomach, with three gnawing tumours, that killed him. A gentleman who fell asleep in one of CL's lectures went home and died of an apoplexy. This is sympathetic magic, though its title invokes a grim Greek deity, and its dedication, to CL's son, invokes a god whose vengeance is a principle of order in a chaotic and dangerous world.

> You have come into a world you know not.
> You see it not, but you marvel at its glory.
> You see confusion everywhere, the like of which no-
>   one has seen or heard.
> You see the fairest lilies choked by weeds.
> But here there dwells a just God who sets everything
>   right.
> *Innocue vivito, numen adest.*

Innocue vivito, numen adest. It was his own motto, carved over his bedroom door. "Live harmlessly. The spirit is close."

HE CAME to a place called Lycksmyran—"lucky marsh"—after a long period of stamping through freezing marshland up to his knees in water; he remarked that if he had had to undergo this misery as a punishment for sin, it would have been severe, and asked *cur non* Olycksmyran, unlucky marsh. Here his Lapp guide, sent out for shelter, returned with "a human being, but whether man or woman I could not tell. I think the poet could never have described a *furia* to compare with this one; she might indeed have issued from the infernal Styx. She was tiny, her face smoked black, the brown eyes shining, the brows black, the jet-black hair hanging round her head, on top of which was a flat red cap. The dress was grey, and from her chest, which resembled frogskin, hung long, limp brown dugs; she wore a number of brass bracelets, a belt and boots.

"At first sight of this being I was afeard. But the Fury took pity on me and cried out, 'Wretched man! Poor creature, what has brought thee here, where none has ventured before! Hast thou not seen how mean are our dwellings?' "

This Fury insisted that the only way to go was back through the swamps. CL begged for food—she offered him raw fish, putrid and breeding maggots. He asked for smoked reindeer tongue, which he had come to like, but there was none. He went back, that time losing his boat, his axe, his pike, a stuffed heron and a stuffed sea-eagle in the rapids of the river. Nevertheless, having recuperated at Umeå he undertook another up-country expedition, and met more Furies, more kindly old women, and magic. He records, in his published Travels, that in Norway he had heard of a curious ruse by which the Lapps could be deceived into surrendering their magic drums—you could sidle up to one, who had refused you his drum, and, without his remarking what you were at, push up his sleeve and open a vein. The wounded Lapp, faint from loss of blood (and apparently unaware of why—CL is vague on this point) can easily be persuaded to hand over the magic object. It is probable that CL's story is a garbled version of the cruel punishments inflicted on the Sami by Christian priests, who tied them down, opened the veins and let the blood run until the unfortunate nomads recanted, were "converted," and gave up their magic objects and practices. We come now to CL himself, and the strange portrait he had made of himself in his Lapp dress, complete with drum and magic drawings, on his return from the uncharted lands. What did the drum mean to him? What did he learn, out there in the wastes, in the skin huts of the Sami?

He was a noticing man, a collector of facts, and he describes their daily life with apparent amiable objectivity. He conducts an examination of the reasons for their strength and resilience—they are pure carnivores, they exercise their strong muscles by sitting cross-legged, they wear heelless boots, they eat frugally and do not fill their stomachs. (He goes into an excursus on teeth, and the carnivorous nature of man, "our species," cf. *Babianos et Simia et Satyros sylvestres*.)

He noted also their sleeping habits, huddled together, quite naked, sixteen at a time, under reindeer skins. Some of their habits disgusted him; they cleaned their bowls and spoons with fingers and spittle, drinking boiled reindeer milk, which was strong-smelling and thick. They did not wash clothes, living in skins, fur inside in the winter, outside in the summer, "rigid sarcophagi" says CL. He was interested also in the strongly scented mushrooms (probably *Boletus suavolens*) which the young Lapp males wore to entice the young females.

"When a Lapland youth finds this fungus he preserves it carefully in a little pouch hanging from his waist, so that its grateful scent may make him more acceptable to the girl he is courting. O whimsical Venus! In other parts of the world you must be wooed with coffee and chocolate, preserves and sweets, wines and dainties, jewels and pearls, gold and silver, silks and cosmetics, balls and assemblies, concerts and plays; here you are satisfied with a little withered fungus!"

There is an analogous case to this borrowed Lapp aphrodisiac in the way in which the male euglossine bee impregnates himself with the musky pheromones of the bucket orchid in order to attract a mate. But certain of CL's jottings lead us to believe that he enjoyed other fungi with other properties. Out of Jukkasjärvi he stayed with a group where he records a conversation with another old woman, whose silver belt with its appendages he described accurately.

1. A spoon in a case.
2. A knife in a sheath.
3. A pipe in a case.
4. A leather thimble to put *digito inditorio.*
5. A needlecase with a brass cap to pull out.
6. Rings, some of them large, in brass.

The belt itself is decorated with tin or with silver beads.

He also made careful notes on her vulva, labia, clitoris and buttocks.

He also described a ceremony in which this person appeared in another costume. This costume corresponds almost exactly to the costume of the prophetess, conjurer, or seer in the saga of Erik the Red. CL records some conversations with this person about *"numen, sive hamr"* in amongst his jottings on ceremonies pertaining to birth, and marriage. He was always interested in ceremonies surrounding birth, marriage and death. He records elsewhere that the pastor's wife in Kemi told him that for a woman to drink a little blood from the severed *funiculus umbilicus* is a good way to avoid *dolores post partum—ipso puerperie multis difficiliores. Hamr,* he records—reconstructing his sketchy notes—was the membrane surrounding the foetus (specifically not the placenta, but the caul, the membrane) which bore, as it were, the shadowed impress, the *double,* of the human creature inside it. There were those whose *hamr* was loosed into the world at the moment of birth and who remained capable of contact with it, of changing shape, of travelling through time and space. I did not see how this could be, wrote the believer in mermaids and "shots" from clear skies. The old woman however told him that he was himself, as she clearly saw—"I have the sight"—*hammramr.*

He makes mention of a ceremonial dress with a hood of black lamb's-hide, lined with white catskin, reindeer-skin boots with long hairs, and catskin gloves, also furred. He writes of the *gandr,* or magic rod, with its knob and its brass and stone decorations. His accounts of the ceremonies, like all these private autobiographical fragments, are in the third person, distancing himself. Thus we read:

"They dance naked, beating their drums, which they say have magic powers, and the wisewomen sing long songs together, and separately, over and over. They drink hydromel and eau-de-vie at these times, and eat special foods. The drums are covered with drawings and signs." The songs, he was told, are the songs of the creatures that make up the drum, the tree (silver birch, *betula*) and the young reindeer, chosen by Fate. They believe that their souls sing and conduct the practicants *ad infernos acque ad supernos.* The singing is strong and persistent; the room is hot and full of smoke and the drumming of naked feet.

The markings on the drums represent many things: the rainbow, skis and sledges, the eyes and wings of birds. They are divided into parts which they told him represent the three divisions of *Mundus*—Caelum, Terra et Regiae Infernae. They believe their spirits may travel to these places, whilst their bodies lie torpid.

Certe est, he saw one of them fall to earth, a dead man *(pulsa non sentitur)* who lay dead for some hours *(duratio temporis incertissime est)* whilst the others danced about him and sang.

HE SAW the huge hairpelt behind the smoke leave the place. They say they may travel for hundreds upon hundreds of leagues, in *utrasque formas;* during that time their names may not be mentioned, nor may the names of their *alter egos, sive entes bestiae,* or they may wander lost for ever. This may be what the priests refer to as *raptus* or *alienato mentis.* Those capable of these feats are known as *mjök trollaukinn*—those whose non-human powers, *troll,* are enhanced, *aukinn.*

He saw also, which gave him courage, but put great fear into him, that the dead man rose again after the *ganda* embraced and called him, striking him with her staff.

"IT IS SAID ALSO that these travellers, who are both still as stone and *velocitates in aeribus et super terras,* can tell accurately what explorers may find in undiscovered countries, such as the location of hot springs, the shape of coastlines, harbours, *et caetera*, meadows and fjords."

Quid dicitur? Scribo ut non? He saw himself also, quite clearly, lying there upon a reindeer skin, a very corpse, white and cold, with staring eyes. And as he saw himself, *id quod vidit, ille qui vidit,* that which saw, he who saw, was able to leave himself there in the smoky place, and go out into the forest. There he was with others, who appeared to him, as in a dream, to be sometimes men wearing the skins of the great beasts, wolf and bear, or eagle feathers, and who sometimes had two pairs of eyes, and sometimes those two pairs melded. And these undertook a great journey, travelling over the high Torneå Fells, to Caituma, hundreds of miles. They travelled also towards Sørfold and from there—let us speak of it as in a dream, but it was no dream, a man may know if his body be dreaming or present, and to this traveller, all was present. For he saw them, in this swift *transitus, cerastium flore maximo,* and *Lycopodium echinat* which later he was to see in his more laborious journeyings.

From there he went even to Lofoten.

He had always greatly desired to see the renowned and terrible Maelstrøm, a wonder of the natural world. Now he found himself on the peak of the mountain, Helseggen, the Cloudy. From there he beheld a wide expanse of ocean, whose waters were so inky a hue as to bring at once to mind the Nubian geographer's account of the *Mare Tenebrarum.* To the right and left, as far as the eye could reach, there lay outstretched, like ramparts of the world, lines of horridly black and beetling cliff, whose gloomy character was made more striking by the surf which reared up its white and ghastly crest . . .

He saw as he watched, the character of the ocean surface change from a chopping character to a forceful current, which tamed into whirlpools, which in turn disappeared, leaving streaks of foam, which combined in a gyratory motion, taking on the motion of the subsided vortices to form the germ of another more vast. Suddenly—very suddenly—this assumed a distinct and definite existence, in a circle of more than a mile in diameter. The funnel, whose interior was a smooth, shining and jet-black wall of water, inclined to the horizon at an angle of some forty-five degrees, speeding round and round with a swaying and sweltering motion, sending to the winds an appalling voice half shriek, half roar . . .

He saw himself lying on the skin as he stood in the doorway of the smoky house. He lay down on his cold body and his spirit entered his still flesh as the fingers of a hand enter a glove and spread and warm the skin. So it was, in truth.

WHAT ARE WE MODERNS to make of this? Some researchers have suggested that his published account of his travels was to some extent mendacious. He had not, they claim, the time to have made the long journey to Kaituma— he would have had to cover 840 miles in a fortnight—and far from undertaking the dangerous sea-voyage from Sørfold to Maelstrøm, he was prevented by storms and rowed about near the beach. He was prone to exaggerate, describing the "Alps" that divide Sweden from Norway as "more than a

Swedish mile high" (considerably higher than Everest). Far from journeying into *Terra Incognita*, he was only travelling where the Christian missionaries had already made trails.

If we look at the painting he commissioned of himself in the Lapp costume he brought back from his journey, it is difficult, almost impossible, to recognise the face of the genial genius in the frizzed and curled wig who appears on medals and in frontispieces, decorated with orders and medals, framed in garlands of flowers and sweetly discreet flying *putti*. He wears his flat pyramidal bonnet and his huge flat-footed fur boots, and looks out of huge, wary dark eyes at the looker-in, as though he was an alert wild creature that might shy away. He wears also his reindeer-skin garment and great fur-cuffed gloves. Round his waist hang the implements of Lapp life, a netting-needle, a straw snuff-box, a cartridge box, a knife, a receptacle also made from furred hide. At his side hangs the Lapp drum, with its mysterious signs facing the viewer, like a clock-face. In his right hand he carries the small pink plant he found near Gävle then named *Campanula serpyllifolia*, but later renamed *Linnaea borealis*, "a plant of Lapland, lowly, insignificant, disregarded, flowering but for a brief space—from Linnaeus, who resembles it."

Naming is a difficult art. The names of magicians who undertake the *hamfar* must not be spoken; nor must the names of the beasts who are their *hamrs*. CL himself, in the fragments, shows his awareness of this, and also of the fact that the creatures were named by circumlocution, indirection and euphemism. He left—if the fragment is his, and autobiographical, and not some record of some old saying, a verse which resembles some of his more conventional poems and paradoxes:

Linnaeus in His Lapland Dress, mezzotint by Dunkarton after a painting by Martin Hoffman, from Thornton's *Temple of Flora*

I ran with grey-foot
With the old man with the fur pelt I ran
Who came from the Stygian depths.
With the winged creature, Voesa, I soared
Over the boiling water-pot.
I flew over the highest mountain,
Where the snow lies, and the grey clouds
Make a mist-cloud for erica and the grey stones.

Northern languages named men for beasts. Björn, the bear, Ari or Örn, the eagle, Hrútr, the ram, Kalfr, the calf, Hundr, the dog, Ormr, the serpent. Did he meditate on these when he made his system of double names for plants and animals, bringing order to the rampant world of creatures and things? Did he muse on his own polymorphous nomenclature? It has been said that he was named originally for flax, lin, linen. It is almost certain his father took his name from a large and venerated lime tree in Småland—Swedish *lind*, Latin *tilia* (French *tilleul*, English linden . . .). Some of the family were called Tiliander. *Tilia* (and *Papaver*, the opium poppy) in CL's sexual system belong to the *Polyandria* with "twenty males or more in the same bed with the female."

Paradise, CL believed, was an island, *the* island, the part of the earth's crust that rose above the waves, as the primal waters receded. In it the Creator had planted two seeds of every species, one male, one female (one seed sufficed for hermaphrodites). The island of Paradise, both because it thrust upwards from the seabed, and because created Nature required it, "was in form a high mountain peak, with the flora and fauna ideally placed in ascending or descending strata, to suit the climate they required. Adam the gardener wandered this mountain, noting and naming all things, plants, beasts, insects, birds, and the fish in the descending funnels and troughs of the surrounding sea." Even as a young man, CL thought of himself, as he journeyed over the fells, swamps and mountains, as the second Adam, the separator, the taxonomist, the Namer of species. Wrapped in his deerskins, he noted the nature and vagaries of mountain climates. After a few days in Norway, he said, he felt heavy, but the mountain air revived him—he was advised to put a wet sponge to his nose, to make the light air thicker. He believed the air only appeared thin because of the compression of his lungs by the effort of climbing—one is breathless *ab accelerata circulatione sanguinis.* But he checked his barometer, and found that the air pressure was weaker. This, for some reason, appeared to him to be *contra rationem,* against reason. But he recorded it. He recorded the delights and salutary benefits of iced snow-water.

He kept those liquid brown eyes open wide in the land of the arctic sun. Early in his journey he had named a pretty plant, *Andromeda polifolia* (bog rosemary), for the chained princess, blushing with blood-red shame ("as soon as she flowers her petals become flesh-coloured") but pale after fertilisation. He had written lyrically of her drenching by "poisonous dragons and beasts—i.e., evil toads and frogs" during their mating. He had made an amateurish drawing of maiden and flower on boggy rocks, and of unrecognisable amphibians. Having created the genus *Andromeda* with this poetic fancy, he nearly, but not quite, failed to see another, in his confusion on a mountain summit. His notes are the precise notes of a scientist:

"At midnight—if such I may call it when the sun never

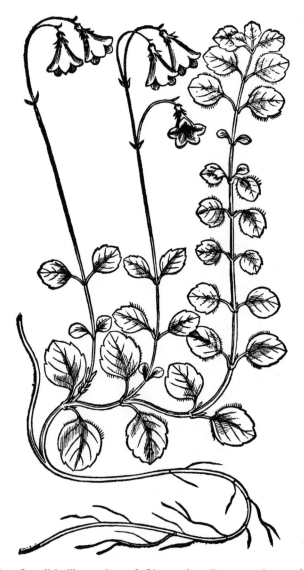

First Swedish illustration of *Linnaea borealis*, a woodcut published by Rudbeck the Younger in *Acta Literaria Sueciae*, 1720–24

sets—I was walking rapidly, facing the icy wind and sweating profusely . . . but always on the alert, when I saw as it were the shadow of this plant, but did not stoop to examine it because I took it to be an *Empetrum*. A moment later, however, I suddenly thought that it might be something new and retraced my steps; I would again have taken it for an *Empetrum* had not its greater height made me examine it more carefully.

"I don't know what it is that at night in our mountains disturbs our vision and makes objects far less distinct than by day, for the sun is just as bright. But from being near the horizon its rays are so level that a hat affords no protection to the eyes. Moreover, the shadows are so extended, and by gusts of wind made so confused, that things not really a bit alike can hardly be told apart . . .

"The *Andromeda* was over, and setting seed; but after a long search I managed to find a single plant still flowering; the flower was white, shaped like a lily of the valley but with five sharper divisions."

II

[The second document, to which I gave the provisional title "G . . ."]

HE WAS INTERESTED in the unconscious mind. What he was interested in was not the Freudian Id, but more what William James called "the deep well of unconscious cerebration." He was a profoundly and delightfully rational man. He conducted many experiments on the activities of the mind, including a word-association test of 100 words to which he submitted himself several times, writing down his immediate responses to each, controlled every four seconds by a stopwatch. He divided the associations (which he found remarkably constant) into groups: those—"abbey, aborigines, abyss"—which gave rise to visual images, those—"abasement, abhorrence, ablution"—which induced represented histrionic scenes, and those more abstract words—"afternoon, ability, abnormal"—to which the most probable responses were purely verbal, quotations or definitions. He was later to conclude that most powerful intellectuals neither formed, nor thought with, mental images, which were much more common amongst women and children. He thought that the paucity and steady recurrence of his personal associations suggested that "the mind is apparently always engaged in mumbling over its old stores, and if any one of these is wholly neglected for a while, it is apt to be forgotten, perhaps irrecoverably."

He concluded:

"Perhaps the strongest impression left by these experiments regards the multifariousness of the work done by the mind in a state of half-unconsciousness, and the valid reason they afford for believing in the existence of still deeper strata of mental operations, sunk wholly below the level of consciousness, which may account for such mental phenomena as cannot otherwise be explained."

His father had greatly desired him to become a medical man, and he spent many years as a medical student and clinical clerk. During his time in the dispensary he made another taxonomic or statistical experiment, deciding to work through his pharmacological supplies from A to Z, taking two drops of each and studying the effects on his own constitution. He was stopped by the effects of croton oil. "I had foolishly believed that two drops of it could have no notable effects as purgative and emetic; but indeed they had, and I can recall them now." A description of his first operation on a young man's jaw suggests an optimistic humour.

"A boy came in looking very deplorable, walked up to me and opened his mouth. I looked awfully wise and the boy sat down in perfect confidence. I did not manage the first proceedings well, for first I put in the key (that is the tooth instrument) the wrong way, then I could not catch hold of the right tooth with it. At last I got hold. I then took my breath to enable me to give a harder wrench; one—two—three and away I went. A confused sort of murmur something like that of a bee in a foxglove proceeded from the boy's mouth, he kicked at me awfully, I wrenched the harder. When, hang the thing,—crash went the tooth. It really was dreadfully decayed—and out came my instrument. I seized hold of the broken bits—the boy's hands were of course over his mouth and eyes from the pain, so he could see nothing—and immediately threw them on the fire and most unconcernedly took another survey of the gentleman's jaws. The tooth was snapped right off. Well, I pacified him, told him that one half the tooth was out and I would take out the other (knowing full well that he would not let me touch it again) and that it was a *double* one. But, as I had expected, he would not let me proceed."

On his tours of the wards he noted healing and decay, communal hysteria in the female wards (infecting the nurses) and the physical and mental effects of *delirium tremens* elsewhere.

"The struggles were sometimes terrible, yet the pulse was feeble and the reserve of strength almost nil. The visions of the patients seemed indistinguishable by them from realities; in the few cases I saw they were wholly of fish or of creeping things. One of the men implored me to take away the creature that was crawling over his counterpane, following its imagined movements with his finger, and staring as at a ghost. Poor humanity! I often feel that the tableland of sanity, on which most of us dwell, is small in area, with unfenced precipices on every side, over any one of which we may fall."

As we shall see, he experienced the falls from the tableland more than once, himself. At various stages in his life he suffered from a kind of nervous collapse. At Cambridge he had to abandon his mathematical tripos and go home for a term.

"A mill seemed to be working inside my head; I could not banish obsessing ideas; at times I could hardly read a book and found it painful even to look at a printed page . . . I had been much too zealous, had worked too irregularly and in too many directions, and had done myself serious harm. It was as though I had tried to make a steam-engine perform more work than it was constructed for, by tampering with its safety valve and thereby straining its mechanism."

He had a more serious episode much later, after thirteen years of marriage. He remarks with his usual judicious good sense:

"Those who have not suffered from mental breakdown can hardly realise the incapacity it causes, or, when the worst is past, the closeness of analogy between a sprained brain and a sprained joint. In both cases, after recovery seems to others to be complete, there remains for a long time an impossibility of performing certain minor actions without pain and serious mischief, mental in the one and bodily in the other. This was a frequent experience with me respecting small problems, which successively obsessed me, day and night, as I tried in vain to think them out. These affected mere twigs, so to speak, rather than large boughs of the mental processes, but for all that most painfully." He had, as this passage shows, an unusual capacity of self-observation, standing beside himself, so to speak, taking his own pulse, observing his own symptoms.

HE SET OFF for Ovampoland in 1849. His father had died in 1844, which had scattered the family and freed him from the medical profession. Immediately after this death, he had travelled to Egypt and along the Nile to the Sudan, where he met the St. Simonian Arnaud Bey, and the wild Mansfield Parkyns, who lived amongst a crew of drug-dealers and slave-traders, dressed in a leopardskin, with a shaven head and Moslem tuft. He had made an earlier student expedition along the Danube to Constantinople from Vienna, where he had been told his own worth as a young male slave. It appears that he may have contracted an infection in the Sudan, after "one night's pleasure," which may have been responsible for his sudden cessation of interest in women. (This great student and exponent of the virtues of breeding men of genius never reproduced himself; his long marriage was childless.) He spent a few years, between the Syrian and the South-West African expeditions, hunting, shooting and fishing in a desultory way—he records a journey to the Shetlands for seal-shooting and bird nesting, with "the weird experiences of a fisher society, living in a treeless land, with whale-jaws for posts, and with no knife in their pockets larger than a penknife, having only tobacco and string to cut with it."

He tells how to shoot and land a seal. He adds, "I would not shoot a seal now, but youths are murderous by instinct and so was I."

One of the aims of the Ovampoland expedition was to shoot hippopotamus in Lake Ngami. His friend, Henry Hallam, gracefully refusing an invitation to join a hippopotamus shoot in the Sudan, had expressed envy, from the point of view of a destroyer of coveys of pheasants, of the proposed target, a large, stationary grey pachyderm. It was not clear whether the lake existed or was simply a dry sandy bowl. There was the further problem of the Boers, who "had been very unruly, and had affirmed their intention of keeping the newly discovered lands about Lake Ngami to themselves and of refusing passage to every Englishman."

He set off, accordingly, on a different route, landing in Walfisch Bay and traversing the territories of the yellow Namaguas, the black Damaras and the Ovampo ("pure negroes of a high type" according to him). The Namaguas, he said, were "yellow Hottentots" with hair growing in tufts on their heads, and speaking a language full of clicks. They had a strain of Dutch blood, and most of them spoke a little of the Dutch language. Their leaders at that time were Jonker, Cornelius, Amiral and Swartboy. They were engaged in continual combat with the Damaras, raiding cattle and selling them. They had decided that no further white man should cross their border. There were also the Ghou Damup, probably a branch of the Ovampo, and the Bushmen, nomadic, good hunters, amongst whom FG spent several days at Tounobis, trying to learn about Lake Ngami. He travelled with a Swede, Charles Andersson, who had come to England to make his fortune.

"His capital wherewith to begin consisted of a crate of live capercailzie, two bearcubs, and the skin of one of their parents. He was then so naïve that, seeing an auctioneer's placard about a forthcoming sale of farm stock, in which was included '20,000 Swedes,' he, not knowing that in the language of farmers 'swedes' meant 'turnips,' confessed afterwards to a thrill of terror lest they should be his compatriots, and lest he himself might be pounced upon and sold as a slave together with them."

FG's *Art of Travel* devotes several pages to a traveller's outfit under the headings of *Small Stores, Various* (fish-hooks, scalpel, bistoury, awls, etc. etc.), *Heavy Stores, Various* (saddles, water-vessels, ammunition), *Stationery* (30 lbs, of ledgers, ink, books to read etc., "say equal to six vols. the ordinary size of novels"), *Mapping Materials* (31 lbs) and *Natural History.*

"Arsenical soap, 2 lbs; camphor ½ lb; pepper ½ lb; bag of some powder to absorb blood, 2 lbs; tow and cotton, about 10 lbs; scalpel, forceps, scissors etc., ½ lb; sheet brass, stamped for labels, ½ lb . . . 16 pillboxes; cork; insect-boxes; pins; tin, for catching and keeping, and killing animals; nets for butterflies . . . 10 lb. Geological hammers, lens, clinometer, etc. . . . 4 lb.

"Specimens. (I make no allowance for the weight of these, for they accumulate as stores are used up; and the total weight is seldom increased.)

"Total weight of Natural History materials (for an *occasional* collector) . . . 30 lb."

He also took some odd and cumbersome things. What are we to make of his decision to make himself agreeable to Nangoro, King of the Ovampo, who were "under strict discipline, secret and very resolute," by investing him with "a big theatrical crown that I had bought in Drury Lane for some such purpose"? It is certain that he offended Nangoro, when invited to eat with him, by refusing to take part in a cleansing ritual in which the host spat gargled water over the face of the guest—a counter-witchcraft expedient of Nangoro's own devising. When the Damara chief, Jonker, would not reply to his request for passage, he mounted his riding-ox (he gives detailed instructions for breaking oxen to be saddled) and, jumping a river, trotted briskly up to Jonker's hut, through the wall of which the ox pushed its head. FG was dressed in hunting pink, cap, cords and jackboots. What possessed him to travel all the way into the desert lumbered with this gear? It intimidated Jonker, briefly, and a treaty was made between the Namagua and the Damara, which barely survived FG's departure, giving way to further massacres.

He may also have offended Nangoro with his attitude to women; he rejected, summarily, his offer of the Princess Chipanga.

"I found her installed in my tent in negress finery, raddled with red ochre and butter, and as capable of leaving a mark on anything she touched as a well-inked printer's roller. I was dressed in my one well-preserved suit of white linen, so I had her ejected without ceremony."

He preferred his women at an experimental distance. He was triangulating the country carefully, using his sextant and landmarks, which had to give way to lunar observations when he went beyond the limit of the landmarks, in North Damaraland and at Elephant Fountain. He spent time at the mission station in Barmen measuring a Hottentot lady.

"I profess to be a scientific man, and was exceedingly anxious to obtain accurate measurements of her shape; but there was a difficulty in doing this. I did not know a word of Hottentot, and could never therefore have explained to the lady what the object of my footrule could be; and I really

75

dared not ask my worthy missionary host to interpret for me. The object of my admiration stood under a tree, and was turning herself about to all points of the compass, as ladies who wish to be admired usually do. Of a sudden my eye fell upon my sextant, the bright thought struck me, and I took a series of observations upon her figure in every direction, up and down, crossways, diagonally, and so forth, and I registered them carefully upon an outline drawing for fear of any mistake: this being done, I boldly pulled out my measuring tape, and measured the distance from where I was to the place where she stood, and having thus obtained both base and angles, I worked out the results by trigonometry and logarithms."

It may be that FG preferred human beings in a net of invisible lines of trigonometric measurement and triangulated distances from the moon. He observed of the Damara that there was "hardly a particle of romance, or affection, or poetry, in their character or creed, but they are a greedy, heartless, silly set of savages."

However, he loved, and closely observed, his cattle. He had nearly a hundred wild Damara cattle, broken in for the wagon, for packs, and for the saddle.

"I travelled an entire journey of exploration on the back of one of them, with others by my side, either labouring, or walking at leisure; and with others who were wholly unbroken and who served the purpose of an itinerant larder. At night, when there had been no time to erect an enclosure to hold them, I lay down in their midst, and it was interesting to observe how readily they then availed themselves of the camp fire, and of man, conscious of the protection they afforded from prowling carnivora, whose cries and roars, now distant, now near, continually broke upon the stillness."

From his observation of these beasts, he formed a whole theory of "gregarious and slavish instincts" which he later—with due demurrers and qualifications—applied to men. The slavish aptitudes in man, he said, "are a direct consequence of his gregarious nature, which itself is a result of the conditions both of his primeval barbarism and of the forms of his subsequent civilisation."

He was a noticing and curious man and a good animal psychologist. He respected the oxen. "The better I understood them, the more complex and worthy of study did their minds appear to be. But I am now concerned only with their blind gregarious instincts, which are conspicuously distinct from the ordinary social desires. In the latter they are deficient; thus they are not amiable to one another, but show on the whole more expressions of spite and disgust than of forbearance or fondness."

He notes the solitude of the creatures embedded in the mass of other creatures.

"They do not suffer from an ennui, which society can remove, because their coarse feeding and their ruminant habits make them somewhat stolid. Neither can they love society, as monkeys do, for the opportunities it affords of a fuller and more varied life, because they remain self-absorbed in the middle of their herd, while the monkeys revel together in frolics, scrambles, fights, loves and chatterings."

His respect for the creatures, which easily refers to their "minds" at a time when many thinkers believed the beasts were no more than machines or automata, is reinforced by his imaginative participation in their emotions.

"Yet although the ox has so little affection for, or individual interest in, his fellows, he cannot endure even a momentary severance from his herd. If he be separated from it by stratagem or force, he exhibits every sign of mental agony; he strives with all his might to get back again, and when he succeeds, he plunges into its middle to bathe his whole body with the comfort of closest companionship. This passionate terror at segregation is a convenience to the herdsman . . ."

He was interested in those independent-minded oxen who grazed apart from the herd, and showed an unusual inquisitiveness and desire to experiment. These, he observed, could be trained to be ridden, or to be lead-oxen; they were not by any means the normal leaders of the herd from within the herd, in flight or simple change of grazing-place, but individuals, with minds of their own. With his usual statistical acuity he worked out that these individuals were about one in fifty, and that a herd could not cohere, or act together, if this proportion were exceeded. He believed, however, that in the case of human beings it might be possible to change whole societies by breeding out slavishness and mere gregariousness, the crowd instincts, in human beings. Human beings, he believed, had been cowed by religious persecution and domination of chieftains with powerful executives, ready to stamp out individual protests.

He hoped, with the aid of eugenics, for better. "A nation need not be a mob of slaves, clinging to one another through fear, and for the most part incapable of self-government, and begging to be led; but it might consist of vigorous, self-reliant men, knit to one another by innumerable ties, into a strong, tense and elastic organisation."

This is one metaphor drawn from a web, or from knitting. So is the converse metaphor for the coherence, or cohesion, of the herd.

"To live gregariously is to become a fibre in a vast sentient web overspreading many acres; it is to become the possessor of faculties always awake, of eyes that see in all directions, of ears and nostrils that explore a broad belt of air; it is also to become the occupier of every bit of vantage ground whence the approach of a wild beast might be overlooked."

It is perhaps interesting, in view of the observations already made about FG's lack of interest in sex, that he points out that his terrified and craven wild animals consisted of "oxen and cows whose nature is no doubt shared by the bulls." Why was he—the precise scientist—so bland about the bulls? Why did he not ask himself why there were none? It seems a simple question.

FG BECAME FAMOUS in his lifetime for his work on anthropometry and eugenics. That last word, since the dreadful events of the last war and before, has come to strike horror into the reading public, and that may be the reason why his extraordinary contributions to knowledge, on so many fronts, are forgotten. His inventions—identification by fingerprint, the weather balloon, the weather-map, the statistical bell-curve of standard deviation in populations, are not generally ascribed to him. Most of all, perhaps, his delicate researches into the nature of consciousness, of thought, of reflection, of the slippage of unremarked mental processes, have disappeared into oblivion unjustly. His fearless eccentricity, his unquenchable curiosity, led to many delicious discoveries. Who else would have thought of measuring the "inclination" to each other of a couple placed side by side at dinner, by calibrating on wax the weight they put on the chair-legs nearest to each other? His capacity to watch himself, to stand outside himself, to make his own consciousness the field and mirror of his enquiries, may appear to have the same innocent charm. But it had its dangers.

He records, in his *Memories,* various such experiments. His first, made in his youth, was, he said, the result of a not uncommon youthful desire to "subjugate the body by the spirit." He made the extraordinary decision to make all his involuntary processes subject to his will, which should "replace automatism by hastening or retarding automatic acts." He nearly killed himself.

"Every breath was subjected to this process, with the result that the normal power of breathing was dangerously interfered with. It seemed as though I should suffocate if I ceased to will. I had a terrible half-hour; at length by slow and irregular steps the lost power returned. My dread was hardly fanciful, for heart-failure is the suspension of the automatic faculty of the heart to beat."

His next effort, after investigating the connections between his mind and his body, was to investigate the mental condition of those who had, as he put it elsewhere, slipped down the unfenced precipice from the tableland of sanity. In this experiment he quite deliberately induced in himself a kind of paranoia, to "gain some idea of the commoner feelings in Insanity. The method tried was to invest everything I met, whether human, animal, or inanimate, with the imaginary attributes of a spy. Having arranged plans, I started on my morning's walk from Rutland Gate, and found the experiment only too successful. By the time I had walked one and a half miles, and reached the cab-stand in Piccadilly at the east end of the Green Park, every horse on the stand seemed watching me, either with pricked ears or disguising its espionage. Hours passed before this uncanny sensation wore off, and I feel that I could only too easily re-establish it."

His third experiment, after consciousness and madness, was with religion. In his attempt to penetrate idolatry and fetishism, he shows perhaps, safe in his London respectability, a certain cultural inadequacy which is perhaps evidenced also in his foxhunting invasion of Jonker or his crowning of Nangoro. (Or is it possible that we moderns, mocking the certainties and the innocence of the Victorians, misinterpret these events also; is it possible that Nangoro smiled with satisfaction under his player's tinsel in the mirror FG lent him?)

He wrote:

"The third experiment of which I will speak was to gain an insight into the abject feelings of barbarians and others concerning the power of images which they know to be of human handiwork. I had visited a large collection of idols gathered by missionaries from many lands, and wondered how each of those absurd and ill-made monstrosities could have obtained the hold it had over the imaginations of its worshippers. I wished, if possible, to enter into those feelings. It was difficult to find a suitable object for trial, because it ought to be in itself quite unfitted to arouse devout feelings. I fixed on a comic picture, it was that of Punch, and made believe in its possession of divine attributes. I addressed it with much quasi-reverence as possessing a mighty power to reward or punish the behaviour of men towards it, and found little difficulty in ignoring the impossibilities of what I professed. The experiment gradually succeeded; I began to feel and long retained for the picture a large share of the feelings that a barbarian entertains towards his idol, and learned to appreciate the enormous potency they might have over him."

He did not like conventional religion, though he submitted it, like everything else, to his questing intellectual stare. He even conducted a statistical survey of the longevity of those (queens, princes, bishops) regularly prayed for in churches, to see if the force of prayer improved their life expectancy. It did not. In his delicate analysis of mental imagery, he moved from systems of number maps and coloured mnemonics, to visions proper, distinguishing carefully between mental imagery, "after-images," "phosphenes," "light dust," and hypnagogic processions, visualisations of named objects or involuntary showers of perfumed and metamorphosing roses. He recorded hallucinations and mirages, phantasmagoric crowds of faces and the curious combinations of dream objects—for instance a rolling, bullet-shaped head on a white surface, which turned out to be a conflated memory of a cheesemonger and his Dutch cheeses. He recorded Napoleon's hallucinatory star and those of other great men. He remarked that all these dreams and visions appeared to be common functions of normal consciousness. "When popular opinion is of a matter-of-fact kind, the seers of visions keep quiet; they do not like to be thought fanciful or mad . . . But let the tide of opinion change and grow favourable to supernaturalism, then the seers of visions come to the front. The faintly perceived fantasies of ordinary persons become invested by the authority of reverend men with a claim to serious regard; they are consequently attended to and encouraged, and they increase in definition through being habitually 'dwelt upon.' "

He wrote a letter to *Nature* about a vision of his own, and apparently thought better of sending it. It is an arresting vision, and peculiarly interesting in his rigorous dissociation of it from the religious associations it might naturally have evoked. He was ill with bronchitis and influenza when it occurred.

"When fancies gathered and I was on the borderland of delirium I was aware of the imminence of a particular hallucination. There was no vivid visualisation of it, but I felt that if I let myself go I should see in bold relief a muscular blood-stained crucified figure nailed against the wall of my bedroom opposite my bed. What on earth made me think of this particular object I have no conception. There was nothing in it of the religious symbol, but just a prisoner freshly mauled and nailed up by a brutal Roman soldier. The interest in this to me was the severance between the state of hallucination and that of ordinary visualisation. They seemed in this case to be quite unconnected."

"If I let myself go." What did he mean? On this occasion, he did not. But, as we have seen, he had a kind of wild courage in regard to his investment of *mana* in cab-horses and Mr. Punch. And in the African interior he saw things, both real and visionary, which he found in some way unbearable—though he recorded some of the real things, at least, in letters to his mother, with whom he was out of touch for two years. There *were*, for instance, the African women victims of one of Jonker's raids.

"I saw two poor women, one with both legs cut off at her ankle joints, and the other at one [*sic*]. They had crawled the whole way on that eventful night from Schelen's Hope to Barmen, some twenty miles. The Hottentots had cut them off after their usual habit, in order to slip off the solid iron anklets that they wear. These wretched creatures showed me how they had stopped the blood by poking the wounded stumps into the sand."

He returned to these unfortunate women when recording his earlier medical experiences for his memoirs. He included them in an observation on the varying tolerance of pain.

"The stumps had healed when I saw them. I asked how they staunched the blood. They explained by gesture that it was by stumping the bleeding ends into the sand, and they grinned with satisfaction while they explained."

In this version, both women had lost both feet.

He recorded also "one of Jonker's sons, a hopeful youth, came to a child that had been dropped on the ground and lay screaming there, and he gouged out its eyes with a small stick."

He records these events, even in his letters to his mother, with no great expression of emotion—indeed, with a curious echo of British schoolboy japes, which may be a commentary on how he felt after his ritual exposure to these.

"The Ovahereros, a very extended nation, attacked a village the other day for fun, and after killing all the men and women, they tied the children's legs together by the ankles, and strung them head downwards on a long pole, which they set horizontally between two trees; then they got plenty of reeds together and put them underneath and lighted them; and as the children were dying, poor wretches, half burnt, half suffocated, they danced and sung round them, and made a fine joke of it. Andersson desires to be particularly remembered to all. With my best love to all the family, relations and friends, collectively and individually, Ever affectly. yours, FG"

Before he set out for Lake Ngami, he spent some time with the bushmen at Tounoubis. They regaled him with stories of the fabulous beasts who lived on the shores of the lake, and in the bush beyond. One had the spoor of a zebra and the horn of a gemsbok, mounted centrally on its forehead. FG wrote to his mother that the skins of this beast, stolen by a party of Kubabees, were quite new to all who saw them. "I really begin to believe in the existence of the beast [the unicorn]," he wrote, "as reports of the animal have been received in many parts of Africa, frequently in the North." The bushmen also gave detailed descriptions of a kind of cockatrice—a climbing tree-snake with the comb of a guinea fowl and a cry like the clucking of a hen, but without the legendary wings. FG observed the bushmen's drawings with interest. "One of their habits is to draw pictures on the walls of caves of men and animals and to colour them with ochre. These drawings were once numerous, but they have been sadly destroyed by advancing colonisation and few of them, and indeed, few wild Bushmen, now exist . . . I was particularly struck with a portrait of an eland as giving a just idea of the precision and purity of their best work." In later life, he collected a description of a wild Bushman, from a tribe living in caves in the Drakenberg, and his method of drawing.

"He invariably began by jotting down upon paper or on a slate a number of isolated dots wch presented no connection or trace of outline of any kind to the uninitiated eye, but looked like the stars scattered promiscuously in the sky. Having with much deliberation satisfied himself of the sufficiency of these dots, he forthwith began to run a free bold line from one to the other, and as he did so the form of an animal—horse, buffalo, elephant or some kind of antelope—gradually developed itself. This was invariably done with a free hand, and with such unerring accuracy of touch, that no correction of a line was at any time attempted. I understood from the lad that this was the plan which was invariably pursued by his kindred in making their clever pictures."

FG offers this, in his discussion of Mental Imagery, as an example of the projection of a complete mental image on to the paper. He follows it immediately with a description of the map-making abilities of the Eskimo, who could draw from memory accurate charts of the icy bays and inlets explored in their canoes. (Explored, it is also claimed, in spirit journeys undertaken by shamans who have never set flesh-foot in the accurately depicted estuaries, peninsulas, pools and promontories.) Karl Pearson, FG's biographer, commenting on his description of the Bushmen's prowess,

86

and his extrapolation of it into the evidences of the mental imagery of our ancestors of the Ice Ages, remarks that FG's artistic interest would have been aroused by the discovery of the cave paintings in Lascaux and other sites, made after his lifetime. These too, it is now generally thought, had shamanistic powers, could evoke presences or lead out souls into the fluid eternal pursuit of hunter and hunted, eater and eaten. Maybe it is not even fanciful to connect FG's observed reference points, "stars scattered promiscuously," with some astrological divination. "Below, the boarhound and the boar / Pursue their pattern as before / But reconciled among the stars."

[Quaere. Delete this ?? S D-S]

It was a dreadful and dangerous journey from Tounoubis to Lake Ngami. It was unbearably hot, and unbearably dry; there was no water to be had for 3½ days out of Tounoubis, and several of his oxen perished, not being fresh, in the remorseless heat. When he came there, he recorded a "waking vision" which came to him as he lay sleepless by the camp-fire at night.

"But in the dark, imagining some fear, / How easy is a bush suppos'd a bear!" So *A Midsummer Night's Dream*, which contains a lucid dissertation on the mental constructions of the lunatic, the lover and the poet. Shakespeare must have had a lively interest in mental imagery. Both Hamlet and Antony discourse upon shapes, whales or dragons, discerned in the random configurations of cloud formations. I have made some study of the mental activities which go on when we observe a stump, or something glistening in the dark holes between leaves, and take them for living creatures, a small dog, a raven, or a pair of bright eyes belonging to a hidden cat, large or small. I have noticed, walking in English parkland, that during the approach to an indeterminate object—say a large rock, with mossy growths, or a small log, the mind continues, from the minimal evidence, or sketched points of reference given, to *construct* the supposed creature. I have created whole ravens—heavy beak, claws, pinion-feathers, watchful eye—from what had to be *reconstructed,* seen again, as a hawthorn root. Here several times I have seen a lion crouched—tufted ears, shoulder muscles, softly lashing tail—where there was nothing but the movement of a bush in a breeze and a light catching on some shiny object, creating a vision of eyes to watching eyes. Something of this kind must have happened to me that night, but on a scale so awful and disgusting that I hesitate to relate it. Indeed I shall relate it only to attempt a rational exorcism. I believe the initial images may have risen in my poor brain, induced in part by our visit to Elephant Fountain, where the heaps of bones of those great beasts have suggested to the natives that it is a graveyard to which they go to die, to lay themselves down amongst their forebears and companions. Be that as it may, I suddenly saw the whole foreshore—on which there were a moderate number of big pebbles, small boulders, driftwood, etc. etc.—spread with bones. These bones were human bones, cloven skulls, severed spines, smashed femurs and tibia, little heaps of tiny phalanges and metatarsals. They gleamed white in the moonlight, and ruddy near at hand, in the light of the camp-fire. Wherever I looked, my gaze

88

seemed, as it were, to invest these dry bones with flesh. I thought irresistibly of Ezekiel in his valley of the dry bones. "Thus saith the Lord God unto these bones; Behold I will cause breath to enter into you, and ye shall live: And I will lay sinews upon you, and will bring up flesh upon you, and cover you with skin, and put breath in you, and ye shall live; and ye shall know that I am the Lord . . . And behold a shaking, and the bones came together, bone to his bone. And when I beheld, lo, the sinews and the flesh came up upon them, and the skin covered them above; but there was no breath in them." Ezekiel made his bones a living army but my creative eye went no further than to invest these with raw, slippery flesh, livid or freshly bleeding, hacked about and mauled, to which unspeakable things had been done. I had performed much butchery on beasts, in my sporting days, and in my explorations, and I was cognisant of the organs and limbs of the human body, from brain to toenail, from my medical days. But I can hardly believe that the horrible tortures, the ingenious mincing and carving up to which this mass of manhood had been subjected, came from my own subconscious. My mind retches at it still. Parts joined together in fantastic conjunctions—nipples with eye-sockets, and other unspeakable concatenations—all in pain, in pain. I walked amongst them, trying to discern a whole man, and came upon a half-flayed, severed head on a pole, out of which—I swear it—*my own eyes looked at me sorrowfully.* As if to say, why have you brought me to this pass?

"These heaps of flesh were inanimate but not immobile. They so to speak writhed or flowed together, moulding themselves into new forms. I was put in mind of some beautiful sad lines of Alfred Tennyson's poem for Henry Hallam's lamented brother Arthur, so tragically cut off. It was published anonymously just as I left for this unknown country: Henry pressed a copy into my hand as we parted. It is a fantastical, fragmentary poem, but its grief rings true, and is a grief for the whole earth, for the loss of a faith.

> "The hills are shadows and they flow
>   From form to form, and nothing stands;
>   They melt like mist, the solid lands
>   Like clouds they shape themselves, and go.

"I wish I had not thought of this then, for now I always see these shadowy hills blood-red, and formed of blood."

He sailed for England in January 1852 and arrived in April, exactly two years after his departure. On his arrival, he learned that Henry Hallam had died in Italy, in 1850, soon after he left, and that Henry's sister, Julia Hallam, to whom he had been—to what extent is not clear—emotionally attached, was a bride of two months' standing. In his *Memories of My Life*, published as late as 1908, he describes his relief on reaching the schooner in Walfish Bay. He sums up.

"This bald outline of a very eventful journey has taken little notice of the risks and adventures which characterised it . . . They must be imagined by the reader, otherwise the following paragraph will seem overcharged, which it is not."

But the following paragraph is hardly charged at all. He begins it: "I had little conception of the severity of the anxiety under which I had been living until I found myself on board the little vessel that took me away, and I felt at last able to sleep in complete security."

The rest of the paragraph is innocuous: summary thanks that he lost no men, survived grumbling and mutinous servants and the breaking-in of cattle, and the help of "an indolent and cruel set of natives speaking an unknown tongue." He mentions tribal wars, "which had to be stopped before I could proceed" and undependable food. He thanks Andersson—who ultimately died in Damaraland—and Hans. His paragraph is *undercharged*. English reticence, or sheering away from what he set out to tell?

III

[The third document, to which I gave the provisional title "I . . ."]

HE WAS a public man, and he made a daily public progress. He set out at two o'clock from Victoria Terrace, and walked to the Grand Hotel. He dressed carefully, always in the same clothes—a black, broadcloth frock-coat, black trousers, concertinaed at the ankles over highly polished, high-heeled black boots, a carefully folded umbrella, a glistening silk top-hat, a little fence of miniature medals. His white beard, and his white hair surrounded his sallow, unsmiling face, like the copious flare of a halo. He was a tiny personage, and carried himself stiffly erect, full of a dignity at once self-important and threatening. His lips were thin; his eyes, under their snowy ledges, have been called, finely, "fierce badger eyes." Cartoonists found him easy to "take"; their images proliferated, all recognisable projections, all the same, all different. He knew he was looked at. He had constructed himself to be looked at. Famous men walk behind, or inside, a simplified mask, constructed from inside and outside simultaneously.

He groomed his parchment skin and his sleek boot-leather to turn back the light to the onlooker. The onlookers, even as they watched the precise, dandified advance, knew they saw the outside, not the inside. They let their imaginations flicker round the inchoate "inside," which remained bland and opaque. He belonged to them, their countryman. They had never been sure if they liked him.

His effigies were round him in his lifetime. In his latter days, his statue stood outside the National Theatre, larger than life, looming through the snow. He was photographed, diminutive and bristling amongst the dignitaries, at ceremonies of dedication. There was a Platz named for him in Gossensass. There was a proposal to make a waxwork double of him to preside over a Freie Bühne festival in Berlin. They wrote to ask for the loan of an old suit. "Be so good as to tell this gentleman that I do not wear 'old suits,' nor do I wish a wax model of myself to be clothed in an 'old suit.' Obviously I cannot give him a new one, and I therefore suggest he order one from my tailor, Herr Friess, of Maximilianstrasse, Munich." Sculptors and painters found him somehow inordinate. He had, he informed one of them, the largest brainpan ever measured by a certain German expert. Another, having asked him to remove his spectacles, was appalled by the disparity between his eyes.

"One was large, I might almost say horrible—so it seemed to me—and deeply mystical; the other much smaller, rather pinched up, cold and clear and calmly probing. I stood speechless a few seconds and stared at those eyes, and spoke the thought that flashed into my mind: 'I wouldn't like to have you as an enemy.' Then his eyes and his whole body seemed to blaze, and I thought instinctively of the troll in the fairy tale who pops out of his hole and roars: 'Who is chopping trees in *my* forest?' "

He was a man *mjök trollaukinn,* with "augmented inhumanity" as one ludicrous translation has it. He wrote:

> To live is to war with trolls in heart and soul.
> To write is to sit in judgement on oneself.

Division and self-division. The trolls ensconced in the blood and under the pelt of the human creature; the writer, watching himself, summing up, delivering judgement. He wrote surrounded by a swarm of red-tongued gutta-percha trolls. "There must be troll in what I write," he said. His monstrous troll came out only *in extremis,* when things were impossibly difficult. "Then I lock my door and bring him out. No other human eye has seen him, not even my wife . . . He is a bear, playing the violin, and beating time with his feet."

So there he was, man and troll, badger and bear, black integument and lined parchment sac containing blood, bones, and busy creatures, proceeding towards the Grand Hotel, in Christiania, in Norway, which he did not want to think was home. "Up here among the fjords I have my native land. But-but-but: where do I find my homeland?" "Ten years ago, after my second absence of ten years, when I sailed up the fjord, I literally felt my chest contract with revulsion and a feeling of sickness. I felt the same during my whole stay; I was no longer myself among all these cold and uncomprehending Norwegian eyes in the windows and on the pavements." In the South, he thought of the North.

He turned his ship's
Prow from the north,
Seeking the trail
Of brighter gods.

The snow-land's beacons
Quenched in the sea.
The fauns of the seashore
Stilled his longing.

He burned his ships.
Blue smoke drifted
Like a bridge's span
Towards the north.

To those snow-capped huts
From the hills of the south
There rides a rider
Every night.

He was a northerner who went south for light, for distance, in order to see the north, in light, from a distance. He
crossed the Alps on May 9th 1864. On April 1, 1898, in
Copenhagen, he spoke of the transition.

"Over the high mountains the clouds hung like great,
dark curtains, and beneath these we drove through the tunnel and, suddenly, found ourselves at Mira Mara, where that
marvellously bright light which is the beauty of the south
suddenly revealed itself to me, gleaming like white marble. It
was to affect all my later work, even if the content thereof

was not always beautiful." He had "a feeling of being released from the darkness into light, emerging from mists through a tunnel into the sunshine."

He was, or had been, a narrow northern Puritan. He was shocked, and then exhilarated, by the excess of energy of Michelangelo and Bernini. "Those fellows had the courage to commit a madness now and then." The Norwegians, he recalled contemptuously, "speak with intense complacency of our Norwegian 'good sense,' which really means nothing but a tepidity of spirit which makes it impossible for those honest souls to commit a madness."

It was his great desire to commit a madness like Michelangelo. Was it for fear of tepidity and dim light only that he fled Norway? Was there a madness, already committed, working away like yeast in the Norwegian small beer of his past, ready to explode the bottle? As a letter-writer, he was inhibited, crabbed, tortuously formal, uncommunicative. After leaving his home town, he never returned there, though on the occasion of his mother's death he wrote a stilted letter to his sister Hedvig, saying that he was just setting off for Egypt, but would like to receive letters. Later, he wrote to his father, who did not preserve the letter, but sent a reply, which was preserved, in which he said, "I tried to read your letter, but I couldn't understand it, I felt ashamed . . ."

It is doubly difficult for a famous man, once returned to his native land, not to make a pious pilgrimage to the place of his birth. Spectators of the public life are interested in its beginnings, in the source. It is patently untrue to claim that he himself was indifferent or uninterested. In 1881 he began an autobiography, rapidly abandoned, expressing surprise that a street had been renamed for him. "Or so at any rate the newspapers have reported, and I have also heard it from reliable travellers." He recorded a grim town—"nothing green; no rural, open landscape"—full of the sound of weirs and, penetrating the watery roar, "from morning to dusk, something resembling the sharp cries of women, now shrieking, now moaning. It was the hundreds of sawblades at work on the weirs. When later I read of the guillotine, I thought of those sawblades." In the tall church, raised by a Copenhagen master builder, the child was exposed, by his nursemaid, sitting in the open window of the tower, high, high up. The unexpected sight of him there caused his mother to scream and faint. In the church, too, lived a demonic black poodle with fiery red eyes, the sight of which, at that same window, had shocked a watchman into falling to his death, bursting open his head in the square below. "I felt that the window belonged to me and the church poodle," he wrote. Then he gave up his autobiographical enterprise. It clearly never tempted him into revisiting those scenes. Something forbade him. He stayed away.

Sometimes he described how he set his characters in motion. How, one may ask, does such a man set about constructing another human being, in some sense *ex nihilo*, an individual who was not there before, and now exists, but whose very identity must leave space for the creative puppet-mastery of a director, the defining touches of a costumier and a *maquilleuse*, the deliberate accidents of directed light-rays and non-functional, even painted, cloth, chairs and tables? Above all, how does he make such a person "real," whatever that is, and yet leave that "reality" sketched and incomplete, to be fleshed out, to be wormed into, to bulge and sag around the unimagined, unaccommodating perhaps, body, voice—and history, and soul, and human limitations—of an actor? And not even one, definitive, magisterial actor, but a succession of these too fleshy ghosts each filling out different pouches and pockets? How could he collaborate, in his work of imagination, with these unknown helpers or opponents?

Such descriptions as he left of this process—few, as always, fewer than one might reasonably hope or expect— are disappointing in this regard. They could have been written by a novelist, or even—stretching the imagination a little—by a biographer. There is perhaps a little more emphasis on the body and the voice, but this is scratching for grains in sand. In a way, his accounts are platitudes, multiplied in other records of other observers. Nevertheless, the precise form of his platitudes, his own platitudes, cannot be without interest; we should, if everything were accessible to know, be interested also in the precise combination of flora in his intestine, or layered convolutions in his brain. Do we have instruments for dissecting platitudes finely enough to yield precise local truths?

"Before I write one word," runs this rare confidence, then, "I must know the character through and through, I must penetrate into the last wrinkle of his soul. I always proceed from the individual; the staging, the dramatic ensemble, all that comes naturally and causes me no worry, as soon as I am certain of the individual in every aspect of his humanity. But I have to have his exterior in mind also, down to the last button, how he stands and walks, how he carries himself, what his voice sounds like. Then I do not let him go until his fate is fulfilled."

Now we may ask—must ask, indeed, since it appears pointless to raise hypothetical theoretical barriers against such a profound and natural human curiosity—where these imagined humans come from? As we shall see, he compares them, ingeniously or disingenuously, to strangers met on a train. He observed those he met on trains, as a naturalist observes new and familiar species. With an overtone of moral judgement, added to pure observation. He is on record as having driven himself into rage and hatred over some unknown fellow-traveller, a woman, who slept in his railway-compartment all the way from Rome to Gossensass, without once looking out of the window. "What a *lazy* woman! To sleep the whole way! How can anyone be so *lazy*? . . . Most people die without ever having lived. Luckily for them, they don't realise it."

But the people he, to use a primitive phrase, "made up" must in some sense be not only watched strangers but spun from his own fabric, sensed inside his own stance, seen through one or the other of those terrible disparate eyes?

"As a rule, I make three drafts of my plays, which differ greatly from each other—in characterisation, not in plot. When I approach the first working-out of my material, it is as though I knew my characters from a railway-journey. One has made a preliminary acquaintance, one has chatted about this and that. At the next draft I already see everything much more clearly, and I know the people roughly as one would after a month spent with them at a spa; I have discovered the fundamentals of their characters and their little peculiarities;

but I may still be wrong about certain essentials. Finally, in my last draft I have reached the limit of my knowledge; I know my characters from close and long acquaintance— they are my intimate friends, who will no longer disappoint me; as I see them now, I shall always see them."

He took things from others, certainly. A very young woman sent him, in Dresden, a sequel to his dramatic poem *Brand,* which she had called *Brand's Daughters.* She called it a religious book. He called it a novel. He bothered, unusually, to give her advice. He liked very young women. He enjoyed their admiration. Something more than talent is required, he told her. "One must have something to create from, some life experience . . . Now I know very well that a life in solitude is not a life devoid of experiences. But the human being is in the spiritual sense a long-sighted creature. We see most clearly at a distance; details confuse us; we must get away from what we desire to judge; summer is best described on a winter day."

Light like white marble, remembered amongst crisp snow under steel skies.

Later he appropriated the same young woman's confusion and folly to construct his doll-wife in his dolls' house; she too had borrowed to pay for her sick husband's travel, she too had forged a cheque. Nora arouses the sympathy of millions. Laura, whose acts were stolen, had periods of madness and shame. He did not choose to make, or keep, friends.

"Friends are an expensive luxury; and when one sinks all one's capital in a vocation and a mission in life, then one cannot afford to have friends. The extravagance of keeping friends lies not in what one does for them, but what, out of consideration for them, one omits to do. On that account, many intellectual shoots are crippled in oneself. I have gone through this, and on that account, I have several years behind me, in which I did not succeed in being myself."

The rigid gnome progressing towards his public table, his brandy-glass, his reserved, non-domestic space, was obsessed with the idea of being himself. He was so very sure, it appeared, that he had a true self to be, despite the dissipation of his appearances in portrait-busts and newspaper jokes. This self depended on the firm construction of frontiers between its consciousness of what it was, and the encroachments, tender, tentacular, boring (in both senses) above all maybe, *judging*, of others. Or maybe it was that he did not want to be, or at the very least did not want to have to see, the mask of the idea others constructed of him, as he, behind his ice-window, through his long-sighted lens, constructed them? Or maybe he did not want to have to be at all? Maybe this so-dreadfully desired, so elaborated real self was an absence of self, a freely-moving, flickering flame of knowledge and language, which should not be forced, or frozen, into any of the gestures required by the social touches and approaches through which most people discover themselves through others?

"I know that I have the failing of not coming close to those people who want to open up completely. I can never bring myself to bare myself. I have a feeling that all I have available in personal relations is a false expression of that which I bear deep within me, and which is really myself; therefore I prefer to keep it locked up inside, and that is why we sometimes seem to stand as if we were observing each other at a distance."

And yet, the paradox. This man made his art precisely

out of those communal motions, bodily touches, meetings of eyeballs, that as a man he could not bear. And he saw this form as another, a different (yet the same) threat to this "real self" so that he could write, excusing his inability to write letters at the end of his life.

"I am almost afraid that I have struggled so long and so hard with the form of the drama, in which to a certain extent it is necessary for the author to kill and drown his own personality, or at any rate hide it, that I may have lost a great deal of what I myself prize most highly in a writer of letters . . ."

Kill, drown. Strong, violent verbs. There was another. Petrification. Trolls turn to stone in the light of day, and monuments are public marble with empty eyes. So the effigy stepped precisely onwards, checking the time on his watch and chain. Blood had gone out of his veins, and liquid stone silted them, he told himself.

Scene: The Grand Hotel. *Various gentlemen, including Edvard Munch, the painter, are sitting at various café tables, in a wintry light. An inner room, at the right, contains a solitary table, behind which a man is sitting, his face and body obscured by a newspaper he is holding up. There is a feeling of expectancy. The gentlemen at the tables are also provided with newspapers, behind which they hide, looking out with suppressed excitement, from time to time. The Strange Customer, by contrast, is unmoving. His newspaper does not rustle.*

HI enters, far L. He closes the door behind him. It is snowing outside. He checks his watch, which is old and battered, and takes a small mirror from the crown of his silk hat; he combs his hair, and returns the mirror. He steps in a straight line between the tables, looking at no one.

MUNCH: I'd watch it, if I were you. He doesn't like company. I once invited him to join us, and he was quite rude to me.

HI: [*Hesitates briefly, frowning. Then he turns back to his path. Faces flicker round newspapers.*]

MUNCH: *Tvertimod.* On the other hand. You do as you please.

HI: [*Walks slightly more slowly, into the alcove.*]
I believe you cannot be unaware that that seat, sir, is mine. Reserved for me. Every day, without fail. They have even done me the honour of engraving my name on a small brass plate, which you will find behind your shoulders.

The Strange Customer slowly lowers the paper. He leans back in the chair and stares at HI. There is an open bottle of brandywine and two glasses in front of him. He is wearing identical clothes, down to the row of miniature medals. He has the same thick white whiskers, bushy white hair, jutting brow. HI stops dead.

STRANGE CUSTOMER: You didn't expect me.

HI: I don't know you.

STRANGE CUSTOMER: Oh, I think you do. I have my papers, they make it clear. I never go anywhere without my papers. They say who I am, who my parents are, where I don't belong.

HI: I see the waxwork man wheedled my suit out of someone. I'll thank you for returning it. It is not worn out.

STRANGE CUSTOMER: There's no copyright in second-best suits. Your wife gave it to a beggar. I was that beggar. She didn't recognise me. Just saw a generic pauper. All the same, I think you'll agree, I have the family face. Comb the hair a bit, beg a clean shirt.

[*He too takes a little mirror out of his hat, and combs his whiskers.*]

HI: I don't know you. I shall ask the manager to have you turned out.

STRANGE CUSTOMER: You don't know me?

Can't you tell the pig by its skin?
Where are your eyes? Can't you see I'm crippled
The way you're crippled, in my soul?

Those are my mother's lines. She can't speak them, because she's dead. I expect you didn't know that. She died blind and a pauper. She never spoke ill of you. Indeed, she said you were irresistible. I have my papers. Do you want to see them?

[*He puts them on the table. HI makes no move to pick them up. The Strange Customer drinks down a glass of brandy-wine, and pours two new ones. He offers HI one, with a gesture. HI remains rigid.*]

You're afraid of me, aren't you? You haven't much courage. You ran away from Rikke Holst's father, on the beach, when he threatened you with a cudgel. She was only fifteen. Everyone knows *that* story. You're afraid of heights. You're afraid of shadows. You're afraid of your poor old Dad and you're afraid of Norway and us crude, quarrelsome Norwegians. But most of all, you're afraid of me. You're afraid of ghosts, walking out of the dark, mopping and mowing at you out of mirrors and firelight. I've read every word you've written, several times. It's all soaked in the sweat of your fear, written with the sour ink of your cringing terror. Of me. Of my trollsnout which is so very recognisably *your* trollsnout, don't you think? Now you see me, you see the likeness. He's a fine figure, your son Sigurd, my little brother—

HI: I forbid you to speak of him!

HENRIKSEN: I was going to say only, he doesn't resemble your secret self, old man, as *I* do.

HI: Nobody resembles a man's secret self. Do you not know, you can walk the whole earth and never find two identical faces?

HENRIKSEN: Or two identical onions? But you can peel them all, layer after layer, down to the centre, down to the juicy quick, and, just as you tear into that, and the last bit of onion-juice stains your fingers, they resemble each other—*enough.*

HI: You have made quite a study of my work.

HENRIKSEN: Oh, I know it by heart. It is pumped in and out of my degenerate heart, along with the gemmules that carry the pith of you through the pith of me. I am tainted with poetry in my heart-juices. As Oswald's brain and his spinal cord were full of the animalculae that swam out of his father.

HI: Your metaphors overreach themselves.

HENRIKSEN: Oh yes? And who wished to go too far—like Michelangelo, like Bernini? We are not respectable Norwegians, neither of us. We have troll-blood in our veins, we are *trollaukinn.* You brought *him* up safe from that knowledge—

HI: You are wrong. And I told you not to mention him.

HENRIKSEN: All your people. All your little imps, all the half-selves you play with, shut away in your room—they have trollsnouts, like you and me. They are like marble busts, but underneath the lovely white surface—so still, so gleaming, so subtle, lurk a pompous horse-face, an obstinate mule, a daft dog, a gross bull, or a sycophant grinning dog.

HI: A farmyard, in fact.

HENRIKSEN: All the poor beasts we men use and pervert, and misshape by breeding for fat and docility. All the poor beasts whose nature the old Lapp wizards knew that we shared intimately. All the things with fur and tails and claws and fangs that fell on Peer Gynt in his trollfather's cavern. Do you know, I have often thought that this very place where I sit—this inner temple, set apart for one who is no mere mortal—is a troll-cavern. Or maybe a loft, where a man may commune with his residual wildness. In the form of a duck, perhaps. Do you remember the old loft where you and your sister Hedvig played at being wild things, owl and eagle, grey mouse and fire-eyed cat, magic swans, white horses and running wolves? You took her, too, very gently, but you took her, and shot her, and stuffed her, and put her on show.

HI: Are you pretending to be my conscience?

HENRIKSEN: And who would have a better right? No, no. I am not the thin person, nor the button-moulder, I'm not interested in judgement. [*He laughs.*] I am the Great Boyg. I am myself. I force you to go round. And round. And round. I am everywhere you look. It would have been better for Peer Gynt to go straight onwards, don't you think? Even to *touch* the nasty thing. Not dead. Not alive. Slimy. Misty. Won't you sit down in our cavern, and drink a glass of your brandywine? It has to be *your* brandywine, because I haven't got a penny to pay for it.

HI: [*Comes forward, sits down, and takes a glass.*] I like the image of the marble busts with the beast faces. That's worthy of being one of mine.

HENRIKSEN: Please, feel free to adapt it.

HI: As you say, poets are thieves. The one thing I never thought you would be—O Boyg—is an intelligent reader.

HENRIKSEN: *Hypocrite lecteur. Mon semblable, mon frère.*

HI: I will concede, I have been afraid of you. I knew you walked the earth, somewhere. Somewhere up there, in the cold. I imagined you with great burning scarlet eyes and a black curly pelt—

HENRIKSEN: The church poodle?

HI: I was only sixteen.

HENRIKSEN: She was only a poor young servant-woman. And generous, to a fault.

HI: You can't know that. You weren't born.

[*Both laugh, and drink brandywine. Henriksen calls for another bottle. Ibsen purses his thin lips.*]

HI: I have heard you were a drunkard.

HENRIKSEN: And I have heard of you being carried shouting through the streets of Munich, quite incapable. And Dresden. And Rome. I have heard of you taunting chained dogs in Ischia, as though they were demons. Malevolent demons, with red eyes and black pelts.

HI: You must have had something else to do with your life. Other than picking up facts, and exaggerations, and naughty tales about a man who doesn't know you.

HENRIKSEN: Oh yes. I have had things to do. I will tell you what I have done, since curiosity has gone only one way in this matter. I have been a smith, in a forge, pumping the flames with the great bellows. You would have recognised me well enough, in *that* shape, with my great leather apron, and my hammer, like Thor of old. I am also a skilled fiddle-maker. The devil has all the best tunes. I blow the flames, I drive on the dancers. My first wife was a quiet soul, with a light burning in her that consumed her quick enough. She had lovely hair and lovely breasts but she turned into a bundle of hot dry sticks and died choking. We lost our lovely boy, Jens, too, to a fever. He had a face like an angel. With the old trollsnout poking through, of course, all the same. Then I married Trina Marie—she liked me. I needed to be liked, and there was another little one, Björn, who took the smallpox from her. Both gone. I followed them to the churchyard. He lay in her arms, on her breast. The flames had gone out of the pockmarks, they were

108

like scuffed marble, my little dead family. Now I am married to Ida. People call her Fru Ibsen, she's so proud. Haunches like a drayhorse, my good Ida, a child-bearing woman. We have five, five little Ibsens, with your eyes, old man, and your stubby fingers, and one with your thin lips. Three in the churchyard, with the soft skin rotted off the sweet skulls, which are still constructed like your mighty brainpan. (I know about that too.) Two sickly girls left to us. Have you never once thought, in all those years, of all this swarming life that came out of an act of yours when you were a boy of sixteen? I have buried five of your grandchildren, Henrik Ibsen, and wept for each one. Have you never thought of them? [*He weeps.*]

HI: No. You are drunk.

HENRIKSEN: They are your grandchildren. I have my papers to prove it.

HI: You are weeping because you are drunk, you are drunk.

HENRIKSEN: So you know one thing about me. I wrote a poem, you know, for the Lillesand Temperance Society. But I don't find good metaphors when I'm sober. I lack courage. I inherited a certain timidity.

[*He weeps.*]

HI: I despise drunks. Including myself, from time to time.

HENRIKSEN: It is good for a man to invite his ghosts into his warm interior, out of the wild night, into the firelight, out of the howling dark. A man should meet his ghosts fearlessly, and embrace them.

HI: And what, on this cold earth, would a man gain by that?

HENRIKSEN: Rest for his soul. Healed sores. Friendliness, calm.

HI: And why should a man want those things? At the price of kissing all those cold lips, of sitting in the stink of brandywine and the splash of maudlin tears? Come, Hans Jacob Henriksen, my son, you know me better than that. I am going to say to you what I was always going to say to you when we should meet, the lines I had written for myself, the old curmudgeon, when you asked me for money, as I supposed you would. I am going to insult you, and we are going to part.

HENRIKSEN: I don't see why. And I really could do with some money, I do have to admit, my children are sick, my wife is hungry . . .

HI: If you don't see why, you aren't my son. There lies the catch. If you are my son, you know how a man must walk his cold road alone, with the imaginary imps and the troll-shapes and the Great Boyg in the darkness behind him, where he likes to imagine them, but doesn't too much like to take a good, direct look. And no, the line I was going to say was not "Get thee behind me." It is a good line. I've had it prepared, for this eventuality.

HENRIKSEN: Can't you just take my hand?

HI: No. Here is some money. Take it or leave it. It

goes with the line, "I gave this much to your mother. It ought to be enough for you."

HENRIKSEN: [*Picks up the money, weeping.*]

HI: You see? You are a drunk. And I am the demon. Now, go home. I am going home. I don't expect to see you in my chair again.

HENRIKSEN: *(weakly defiant)* You never know.

HI: You can't repeat a scene like this. I was always particularly good at last acts.

Take your money, my son, and go home.

I wasn't sure what to make of these three odd pieces of writing. I found them both intriguing and irritating. The irritating aspect—well, the *most* irritating, there were others—was the air of perfunctory secrecy or deception about the whole enterprise. What was the point of withholding the identification of the protagonists (if that was what they were) for so long? I had no trouble identifying Ibsen, even before his name crept in at the end. There are not so very many great Norwegian dramatists with white whiskers. I also had little trouble with Carl Linnaeus, since if you look up *Linnaea Borealis* or *Systema Naturae* in any decent encyclopaedia you find potted biographies of the great taxonomist with no trouble. I took longer sorting out Francis Galton, grandson of Erasmus Darwin, cousin of Charles Darwin, now forgotten because the idea he believed to be his great contribution to humanity— the idea of eugenics, as a statistical, scientific, progressive, political and ethical way of life—is regarded with horror by all right-thinking men after what the National Socialists made of it. I discovered that there still exists a Galton Professor of Human Genetics. I discovered, in fact, all sorts of leads about all three heroes of these fragmentary narratives—no doubt, at some point in *this* narrative, I shall find myself impelled to reveal some of these discoveries. Nobody likes keeping discoveries to himself. But my project was not to start projects of research into Linnaeus, Galton and Ibsen. My project was to discover, to come to grips with, Scholes Destry-Scholes. I had now read three unpublished pieces by him. In a sense I knew a lot more about him than I had. And in another sense, I knew nothing at all.

I could start work on Ibsen, Galton and Linnaeus, as I had worked on the movements and preoccupations of Sir Elmer Bole. There were tiny factual connections, which might lead directly to Destry-Scholes. Linnaeus had visited the Maelstrøm. Destry-Scholes's letters to his publishers asking about grants to go to South Africa may have been to do with Galton's youthful trek into Ovampoland. Or I could do a semiotic analysis of those teasing half-concealments, in an attempt to reconstruct the man who invented them. There were also odd moments where the professional biographer revealed his own preoccupations. I might track him through his unconscious (or conscious) assumptions. Even that became almost immediately almost impossible. For one thing, a semiotic analysis shows only the choice of available sign systems, from the culture in which the signs were made—in Destry-Scholes's case, a 1950s prestructuralist culture. A semiotic analysis is not an instrument designed to discover a singular individual. Indeed, it assumes that there is no such thing. It could be argued (a dreadful phrase I find myself using, still, *in extremis,* when I want to hedge or hide or prevaricate)—it could be argued that Destry-Scholes himself, in evading the identification of his "characters" for so long, was intending to show that identity, that the self, is a dubious matter, not of the first consequence.

It could equally be argued that he made such a to-do about it because the identity of his people *was* of consequence, because the events he narrated only made sense if the narration concerned these people precisely, and no others.

I found myself, ludicrously, reacting as if Destry-Scholes had put together the three faded blue carbons under the hanging folders in the Lincoln University archive, in order to baffle and intrigue me, me personally, Phineas G. Nanson. All this writing was a conundrum bequeathed by him to me.

I wasn't born, when he drowned, if he did drown.

It has been dinned into me that objectivity is an exploded and deconstructed notion. But subjectivity—the meeting of two hypothetical subjects, in this case Scholes Destry-Scholes and myself—is just as suspect, since it can't be looked at objectively.

A drowned, or possibly drowned, biographer, in 1965, could have had no conceivable reader in mind for this limp cache of unbegun and unended stories.

I also could not help thinking about the three stories, or parts of stories, as though, taken together, they were all part of some larger work in progress. They presented a single problem to me; it was very tempting to turn them into a singular object. They had intriguing, pointless symmetries. The appearance, early on in the Galton and Linnaeus tales, of jawbones and teeth. Animals. Magic. There appeared to be a real, urgent voice in the storytelling when the narrator got on to magic, in all three cases.

I have always been intrigued by those very large advertising installations, which show you an image, made up of a series of vertical stripes, for a calculated number of minutes, and then flick, or revolve, the stripes, to constitute (to reveal) a quite other image. So there may be a silver car on a snowy mountaintop, which can flicker, in its orderly way, into a soft-drinks bottle full of rising bubbles, which in turn can become a pair of huge breasts in a black lace brassière. Between scene-shifts, or metamorphoses, there is an illusion that the vanishing vision is partly obscured by bars of smoky steel and then time's revolution brings in the car, the bubbles, the breasts, also briefly barred.

I had the fanciful idea that the three personages were like stripes or bars behind which lurked the figure of Destry-Scholes. There is a sense, also, in which those things remind one of Venetian blinds, though they do not work on the same principle. I wasn't clear whether I thought that Destry-Scholes was the grey shadow, or metal, which connected all the bright pictures, or whether he was the brightly painted surface of the blind, through the interstices of which the empty sky—grey, or blue, or even roseate as it might be—could be glimpsed in orderly strips. The image doesn't really work, though it leaves the residual pleasure of the idea of a beast behind bars who is simultaneously the gaps in a flat screen. I should never have made a real writer; I can't think my images through. This one connected to the rather moving idea—imposed, as far as I could see, by Destry-Scholes upon Ibsen—of the famous man walking the streets behind a pasteboard mask of himself. (Maybe the idea was Ibsen's, quoted by Destry-Scholes—he seemed to work like that.) It is partly because of this idea of masks and effigies that I have taken to thinking of the "three" as *personages*. The other, more urgent reason, is because "personage" is not, as far as I know, a literary critical term in current use or abuse. (I can't call them "characters," or "persons," or "men.")

Another way of looking at those billboards is to think of them as the picture bricks we all had as kids. If you get the right sides of the cubes facing out in your tower, suddenly you have four pictures. A grenadier, a clown, a dragon, a magician. Three personages, and Destry-Scholes.

But if he was *in* the picture, the construction-work became not his, but someone else's, mine. And the last thing I have any interest in writing—I mean this—is an autobiography.

I am interested in Scholes Destry-Scholes because he was interested in Elmer Bole, because he wanted to find out *facts* about Elmer Bole. I am not interested in myself. It was difficult being a literary schoolchild—I was often nearly put off what turned out to be my vocation by the urgings of pedagogues who assured me I would "discover myself" by reading, that I would "understand myself" by "identifying" with— well, whom? Robin Hood? Hamlet? Gregor Samsa? Prince Myshkin? No, no, the true literary fanatic, the primeval reader, is looking for anything but a mirror—for an escape route, for an expanding horizon, for receding starscapes, for unimaginable monstrosities and incomprehensible (strictly) beauties. Also for meaning, for making sense of things, always with the proviso that complete sense cannot probably be made because of the restrictions of small things like death, and the configuration of the folds of our electrically charged, insensible grey matter. I got into post-structuralism out of a true intellectual passion for coherence and meanings. I am trying to record the events which followed my decision to give up that way of looking at things, as an intellectual ordering of this search for meaning. I am not writing an autobiography. I am writing in the first person for the sake of precision, because this procedure allows me to say certain things I am reasonably sure of. I have once or twice started a sentence in this last paragraph or two with a more or less automatic address to an imaginary reader. "Have you noticed those billboards . . ." I wrote, and crossed it out. Worse, I ascribed opinions to this person. "You might think everyone has to be interested in himself," I wrote, and scratched it out. Who is this "you"? No one. Or me, and I know what I think, I think.

I was for this reason very interested in Destry-Scholes's presentation of Ibsen's paring-away of his human relations in search of his Self. It seems likely to me that if I had been born into an earlier generation I might have had to have some idea of my Self, might have had a go at the Nanson onion, or the Nanson king of infinite space bounded in a nutshell. I do exist on the earth, and would like to be of some use, and find a meaning or two. (*The* meaning is beyond all of us.)

I am not very good at finding out who Scholes Destry-Scholes was because I am not very interested in finding out who I am.

He, on the other hand, was very good at finding out other personages, but left no tracks of who he was. Because of not knowing who he was? Or not choosing that anyone else should? Or am I just the wrong, incompetent, seeker?

If I were to write about myself, where would I start? Arbitrarily, let me decide, with my socks. Socks are a fact. Mine are not new, and all have matted patches under the ball of the metatarsal joint, which in my case is protuberant. Unlike many people I know, I don't have lots of odd socks, because I take them off and roll them immediately into a single ball, which I put in the laundry-bag until I empty that into the launderette, and I repeat this process before leaving the launderette. It is nonsense to say you always have odd socks. This reads like a bit of Beckett, not like an autobiography. It is a fact, but it has a displaced, odd, surreal look. What colour are the socks? Most are stained navy. Some were once white but couldn't now be said to be white; they are white with dust and earth strained repeatedly through them. I have two pairs with red white and blue (thin) stripes above the white/earthy necks (is that the right word? If a sock doesn't have a neck, like a womb or a bottle, what *does* it have?). Red, white and blue is a surprisingly frequent combination in national flags, something I've never understood, since I find it neither striking nor beautiful. Yellow, red and blue would be better, but only children's socks, or very expensive socks, are those colours, and not many flags. I suppose if I offered this paragraph to a psychoanalyst as an example of free association, he/she would say it was *evasive*, but the truth is that I am more interested in things like *why* choose red, white and blue than in my own feet (or psyche), and what I have learned from this paragraph is that writing down one fact leads to another unrelated fact (socks, national flags) and this is restorative to the baffled minds of despondent researchers.

I could go on to some other aspect of my daily life. Bookshelves, for instance, except that those could be seen as a portrait, a taxonomy of the mind. The truth is I began to feel very despondent. I had no idea where to go next. I did have a strong urge to follow up all the clues in the three documents, to pursue Linnaeus, Galton and Ibsen jointly or severally, as I had tracked Destry-Scholes through the life and works of Elmer Bole. But where would it stop? Linnaeus would lead to Swedenborg, Galton to Darwin, Ibsen to Strindberg or Shaw, and I would run like a ferret from library to library, shelf to shelf. There is no end to the pursuit of knowledge, no limit, no bound (socks, washeterias, seraglios, shamans, beehives, apparitions, overcoats, mosaics, starry skies . . .). Also my income was diminishing, as were my human contacts, and for the same reason—I had lost my few teaching assignments with my change of thesis and director. And I had no knowledge of Ormerod Goode's research field, the Anglo-Saxon place-names, the ancient Icelandic myths. I took the typescripts about the three personages to Goode, however. I had told him a little about my search through the life and works of Bole. He had not really offered much of a comment. Indeed, he seemed faintly detached, as though his expectations of my project were diminishing.

He turned over the three part-manuscripts. I described them as he did so, identifying L, G and HI for him. "Quite, quite," he said, not looking up, as though there was no problem about this. I said that I was further forward, in that I knew something, and no further forward, in that I did not know where to look next. He had not offered me a drink at all, on this occasion. He said, still sifting Destry-Scholes's papers,

"I see. A taxonomist, a statistician, a button-moulder."

He added, "I thought of writing on Ibsen myself, at one point. His use of the folk tale. I was deflected."

I said that I did not see what to do next.

He agreed that it was difficult to see what to do next.

I said I could clearly look into these three lives, but where would that lead?

He said, "Have you got a life yourself, Nanson? What do you do with your *spare* time."

It looked as though it was all spare, I replied, evading the question, which he had no right to ask.

"You don't look well," he said, though I had not been aware of him looking directly *at* me throughout this encounter. "You look peaked. You should take a holiday, perhaps. Get away from all this for a break. Go hiking, perhaps, or take a train, or a boat, to somewhere else. With a friend."

I said that I had insufficient means to go anywhere at all. Especially since I had lost my teaching.

There was something to be said, said Ormerod Goode, for a part-time job, if one could be found. "Personally I have never objected to a little manual labour," he said, not making it clear whether he meant for himself or for his students. "Puts things in perspective," he said, vaguely. I chose to believe he was saying I was a failure. I said I would think about it, and rose to leave. He looked at me, then.

"There is something shifty about all that shamanistic stuff in the Linnaeus document," he said. "Something decidedly shifty."

"Shifty?" I repeated.

"If you look into it," he said, "I think you'll find that that's so. But I don't know that you will be much the wiser."

I was perhaps stung by this last remark into making a decision to visit the Linnean Society. I had noticed its existence once or twice already, on my way to exhibitions in the Royal Academy. It has a secret-looking door *inside* the arch of the Palladian grandeur of Burlington House. I telephoned, and asked if the Society's collections were open to the general public. By appointment, I was told. Use of the Society's library was also available by appointment. Linnaeus's own collections were held in an atmospherically controlled strongroom, but someone would be happy to show them to me. His collections? I asked. The Society was founded in 1788 when the collections were purchased, after Linnaeus's death, by James Edward Smith, who became its first President. It moved the collections to Burlington House in 1857. Many of Linnaeus's specimens had been destroyed or dispersed, but what was left was substantial. What was I particularly interested in? The fish, the insects, the library? As I thanked the courteous voice on my telephone, it came to me, I remember, that this would be my first contact with *things*. Not Destry-Scholes's things, but *things*, nevertheless. I felt a thrill in my fingertips.

I set out on foot from King's Cross, where I lived, to Piccadilly. I was watching my pennies, which was increasingly necessary, and getting some exercise, both. Keeping fit is a major problem for sedentary scholars. Ormerod Goode was right that I was "peaked." An odd word. I wondered what its derivation was. The post-structuralist I had been would have taken pleasure in a pun—Goode had perceived, without looking, that I was piqued by his lack of interest, by his non-offer of a drink. I looked up "peaked" in the *OED*. I have one I bought in a sale, which is compact, that is one volume, but very large and cumbersome, and can be read with a lens which has its own little light that makes an island of a word in a sea of invisibly tiny print. I have to read it crouched over it, on the floor. "Peaked," to my disappointment, had no etymological source, but was said to be colloquially derived from "peaked," meaning the point, or summit, of a mountain, or hill, thus a face sharpened or thinned by illness or malnutrition. I do have a sharp face. It is a word I would apply to it. I also think it is a word Goode would apply, being a place-names man with a prejudice in favour of the Anglo-Saxon. I believe, though, I did look *peaked,* not only because I am naturally thin and sharp. It is difficult, in view of all the subsequent events, to remember clearly the sense of aimless desolation with which I set out to walk to Piccadilly. Aimless is the wrong word. I had *too many aims,* towards all points of the compass, including the entirely arbitrary one of Piccadilly.

Desolation, however, is not the wrong word.

I was in one of those little streets around Bond Street when I saw the Maelstrøm. It was in the window—narrow but deep—of a small shop which advertised itself, in sky-blue lettering on pine green, as Puck's Girdle. The Maelstrøm was made of a kind of bravura and exaggerated origami, a funnel of scissored and foaming navy-blue paper with spiring silver coils and feathery snipped and streaming froth. It was suspended on nylon thread in a slight current of air, and swayed in a gyre. Balancing it on the other side of the window was a creamy paper replica of the Alhambra, with delicate windows and tracery, colonnades and courtyards. In the middle was a small jungle, a paper rainforest with a parrot or two, some golden frogs, several winding paper snakes and receding jungle paths under the canopy like a set for a children's theatre. Whoever was good with the scissors was good with lettering. They had scattered shadowy grey bird-like words over the top half of the glass. GET AWAY. LOOK FORWARD TO. GO OUTWARD. CLIMB. DREAM. LOOK. LISTEN. SUN. RAIN. WIND. ICE. WATER. FLY. FLOAT. HURTLE. PERIPLUM.

I liked hurtle. I liked periplum.

The floor of the window was deep in small things. Pebbles, little lamps, glass bottles, feather butterflies, wax fruit, winding ribbons of sand, snowflake crystals in plastic.

I stared. The only conventional poster said, "This is not a bucket shop. We sell solid pleasure at reasonable prices."

There was another notice, handwritten.

"Part-time person wanted, frankly as a dogsbody. With possibility (eventually) of travel."

Naïve critics are accustomed to saying that life is random, things do not turn out, or present themselves, in life with the glittering appositeness and fated inevitability that they do in literature. Everyday experience contradicts this silly wisdom every day.

I went in.

Inside was also decorated in the very agreeable mixture of sky-blue and pine-green, with touches of a paler, apple-green, and a ceiling studded with little halogen lights like stars, on a midnight ground. The counter was a crescent moon, behind which, one at each end, were two men, one large and blond, one slight and dark. They both wore oil-coloured seamen's sweaters, wide-necked and cable-stitched. They both wore

124

large, round spectacles, with frames in that iridescent multi-striped light-weight metal (is it titanium?) that is fashionable in Sweden. They asked simultaneously if they could help me. I said I was interested in being a part-time dogsbody. If the job was still available.

They said, again simultaneously, that the notice had only just been put in the window. They introduced themselves as Erik and Christophe. "We sell odd holidays," said Erik. "Literary holidays—the golden road to Samarkand, haunts of the Lorelei, Treasure Islands. Brontës' Brussels. Anywhere that isn't a Heritage site. The battlefields of the Hundred Years War. Green Hells. And so on. Sometimes we employ individual guides for little groups, but the dogsbody we want would only be required to play around in here with a computer and a filing cabinet."

I said I had been drawn in by their window. By the origami Maelstrøm, by hurtle and periplum.

"That's good," said Christophe, the thin one. "Our *favourite* customers are tempted by words and images. We do have a vulgar brochure or two of beach umbrellas and pedalos for those who have an aesthetic taste for the banal. We have a Fourieriste ambition to cater to all tastes. I had the idea, speaking of Fourier, of a world tour of nineteenth-century glassed-over shopping arcades . . ."

I said it was unlikely in the extreme that they would have an applicant dogsbody who had read Fourier, and his dreamed phalansteries under glass arcades, but that I did happen to have done so.

They had a mild look, of satisfied pleasure, which they shared with each other. I thought they were almost certainly a couple, from the way they looked at one another. I had—for almost the first time in my life—the sense that if I said what came into my head it would be the right, not the wrong, thing. I said I had come in because I had been reading various accounts of the Maelstrøm and had been attracted by the cutout. Also, as I had said, by the words, by hurtle and periplum. I supposed, I said, that they risked disappointment in clients seduced by words and images. Not really, said Erik. People who live amongst words and images take them around with them like baggage. He asked if I had ever been to the Cimetière Marin of Valéry. I had not. I have travelled very, very little. It was, said Erik, not as he, a northern European had expected. He had expected greensward (he used exactly that word) and low headstones. Not a cramped stone town of dog-kennel mausoleums, with stony streets and blind, blank frontages. But the sea was the same as the image he had taken there. *"La mer, la mer, toujours recommencée,"* they said, in unison.

I said I would very much like to be their dogsbody, if they would have me. Erik asked what else I did. I told the truth, more or less. That I was thinking of writing a book that had run into the ground for lack of information. That I wanted eventually to see the Maelstrøm, though I was not quite sure why. My "subject," I said, had possibly, not certainly, drowned in or near it.

They consulted each other with silent stares and smiles, a flick of an eyebrow, a movement of a mouth. I wondered if this couple was asking itself how I would fit into their intimacy. I have noticed that I arouse questions in the minds of those I encounter—those who are interested in me *at all*, that is—as to my sexual orientation. I think these things may be harder to diagnose in the very small. I stood equably there, offering no help on the sexual front, but expressing, I hoped, silent enthusiasm for the general aesthetic of Puck's Girdle.

"Would you change the name of the shop?" asked Christophe, as though he read my thoughts.

I replied that I had wondered. It was hard to know how to take a word like "girdle" on a modern shop. But I had decided it was totally memorable. Once seen, never forgotten. And representing exactly the desired travel connotations. "You could call it 'Periplum,' " I found myself saying, "but that *does* look exclusive. That might be thought to be arcane."

"You'll do," said Erik. I think he was reserving judgement on my sexuality. I didn't mean him to solve the problem; it was not his business.

When I left, I had learned that they were an ex-artist and an ex-athlete. The artist, who had constructed Maelstrøm, trees and paper colonnades, was the burly Erik, who was a Dane. The athlete was Christophe, who had been an 800-metre runner—until the Kenyans came, he said, and until my hamstring went for the third time. He watched me flinch in my own body at this thought. "We met in Kashmir," said Erik. "Where we had gone to think our way out of separate *impasses*," said Christophe. "And we found a joint way out."

It was agreed that I should begin work in two days' time, for a probationary month, to see if we suited each other. Did they do visits to the Maelstrøm, I asked, my hand on their spherical steel door-knob. "Frequently," said Erik. "It is a regular request."

I went on my way towards the Linnean Society, considerably encouraged. The entrance, as I said, is in the shadow in the

127

gateway to Burlington House. I went in; there was a small entrance hall, with a glass case containing memorabilia and portraits. A very steep spiral staircase went up inside the building. I was surprised to see that both hall and stairway—essentially austere—were decorated with very large mushrooms and toadstools constructed, solidly but fancifully, from velvet, tweed, lace and *broderie anglaise.* Several of these monster fungi—as large as two-year-olds—sprouted in the stair-corners and squatted on the landings. They made me uneasy, though their general appearance was sprightly. I was not at all sure what I wanted to ask the librarian, who had kindly agreed to show me round. I wanted to find a whiff, a trace, a smudged fingerprint, so to speak, that would indicate the presence—in the past—of Destry-Scholes. After all, I thought, as I circumvented the velvet fungi, if he had drowned in the Maelstrøm, the exiguous evidence I possessed suggested he had gone there in search of Linnaeus. Who had gone there, according to the document I had a copy of, which Ormerod Goode said was "shifty." I had decided to explain myself briefly but truthfully—to say that I was investigating someone who appeared to have been researching Linnaeus at the time of his own death. I had brought my folder containing the fragmentary narratives about the three personages. Much depended on the nature of the librarian.

I need not have worried, as it turned out. Several people were gathered in the library office to be shown the library and the collections. I was merely an anonymous extra in the group, all of whom were attending a conference on pollens and spores, which was indeed advertised in the downstairs lobby. There were two Englishmen, an American, a Dutchman and a Swedish woman, who reminded me of a Picasso ceramic. Not the long-necked, leggy, swanlike kind of jug, the stocky, stout kind. Like a squat S, with breasts pushing forwards and buttocks pushing backwards, and solid calves under a denim skirt with a leather belt. The most striking thing about this woman, however, was not her resemblance to a jar, but her hair, which had a life of its own, appearing so abundant and energetic that it was almost a separate life-form. It was dull gold and frizzy and springy, and long. It would have stood out from her head like sun-rays if she had not caught it back and confined it, on the shelf of her skull, in a plum-coloured elasticated velvet band. It flew out behind this compressed bottleneck like a comet, defying gravity, rushing, so to speak, behind her. I did not notice her face, having taken in her form. I suspect this usually happened. She was introduced to us as Fulla Biefeld, pollination ecologist. We were shown the elegant little library, which had a vertiginous narrow gallery, with a quite inadequate iron rail, that looked as though it might detach itself at any moment. I asked the librarian whether she would have any record of any visit by Scholes Destry-Scholes, and she said it was possible, but not certain. She would have to retrieve and consult the archive. I said I believed he had been considering a biography of Linnaeus when he died. She offered to search the Society's correspondence files.

The party then moved down to the strongroom, which houses what is left (it is a good part) of the Linnean collections. We were asked if there was anything specific we wished to see. The room is richly dark—one wall has Linnaeus's library, leather-bound, gold-lettered on warm skin, polished and stamped. I ran my eye along the shelf, Virgil and Aristotle, Descartes and Rousseau, and Vaillant. It was a large library for a gentleman of that time, and considerably smaller and more compact than my own rambling and ramshackle heaps of paperbacks. Another savant's library of that time would not have been dissimilar. There was a central desk with specimen cabinets in the space, which had the airless feel of a mausoleum. (I have never gone into a mausoleum, but was thinking about houselike tombs because of Erik's revelations about Valéry's marine cemetery.) Fulla Biefeld said she wanted to see bees. She wanted to know very precisely the physical state of the Linnean specimens of certain solitary bees—though she was also generally interested in butterflies, moths and wasps—from the region round Izmir, and from certain parts of Mexico. She hoped to get permission to put them under an electron microscope to study ancient pollen caught in their hairs, or fur, or scales. For a moment or two we all clustered round the fine drawers of bees, with their twisted corpses contorted on their eighteenth-century pins. One of the men said he had heard that the fish specimens were interesting. I followed him to these drawers, where the fish lay in neat files, one above the other, bisected laterally and pressed like flowers, with their spines displayed and their gaping faces turned sideways to show cheeks, teeth and faded colours. Some of these, the librarian said, were Artedi's fish. Artedi would have been the greater man, said one of the scientists. I did not know anything about Artedi, beyond that he was Linnaeus's friend. I was beginning to suffer mildly from claustrophobia, amongst all this long-dead life. What did I want to see? the librarian asked courteously.

I thought about Destry-Scholes's narrative. The journey to Lapland, I said, was what interested me. They had the manuscript itself, they said, Linnaeus's own account of his journey north. They fetched it out—leather-bound, its ink now root-brown on onion-skin tawny paper. The Maelstrøm, I murmured, would interest me. And the last part of the journey, the climbing in the Torneå fells. Fulla Biefeld looked up from her trays of dead bees. "He didn't go there," she said, in her flat, singing, Swedish voice. "He never went to the Maelstrøm. He never went to Torneå."

Shifty, Ormerod Goode said.

I said I was sorry. The document I was working on had a very circumstantial description of those parts of his journey.

"He *said* he went there," Fulla Biefeld said. "It is Linnaeus's little untruth. Big lie, maybe. The weather stopped him from going to Maelstrøm. He just rowed about in a little boat and did a trip to Rörstadt. And the Kaituma trip, you know, was another 840 miles, in less than two weeks available. He never went. He romanced it."

I said nothing. I thought about Destry-Scholes, who, it was beginning to appear, had romanced further what Linnaeus had already romanced. I looked at Linnaeus's scribble. The librarian with practised hands turned to Linnaeus's curious drawing of the plant he named *Andromeda—Andromeda polifolia*, marsh andromeda or bog rosemary, previously known as *Chamaedaphne*. I attach a photocopy of a copy of his drawing, as I find myself unable to describe its particular kind of incompetence, neither endearing nor ridiculous. The legend in the middle, between the human personification and the botanical representation, reads:

Andromaeda

ficta et vera
mystica et genuina
figurata et depicta

His description of the relations between mythic woman and flower was both far-fetched and in a way sexy. One of the pollination-men read it out to me in English, mellifluously.

"I noticed that she was blood-red before flowering, but that as soon as she blooms her petals become flesh-coloured. I doubt whether any artist could rival these charms in a portrait of a young girl, or adorn her cheeks with such beauties as are here and to which no cosmetics have lent their aid. As I looked at her I was reminded of Andromeda as described by the poets, and the more I thought about her, the more affinity she seemed to have with the plant; indeed, had Ovid set out to describe the plant mystically *(mystice)* he could not have caught a better likeness . . .

"Her beauty is preserved only so long as she remains a virgin (as often happens with women also)—i.e., until she is fertilised, which will not now be long, as she is a bride. She is anchored far out in the water, as always on a little tuft in the

Andromeda polifolia

marsh and fast tied as if on a rock in the midst of the sea. The water comes up to her knees, above her roots; and she is always surrounded by poisonous dragons and beasts—i.e., evil toads and frogs—which drench her with water when they mate in the spring. She stands and bows her head in grief. Then her little clusters of flowers with their rosy cheeks droop and grow ever paler and paler . . ."

The flower, I observed, looked sexier than its mystic counterpart. One of the things I did know about Linnaeus was that his taxonomy was based on the sexuality of plants. We had all read our Foucault, *Les mots et les choses*. I had looked it up again when I first made the identification of Destry-Scholes's arctic pilgrim.

What follows is not of course what went through my head as I stood amongst the pollination people in the Linnean strong-room. It is what I have later revisited and adumbrated for this document. I have resisted the temptation to insert several pages of Foucault. One of the reasons why I abandoned—oh, and I *have* abandoned—post-structuralist semiotics, was the requirement to write page upon page of citations from Foucault (or Lacan or Derrida or Bakhtin) in support of the simplest statement, such as that a scene of Shakespeare may be simultaneously comic and tragic—which earlier critics were able to say without all this paraphernalia. But it would be very wrong of me not to give these thinkers their due where it matters—and Foucault did fit Linnaeus's desire for a complete taxonomy into a view of language and languages which extends beyond and includes it. The pleasure, for me, I suppose, as I write, is that this time I was thinking of Foucault, and even more of Linnaeus, amongst *things,* shaved fish-skeletons, great blue butterflies, leather bindings, drawings done by the man himself even if the drawings involved (why not?) levels of meaning, analogies between plants and other creatures, real and invented, accurate and far-fetched.

Linnaeus calculated that the 38 organs of generation, containing 4 variables of number, figure, situation and proposition, allowed 5,776 combinations which were sufficient to define the *genus.* From the precise definitions afforded by the 5,776 combinations, it was possible to give precise names to the entire vegetable and animal kingdom, and these names would indicate all the relationships, all the connections (manifest or hidden, Foucault says) between the plants of the same kind, and further, of related kinds. Natural history, for Linnaeus, according to Foucault, was fundamentally designed to order and to name the world. The French word I have translated as "order" is *"disposition,"* and the translation isn't quite right. It means "place," "arrange"—*order* is too strong. Linnaeus took the sex of plants and the sexual organs of other living things as the basis of his system. This wasn't inevitable. Cuvier, for example, was interested in the morphology of bones as a starting-place. Foucault makes the point that we moderns do not like the idea of an *immobile* nature, which is to some extent implicit in a classificatory system—we like, he says elegantly, "a swarming continuity of beings who communicate amongst themselves, mingle and perhaps transform themselves, shift shapes, one into the other." He himself remarks precisely that the essence of the idea isn't in the conflict of these two visions of nature, but in the relationship, precisely between words and things. It all resides, he says, *"dans le réseau de nécessité qui en ce point a rendu possible et indispensable le choix entre deux manières de constituer l'histoire naturelle comme une langue."* His two ways of making a language were the System and the Method. The System is Linnaeus, the taxonomy, the mapping and naming of a finite structure. Linnaeus published his thesis—*Praeludia Sponsaliarum Plantanum*—in 1729. It expatiated in a learned way on stamens and pistil, pollen (sperm), seeds (ova), castration and infertility. Also on polyandry, polygyny, incest, concubinage and marriage-beds of petals, with a strong erotic charge. He aroused considerable moral opprobrium with this work. I looked at his sad little Andromeda, with her far-fetched fictive, mystic and figurative senses. The network of myth and legend intertwines like vines or ivy with the branches of the Linnean system, through his predilection for classical nomenclature. His butterflies are Greek and Trojan heroes, and here was a curious concrete image of the net of connections, even containing drawings of an inadequately attached chain of links, a crossing-place of languages. I murmured something anodyne about the sexuality of plants and the librarian opened another volume for me, showing me the complicated plans of the flower, leaves, sepals, petals, as bridal chambers for monogamous or polygamous weddings, "public" and "clandestine." The whole family of ferns, mosses, algae, fungi, he called *Cryptogamia* (plants that marry secretly). The Dutchman said, surprisingly, that many of Linnaeus's drawings of polygamy and cryptogamy were felt to be satirical representations of the clandestine relations of the Swedish court. I bent my head over the spidery black petal-divisions, tiny lettering, linking lines. Other heads bent beside mine.

We were plunged into darkness.

There was a sound of ratcheting, or switching, and a further, more ominous sound of locks rolling into sockets. It was a violently thick, absolute darkness; if the eyes waited to adjust to it, all they were exposed to was black and more black, complete absence of light. I am a mildly claustrophobic person—I try to keep it in control—and I began immediately to persuade myself that I perceived an increase in the mustiness or fustiness of the air. Things rose in my throat—unuttered, battened-down howls or sobs of fear, a gulp of burning acid. I backed away from the group—I instinctively seek solitude at extreme moments. I felt my way along Linnaeus's leather-bound volumes, to where I believed the strongroom door to be—whether because I thought I might open it, or because I desired to be first out when it was opened from outside, I don't know. It was a primitive and ignoble rush towards an exit, even a locked one. Someone said there was a power-cut. Someone else asked if there was anyone in the building who was not locked in with us. Someone else said that it was possible the janitor had gone home. I began to tremble, and continued to shuffle round the wall . . .

My questing face, my gaping mouth, my desperate nostrils were suddenly muffled in softness—I thought of bats, but it was more as though I had plunged into thick fine moss, which smelled ferny and animal at once, and was suffocating me. I beat out with my hands and encountered yielding soft flesh (under cloth). I slipped to my knees, losing consciousness, and my hands ran down solid thighs, strong knees, warm, muscular. The door opened, and I found myself at the feet of Fulla Biefeld, staring up inside her skirt at the slight wiriness of her pubic hair pressing against what appeared to be alter-

nately crimson and emerald knickers (no doubt an effect of
the lack of oxygen to my brain). The stalwart legs were furred
with strong, brass-gold hairs. I let myself lose consciousness
completely—I felt it coming over me and went along with it,
it seemed the best thing. My nose was alive with Fulla
Biefeld's sex. Linnaeus knew nothing about pheromones.

She bent fiercely and solicitously over me. Her hair was a
great cage of zigzag lines of honey-light, after the dark. It had
odd scarlet flashes in it, as my eyes adjusted. I closed them
again, and murmured, deliberately exaggerating my weakness, "Claustrophobia."

"I thought you meant to trample me down," she said.

I kept my eyes closed, and my posture submissive.

Someone else brought me a glass of water. After a time I
was able to come out, blinking, into the light. The party was
breaking up. I arranged, with the librarian, to return, to see
whether their archive would produce any sign of the passage
of Scholes Destry-Scholes. Fulla Biefeld was hovering near my
shoulder. If I wished, she said, she would look over the document I was researching, which appeared to have some anom-
alies. Who was its author?

Why did I not want to tell her?

"Scholes Destry-Scholes," I said. "He wrote a biography of
Sir Elmer Bole."

"I don't know that name."

"He was a Victorian polymath. Among other things—
many other things—he studied leaf-cutter bees near Troy."

She did not show any particular interest in either Destry-
Scholes or Bole. I said I could not give her the typescript,
which was not mine, and was my only copy. She said that in

that case, if I accompanied her to a pâtisserie in Piccadilly she would glance over it for me, and suggest—if relevant—leads I could follow up. I demurred. She pointed out that I would not meet so very many Swedish-speakers and taxonomic specialists who had also written term papers on Linnaeus's Lapp journey. This was indisputably true. So I followed her into Piccadilly and sat down to a cappuccino, over a starched tablecloth, under pink lights, surrounded by slightly swooning Muzak. Fulla Biefeld put on wide, narrow oval-lensed glasses, surrounded like those of the male couple in Puck's Girdle, with iridescent titanium. She frowned over Destry-Scholes's carbon.

"This is a tissue of truths and half-truths and untruths, I rather suspect." The Swedish sing-song was more pronounced out of the strongroom. "It is true Linnaeus was interested in superstition and magic. But all this spirit-journey is most unlikely, most. On the other hand, the *Furia Infernalis* is authentic. There are inauthentic fabrics here suspended from authentic hooks. Why would anyone do that?"

I said I didn't know. I didn't. Maybe Destry-Scholes was trying to become a fiction writer. I did not mention the feeling I had had, evolved from the readerly solipsism, that he was trying to deceive or illude me, me personally. I reflected that I had become quite unused to reciprocal conversation. I said flatly that I wasn't sure where to go next. I might have to give up this project for lack of information. I expected it would be no great loss, I heard myself saying, more especially if what I had found was all a tissue of lies. Fulla Biefeld agreed with this, more forcefully than I could have wished. Conversations, I thought grindingly again, went two ways. Courtesy required me to ask her a question, a quid pro quo. I asked her how she had become a palaeoecologist. She replied, rather crossly, that she did not call herself a palaeoecologist. She was a bee taxonomist. She was a bee taxonomist in training.

Interesting, I said limply. She stared wrathfully at me. Her face is not beautiful. Her nose is sharp, her eyes too deep under the bristling ledges of her pale brows, her mouth too big for her (smallish) face, and set in what is almost a permanent expression of disapproval. Her eyes are not blue but greenish, flecked with brownish streaks. Her eyelashes are actually quite thick, but so pale that they are only visible in certain lights.

"I do palaeoecology as an adjunct to pollination studies," she said. "Reciprocities between insects and plants and other pollinators have developed over millions and millions of years. Recently there was a very clever disproof of the idea that rats pollinated the *ie-ie* vine, worked out through the study of bird-specimens collected by nineteenth-century naturalists. There are crops, and wild plants, whose histories we most urgently need to know if we are to preserve them and their habitats. What isn't fertilised dies out. What is inadequately fertilised doesn't grow, doesn't fruit. Too little is known, and whilst we try to find out we lay things waste with crop-spraying, clearance, weedkillers, poisonous plants we have ourselves engineered, imported pollinators, or controlling predators, which in their turn become pests and destroyers. Have you read *Silent Spring*, Mr. Nanson?"

Indeed I had, I said. I had written a paper on literary and popular-cultural images of induced panic and mass fear. I had contrasted seventeenth-century evil spirits with the idea of Napoleon the bogeyman, and fear of the Bomb and heaps of dead birds in a wasteland in our own time.

"Literary and popular-cultural images," said this fizzing woman, "are neither here nor there. As you say in English. Neither here nor there. Whereas both *here* and *there* and *now* this species is destroying, every day, 6,000 species perhaps, many unknown, some perhaps essential—certainly essential—to the survival of a whole chain of others."

"You are an eco-warrior," I said, with disastrous flippancy. I thought I knew her type. Earnest, covered with natural body-hair, intent on organic living, opposed to modern machines and comforts, believers in Gaia and beyond that in a whole-wheat Whole Earth, absolutely no compromise with commerce or experimentation on animals or embryos, makers of sustainable homes with organic earth closets and gimcrack recycling machines, mysticism of minerals, aromatherapies, ley lines, druidic wisdom of the mistletoe, respect for Aztec flesh-ripping with obsidian knives. I am a modern man, if not a postmodern man. I am an urban animal. Cities are a miraculous invention. We have evolved into city-dwellers, with sewage and electric light. It isn't natural to live in moss-huts. It's profoundly *un*natural. The earth never was as these Gaia mythographers believed it had been. It was red in tooth and claw. We have the best teeth and claws.

"There are only thirty-nine in the world," she said.

Hardly a successful life-form, I thought.

"Thirty-nine *what?*" I asked.

"Bee taxonomists," she said. "Their average age is sixty plus. Only two are training a new generation of taxonomists. Both are over eighty, and both are in the New World, where the situation's less dire. All are men."

"Does that matter?" Not only an ecologist, a feminist. Feminism was one of the secondary reasons why I had given up post-structuralist theory. There is an (almost) irresistible urge to distort or misrepresent or ignore or overemphasise facts and items of information, in feminist theory. It is also not really possible to say so.

"No," she said. "It's just interesting. What matters is the lack of knowledge. The American alfalfa yield plummeted because they thought they could use honeybees instead of the alkali bees that are its natural pollinator. There is a miracle crop—sesbania, a legume—which could feed Ethiopia and hold back desertification—it enriches the soil—but no one has studied the local pollinators, the bees, no one has studied whether there would be enough, or whether any introduced pollinator could live there, and what effect it would have on indigenous bees and other creatures."

"Well," I said pacifically, "it's good that you're around to rectify that."

"Thirty-nine," she said. "It's urgent. You haven't understood."

"In the steps of Linnaeus," I said.

"Linnaeus," she told me, "knew nothing about insect pollination. He invented anthropomorphic fairy tales and thought the bees were blundering about damaging the marriage-chambers, accidentally deflowering the virgins, and robbing the seed-stores. He didn't see—he didn't need to see—the interdependence of things."

There was a pause.

"If you could get this document photocopied," she said, "I could look into it, while I'm working here for the next few weeks."

I said I wouldn't wish to take her away from her important

work to look into a mere literary puzzle. I said I could do my own research.

"I suppose you mean to spend a few months learning Swedish?" she said scornfully. "I do not see where this project will end. Can you read Latin?"

"Sort of," I said, truthfully.

"I'm not trying to steal your project," she said. "Only to be normally helpful. If you don't want help, that's a matter of indifference to me."

I was . . . I was about to write *ashamed,* but that isn't true. I was embarrassed. She was quite right, on all counts. She was a piece of luck, not a threat. Was I afraid she would notice the threadbare thinness of my project? That didn't really matter, either. She would soon be off to Ethiopia, or wherever. I said I would be very grateful, and would make a photocopy.

"We could do it now, in the Linnean library," she said. I tagged after her and watched her reproduce my treasure-trove. She folded it, and stuffed it into her capacious hand-bag. I gave her my address.

"You'll hear from me if I think of anything," she said. And strode bouncing away down Piccadilly, the burning bush of her hair simmering behind her.

I began my work (two days a week) at Puck's Girdle. I have to record that (apart from my haunted desks at the British Library) it was the first human space I had ever enjoyed shar-ing. It was, as I said, blue and green, with starry lights in a midnight sky—and delicately spangled little desk-lights on threads of metal, cone-shaped, crescent-shaped, making little pools and pencil-streams of brilliance. Not much daylight filtered in through the cardboard Maelstrøm, the Paradise jungle and the Alhambra arcades, though some did, on bright days. Have I said it was spring? We lived in our own softly luminous artificial pool, and moved around it calmly like exploratory fishes. I loved the coffee pot, streamlined stainless steel and glass, that produced endless delicious cappuccino. Along the two sides of the space not occupied by the window and the counter, ran shelves, with books—not brochures—encyclopaedias, atlases, guides to the flora and fauna, the cathedrals and railways, the ships and geysers, the art galleries and sculpture gardens, the temples and arboretums of the world. These expensive and lovely books were attached to the wall with fine stainless-steel chains, and lit by their own downlighters. There were silver-legged stools for customers to perch and browse, stools in many greens, from jade to olive, from apple to evergreen. There were even magnifying glasses, on finer chains. Erik said that they had fitted the chains because of theft, it was true, but he thought they were elegant, and invited long sessions of thought, which he encouraged.

In the back, behind the counter, were a white windowless kitchen and a small bathroom, both minimally and perfectly provided with what was necessary.

My first task was to learn to use the database on the computer. My own is old, grey and cranky. These were new and humming and speedy. My screen was full of sapphire light. I learned to find trains, planes, buses, coaches, horse-caravans, guides, mules, jeeps, car hire, monoplanes, yachts, barges, anywhere, everywhere in the world. I leaned to consult Puck's Girdle's extensive list of trustworthy hotels, inns, bed-and-breakfasts, tents, caravans, châteaux, monasteries, caravanserais in every category, and how to update it with customer comments, commendations and complaints. I watched Erik and Christophe feed and expand the imaginations of their customers, casual new ones, and old regulars, of whom there were many, from an expert in medieval stained glass tracking a particular glazier from England across Europe to Assisi, to a bird-watching taxi driver who had been through the Indian jungle, the African savannah, the Amazon, on elephants, in Range-Rovers and dug-out canoes, and wanted something new. A man who wanted to do Italy in a new way was encouraged to retrace Goethe's *Italienische Reise*. Another followed the footsteps of Wordsworth, Dorothy and Coleridge in Germany. There was the man who had done all the battlefields of the Napoleonic Wars and was embarking on the Hundred Years War. There were followers of Mary Wollstonecraft and Lady Mary Wortley Montagu, Berengaria and Guenivere. There was also someone who wanted to retrace the journeys of Alfred Russel Wallace. Christophe was trying to interest people in Humboldt in South America. We played games over lunch in the kitchen—Christophe made delicious salads and my complexion improved remarkably—inventing truly extravagant tours, and inventing the customers to whom we would sell them. I say "we." I am not sure I have ever in my life before said "we" about any group to which I might be thought to belong. There was an ease of belonging between Erik and Christophe, which I have rarely seen. They brushed hands, they touched each other, as they moved about kitchen and office. They appeared to know what the other was doing, without his being in their line of vision, by some perfection of timing and attention. They included me, most gracefully, not as an equal, but as someone involved in this benign purposefulness. One or the other would ruffle my hair, or touch my shoulder as I peered into the screen. I did not make any reciprocal movement of approach. I did not want to. But I was grateful for the brush of fingers, the acceptance. I have to say, I was grateful.

In time, I came to make suggestions. I found my Destry-Scholes research to have surprising uses. We constructed a tour to look at mosaics, taking in the glories of Istanbul and Ravenna, and some arcane churches in Serbia and Macedonia. Erik found a school in Ravenna where travellers could *make* mosaics according to the ancient methods, cutting the stone and placing the tesserae. We went on from there to construct a tour following Turner to Venice, with practice in his peculiar way of making watercolours, dabbling his fingers in drenched colour on paper. Christophe said we were making schools for forgers, and Erik said forgery was a human pleasure that should be catered for, according to Fourier's principles. It wasn't all art—we arranged for someone to be a castaway on an island, and for someone else to prospect for wrecks off the Azores.

Staples of the tours we offered were art-history with a difference. Specialist comparative viewing of Nativities in Germany, Austria, France, Italy and Flanders. Paintings of the Paradise garden across the world. A century of stone angels. At the time when I arrived, Erik and Christophe were researching a tour of Last Judgements on church walls, from Michelangelo to obscure Northumbrian Anglo-Saxons, from

146

Bavaria to Constantinople. Whilst we were discussing this, an angry-looking man in a raincoat came in and said he did not suppose we could organise a tour of suicide leaps? Places people had jumped from? Erik said he didn't see why not. Beachy Head, the Reichenbach Falls, Paul Celan's Paris bridge, certain skyscrapers. Money, said the man in the raincoat, was no inhibiting factor. It was not a very good, nor a very clean raincoat. When he had gone, Christophe said that he had probably sold everything and intended to jump, himself, from one place or another. Should we help him? Erik said (a) people had a right to jump if they wanted to, (b) the travel might quite likely weaken his purpose, and (c) it was an original idea, it added a new dimension.

Death, judgement, heaven and hell, I said. The Four Last Things. Something was tugging at my mind. A new idea, said Erik. A tour of the Four Last Things. Like a pilgrimage. Tourism had taken over from pilgrimages, said Christophe, that was a cliché. Travel was what was left of religion. Art galleries were the new temples, it was true, said Erik. Once people travelled to see the artifacts in the galleries. Now the galleries themselves—Stuttgart, Nîmes, Houston, St. Ives—were the ends of journeys, spiritual centres of contemplation, as the great cathedrals had been, and before them the caves of the oracles. Great nineteenth-century monumental buildings of the industrial revolution (the Bankside power house, the Gare d'Orsay, the Hamburger Banhof in Berlin) now housed collections of art, canvas and sculpture, wax and glass boxes.

Something tugged more insistently. It was Destry-Scholes's personages. All three were travellers. He appeared to have embellished all three journeys with invented "spiritual" visions. All three personages had, so to speak, hallucinated themselves, their doubles, their spirits, after strenuous journeys. Ibsen perhaps didn't quite fit. I needed to do more work on his biography, on his real contact, or lack of contact, with Henriksen, his illegitimate son. But the biographical playlet presented the son as a double, an alter ego, a ghost. I had gone off Linnaeus since Fulla Biefeld had departed with the spliced-faked document. I wondered if it was time to start serious work on what Francis Galton had seen in Ovampoland. *Why* had Destry-Scholes taken to inventing spirit-journeys? The truth was, at that time, I had taken to spending more and more of "my own" research time in the British Library producing refinements of tour-plans that Erik and Christophe had in hand. It was nice to come up with an unexpected site full of archaeopteryx bones that could be reached from a better-known one by a trek across the Peruvian wild, or a painting of the Earthly Paradise by Brueghel the younger in an otherwise undistinguished minor Swiss gallery. Erik and Christophe were so encouragingly enthusiastic about my finds and my projects. They pointed out the uses of the Internet for research, and I took to it with pleasure, but it did not beat the library, not yet, with its catalogue and its books full of bibliographies full of books full of bibliographies. It was interesting that Destry-Scholes was becoming more substantial even whilst no progress was being made. I wondered if there was a Galton society like the Linnean?

I wondered also—how could I not—about travelling myself. The fortunate notice in the window had mentioned a possibility of travel. I asked Erik and Christophe—they were so easy, so relaxed, it was not difficult—what they had meant. They said that every so often a particular tourist needed a companion—for reasons of health, or frailty, or loneliness.

Sometimes tourists could be amiably paired, satisfying a double need. But now and then—not often—one of them—one of us—might be the best and most reliable travelling companion. Christophe said I would need to know the trade backwards—to have proved my worth—before there was any possibility of such a jaunt. Where would I ideally wish to jaunt to? I mentioned, again, the Maelstrøm. The man I was researching, I said, had disappeared near, or in, it. Erik remarked that it should perhaps be included with the death-leaps or in the Four Last Things. Christophe said there would be nothing to see. Erik said that depends on him. Meaning me. But they did not offer to facilitate my journey to the Maelstrøm and I did not mention it again.

I cannot now remember what came next, the letter or the first visit of the Strange Customer. I called him the Strange Customer, to myself, from the beginning I think, after Destry-Scholes's rendering of Henrik Ibsen's doppelgänger son. Who had been named for the Strange Passenger, in Peer Gynt's last voyage. He came in when I was alone, the first time, and the subsequent times. The first time I think I did not notice his tall shadow pacing the pavement outside the proscenium of the window with its paper whirlpool. Subsequent times, I did. I came to suppose that he was prospecting, so to speak, to see whether I was alone, but the first time that was a long way from my thoughts. I thought he had come in on an impulse, as I had myself. He was very tall, well over six feet, with sleek black hair, beautifully cut, short and conventional. He wore a suit—double-breasted—also beautifully cut, with the merest hint of an exaggerated nipped waist, the merest gesture towards a flamboyantly wide lapel. He wore a white rosebud in his buttonhole, and carried a black lacquered cane with a bone handle, which he propped against the counter. His face was a little too long for its proportions. His lips were large and full, but pursed a bit tightly, not loose, not even relaxed. His nails were square and dreadfully clean. I took a long time to notice or remember his eyes. When I called him up to memory, that part of his face, which should be the most striking, always remained a grey rectangle of smoke or cloud or something. I think he may have worn dark glasses, or other sorts of glasses, and possibly not always the same. I was not very used to being left alone with the shop on the occasion of his first visit. So I pretended to be busy—well, I *was* busy, I went on being busy—with my blue screen and dancing alphabets. He stood in the doorway—he always stood in the doorway—I could feel his weight like a barrier if I should wish to rush out into the street. His shoes were beautifully polished.

Erik and Christophe had told me not to disrupt any customer who showed signs of wanting to browse without approaching the counter. He looked at me for a moment, and then went and sat down on one of the stools, leafing through books on Greek art and Thai temples. I had developed the conceit that Puck's Girdle was a chapel for meditation, with its starry ceiling and chained bibles of tourism. There was a certain reverence about my Strange Customer, who bowed his head over the pages and put the tips of his fingers together. He spent a long time there, moving along the rows, opening and closing the books. Finally he approached me. He asked where Pim (or Pym, perhaps. I didn't know) was. I said I didn't know Pim.

His voice was clear and belling. Not like those voices in

Fitzgerald, full of money, but full of a thick-blooded mixture of confidence and desire (a word used, partly at least, in the sense of my postmodernist French theory). I don't mean that he desired *me*. I mean that he gave me the impression of wanting to eat huge meals with gusto, and fly first class at great speeds. He said that perhaps Pim had left, perhaps I was Pim's successor? Pim had arranged some unforgettable experiences for him, he said, leaning briefly towards me across the counter. I hadn't thought about whether I had had a predecessor, but let it lie. I said we tried to think of unusual things. We succeeded beyond expectation, he agreed cordially. He added, to my surprise, that though many travel agencies might be said to run on adulterated or bastardised Fourierist principles, Puck's Girdle was, so to speak, the distinguished thing itself, wouldn't I agree? I agreed enthusiastically (for me, I don't let much expression show in my face, even when I'm excited, that's my nature). I could hardly believe I was living in a real world, where Englishmen in suits with buttonholes came in and chatted knowledgeably about Fourier. He would be back, he announced. He liked a long period of anticipation. He had one or two things in mind. Brewing. He'd be more specific when the time was ripe. I said I hoped we should be able to satisfy him. He said he was sure we would. I think that is all I have to record about my first encounter with him. I think all the rest came later, including his name, which he didn't offer me on that occasion.

The letter was a complete surprise, not least because I don't get letters, I don't have correspondents. In recent weeks I had had two or three (or more—there were more) brief notes from

Fulla Biefeld, who had gone to the Hope Entomological Institute in Oxford to work on bee systematics. She had sent me a bibliography of further reading on Linnaeus. This I found a little insulting, partly because the one expertise I pride myself on is my way with catalogues and bibliographies, and partly because she made the wrong assumption that I was unable to read material in French or Latin or German. She also sent me some material on the crisis in pollination studies, and what she referred to as the TI (Taxonomic Impediment) and TD (Taxonomic Deficit) in the study of natural resources and ecology. Other things that came through the post almost certainly through her agency were an invitation to join a Europe-wide Bee Watch, sponsored in London by the Wildlife Trust, and a taxonomic study of the flora and fauna of Richmond Park. "You might like to use some of your spare time on what may (probably will) turn out to be a matter of some urgency," she wrote. I was vaguely insulted by her assumption that I had spare time. I began to notice bumblebees on pavements and honeybees in hedges as I walked to Piccadilly. I wondered if it would be interesting to add Bee Watches and pollination holidays to the fan of possibilities displayed at Puck's Girdle. I even thought with evanescent pleasure of looking at wormcasts and birdnests in Richmond Park. No one could say these were not *things*. There were things in Puck's Girdle, but most of these things were images of other things, photographs of glaciers, standardised descriptions of hotel rooms (TV, central heating, bath/shower, large/small/queensize/kingsize bed and so on). The chained books were things, and the screens of the computers, but things containing the codes to access thingier, denser *things*.

I digress. The letter came from Willesden, and was

nothing to do with Fulla Biefeld. It was written in beautifully neat, minuscule writing, clear enough, but clearer under a magnifying glass.

Dear Mr. Nanson,

Someone brought your query to the *Times Literary Supplement* to my attention some time ago. I don't see the *Supplement,* I'm afraid. I am the niece of Scholes Destry-Scholes—my mother (now dead) was his sister. It is possible that I am his only living relative, I don't know, we are not a close family and never have been. Certainly my mother was his only sister. At the time I didn't bother to write to you, because there seemed nothing to say. I never met my uncle and I don't really remember much mention of him. But it seems from your query that he might have had some kind of importance. I have been clearing out some junk in my attic and found a suitcase of his things. There are a lot of index cards you might find interesting. It seems a pity for them just to gather dust if anyone at all is interested in them. Let me know what you think. I'll quite understand if you think my "find" is too insignificant to bother with.

Yours faithfully,
Vera Alphage

Naturally, I was intrigued by the connection of Scholes Destry-Scholes with a suitcase full of authentic *things*. I did not form any very clear impression of Miss or Mrs. Vera Alphage. I wrote back to Willesden in a businesslike way, saying that I had formed the project of writing a biography of

Scholes Destry-Scholes, having been very impressed by his own work on Elmer Bole, but that I had been finding it very difficult to discover any information, and was therefore delighted to have the possibility of meeting a relative, or seeing any archival material at all. I had formed the impression, from her style, that she was a comfortable, slightly naïve housewife in her late forties. I saw her plump and cheerful. Matter of fact. She replied, however, that she could only see me in the evenings, when she got back from work, which could sometimes be quite late. I replied—always by post, neither of us vouchsafed a telephone number—with my own timetable of work and research time. So I ended up travelling to Willesden at about eight o'clock of a summer evening, forewarned that Ms. Alphage "would not call a few index cards an archive exactly."

Number 10, Fox Crescent, resembled the Askham Way birthplace in many ways. It was small, in a terrace, with a little wicket gate into a front garden with a border of phlox and delphiniums and a strip of lawn like the area between wickets in cricket. (Which I know only from the television, it is not played at the sort of school I went to. I thought of saying, two complete revolutions of a roller, and then thought, I had got the roller from cricket, and needed the reference.) Unlike the Pontefract house, number 10 had a porch with a pointed roof, over which an abundant creeper sprawled, so that the door inside was shadowed. I knocked, and was let in. Vera Alphage is neither middle-aged nor all those other ordinary things I had supposed. She is young—in her late twenties—and quite shockingly beautiful. You do not notice this at first because she keeps her head down, and her fine black hair, including a falling fringe, is very long. Her legs and her fingers and her slender neck are long, too. Her skin is pale. I formed the immediate impression that she shunned bright light—her windows were veiled with lace curtains as well as shaded by tendrils of creeper. Her voice was very soft, and shy. She offered me tea—or sherry—I settled for tea—and a place on the sofa, which was covered with a pattern of violets on ivory linen. The room was a small box of a room (I grew up, and have always lived, in small boxes of rooms). It was uncluttered and minimally furnished, with white shelves on white walls, holding a few books (twenty or so, nothing in my reckoning) and a few pretty cups and saucers. I noticed also that Ms. Alphage wore no wedding rings, indeed, no rings.

We chatted. We are both shy, it was not easy, almost painful, indeed. She kept her head down over her tea, what I saw was the falling fringe. She said that her grandfather, Destry-Scholes's father, had been a tax-inspector.

"They weren't called Destry-Scholes, as far as I know, just plain Destry. My mother always called herself Joan Destry, quite plainly. She believed in plainness. She wasn't romantic. She died about six years ago. She didn't talk about her brother—I don't think she ever mentioned that he had written a book—perhaps she didn't know? She was quite miffed, I think, that he was sent to university and she wasn't. She made sure I got a good education, but I was an only child anyway."

"Did he marry?"

"I don't *think* so. I don't know. Mummy burned most of her letters before she died—out of tidiness, I think, she had bone cancer, she had time to think, not out of any desire to hide any secrets. I didn't mind, I didn't think to stop her. I wish I had now. I have a very *thinned-down* sense of my family, of any past—something people seem to like to have. You know, if I were to marry, there'd be no one I really need invite to the wedding, except a few colleagues. No family. I'm sorry to be so unhelpful."

I reminded her about the suitcase of Uncle's things.

She said it was in the loft, and too heavy for her to lift alone. Would I mind coming up, and helping. I could see her dubious look at my small size and delicate hands. She must be six inches, or more, taller than I am. I stood up briskly, to show that I was ready for effort. Her staircase is little and boxed, like the rooms. The loft is approached from a trap door in the ceiling of the landing. She fetched a stepladder, and a broom-handle, with which she pushed open the trap door. I followed her up. The loft is full of light—she has had a Velux window let into the roof—and full of neatly arranged packing-cases and bales. There is no dust. She had pulled the suitcase—battered, russet leather—out under a window. Someone—I presumed it was Vera Alphage herself—had stuck a label on it: UNCLE'S THINGS. I knelt beside it. I was about to write I knelt *reverently,* because the adverb tripped off the pen. But that wasn't true. I knelt greedily, if you can put those words together. Vera Alphage produced a little key, and opened the lock (which she had oiled, it was clear).

There were two shoeboxes, made of shiny, durable cardboard. One a kind of dove-grey, and one a navy-blue. There was also a pair of rather battered lace-up shoes, ordinary brown, unexceptionable lace-up shoes—not very large shoes, I noticed, the shoes of a smallish man, unless his feet were disproportionate. There was a collection of corkscrews and bottle-openers, tied together with red cord, and other instruments—a cheese-grater, a nutmeg-grater, a box of tin-tacks, a Swiss Army knife, a pouch which when opened turned out to contain surgical instruments—scalpel, needles, scissors, a small saw. There was a contraption of leather bands and screws and spikes I could make nothing of. There was also a soft scarlet leather bag, which drew up at the neck with a cord, designed perhaps as a sewing-bag to hold needles, threads, etc.—Vera Alphage referred to it, later, as "the dolly-bag." This rattled, as though it was full of little stones. I had hoped for heaps of documents—letters, drafts of further instalments of the lives of the personages—but there was nothing. There were several pairs of well-worn socks, and some rather voluminous jersey underpants. Two balls of twine, of different thickness, and a very small geological hammer. Vera Alphage said, "The index cards I wrote to you about are in the grey shoebox. The blue one is full of photos." I lifted the lids. Both boxes were packed neatly, one with large-sized index cards, narrow-ruled, and one with photographs. The photographs, ruffled through, appeared to date from many periods—Victorian, Edwardian, 1920s, 1930s, 1950s—and to vary from family snapshots to sea-side postcards, heavy daguerreotypes to fading Kodak prints perhaps two inches square. Some were even pasted cutouts from newspapers or what appeared to be plates from books. At first glance they were in no order—blurry babies in woolly bonnets came next to impressive opera-singer-like dames in corsages, next to freaks with elephantine proboses or pendulous buttocks. "I haven't touched them," said Vera Alphage, as if to exonerate her tidy self from responsibility for this disarray. I asked if any of the collection were family photographs (hastily flicking past a close-up of a canker to settle on a pretty 1950s debutante in a Juliet-cap). She said she had only cast a cursory glance over them, and had recognised no-one.

"They are like a freak-show," she said. "Even the ones that are normal at first sight."

This remark interested me.

I turned my attention to the box of cards. It was possible that here, at last, (unless you counted the brown shoes and the greyish underpants) was Destry-Scholes himself. They were handwritten, in a maniacally tidy script (what do I mean, maniacally? I mean, simply tidy, tiny and tidy) in blue ink, with a fountain-pen. They appeared, at very first glance, to be a file of disjunct quotations or jottings—again in no immediately apparent order, and again with no apparent system of reference or categorisation. My own notes on Destry-Scholes, like my notes on female personae in Firbank, Maugham and Forster, are all carefully referenced, with the source, the edition, the page. Here there was nothing. Careful annotation and analysis would be required. I ruffled through the cards. Almost at random, I pulled out two—not quite at random, they were both in verse, not prose. I noticed Vera Alphage's reflex gesture to prevent me destroying the order, which pleased me. She had a scholarly temperament, it was clear. I had not asked what her work was, that kept her late.

When I was a boy, I remember
Two thoughts kept occurring to me, and made me
    laugh.
An owl frightened by darkness, and a fish
Afraid of water. Why did I think of them?

158

Because I felt dimly the difference
Between what is, and what should be; between
Having to endure and finding one's burden
Unendurable.
    Every man
Is such an owl and such a fish, created
To work in darkness, to live in the deep;
And yet he is afraid. He splashes
In anguish towards the shore, stares at the bright
Vault of heaven, and screams: "Give me the air
And the blaze of day!"

And:

Almighty God, Creator and Preserver of all things, who
On Lapland fells suffered me to ascend so high
In Falun mines to descend so low,
On Lapland fells showed me *diem sine nocte,* day with-
    out night,
In Falun mines *noctem sine die,* night without day,
On Lapland fells suffered me to be where cold is
    never-ending
In Falun mines where heat is never-ending,
On Lapland fells suffered me to see in one place all the
    four seasons
In Falun mines not one of the four seasons
In Lapland led me unharmed through so many mortal
    dangers
In Falun through so many perils to health
    Praised be all Thou has created
    From the beginning to the end.

159

For a wild moment, I thought that Destry-Scholes himself had written these poems, that I had, so to speak, met him naked. Then I thought that the second, with its references to Lapland and Falun, was much more likely to have something to do with—even to be written by—Linnaeus—and I do not wish to obfuscate things, or deny my own good intuition, so will state here that I later very quickly ascertained that Linnaeus had indeed written this paradoxical paean at the end of his (partly fictive) Lapland journey. Much later, I found out that the odd owl/fish paradox was by Ibsen. Heights and depths and confusion in both. Teasing and (perhaps pointlessly) suggestive.

Vera Alphage asked if I would like to take this box—and possibly also the photographs—downstairs, to be looked at at leisure, in more comfortable circumstances. Her thin white fingers were pulling at the knot that held together the neck of the scarlet leather dolly-bag. I agreed that taking down the cards and the photographs would be a good first step. I picked up the contraption of straps and screws. I wondered, I said idly, what it was for.

"Oh," said Vera Alphage. "I know what that is. That is a trepanning instrument."

I was not quite sure what trepanning was. I associated the word with dangerous operations on board Napoleonic battleships. She elaborated.

"It makes a small hole in the skull. It relieves pressure and was believed to increase intelligence and even to produce visionary states." She spoke with a certain authority. "I don't know why he would have had one."

Perhaps to enjoy visionary states, I suggested. It had elements of Russian roulette, she replied, almost tartly. Her fingers unloosed the last recalcitrant thread of the knot in the dolly-bag. It proved to contain—we counted them later—366 glass marbles, some obviously very old and beautiful, of many sizes, colours and patterns. There was also, in the dolly-bag, a small notebook, an old-fashioned cash book, in which someone had written: The Names of the Great Families, the Decads, the Sexes and the Hands, in order, with the Comings and Goings Thereof, the Signs, the Blazons and other Matters of Import to the Governance and the Issuing Forth and Return of the Sally-forces and the Defenders of the Posts and Portals. The writing was a schoolboy's writing. It could have evolved—must have evolved—into the neat script of the index cards. Vera Alphage handed me the little book. It was almost entirely a list of names.

Cyanea Spinel Arsenikon Radiolarion, Maidenhair Horsetail Cirrhus Bum Lung Oroubouros Crimsonwisp Cramoisie Nightshade Lamplight Tendril Goosefeather Plume Penna Argus Cuttle Spindrift Bloodrift Rust Amalekite Rahab Rapunzel Hemlock Goosegob Florian Hesper Jasper Whisper Pomegranate Pard Rip Portwine Gyr Tyr Fang Gentian Millipede Fumato Argile Nieve Schneewittchen Popocatapetl Spitfire Uvula Metatarsal Omoplat Cocky Nepenthe Kekule Claw Jormungandr Amphisbaena Moly Gloop

These are only a few of the names from one of the lists. Vera Alphage said, "They all had names. They were all arranged in groups and armies." She held one up to the light, a large, clear one, with a spiral lattice of cobalt in its centre, surrounded by a crimson and gold and white ribbon-system. "I love these," she said. "I shall bring these down with the other things. I wonder if it would be possible to guess which name went with which marble?"

We carried the two shoeboxes and the bag of marbles down the ladder into Vera Alphage's white living-room with its lavender-coloured shadows. I made a quick prospecting foray through both the photograph archive and the card index. Neither showed any signs of order, even on examination. Some of the cards were in verse—I recognised fragments from *Peer Gynt*—and some were small narratives—a man taunting a dog through an iron gate, a man identifying a dead man on a mortuary slab, a fall from a paddle-steamer. There were also reflections on psychology, philosophy, evolution, hybridisation and so on. All on separate cards, with an illusion of equivalent importance given by the geometry of the cards themselves, the 8″ × 6″ rectangles, the fine shadowy feint of the grey lines, the single red line at the top, on which the heading should have been, and wasn't. I caught a glimpse of a card about categorising the colours of glass eyes, which made me think of the marbles. Vera Alphage had laid out a row of the larger ones—some with formal lattice work, some with random coilings of different colours, and was holding them up to the light, one by one, and peering through them.

"This brown is really a very deep purple," she observed, "with golden worms in it."

I turned my attention to the photographs. There were several formal silvery Victorian portraits, and a few naughtyish Edwardian postcards of ladies in frilly knickers with their foot raised suggestively on a pouffe or a ladder. There were photographs either by, or in the style of, Nadar and August Sander. There were *Picture Post* photographs of soldiers bivouacking, and *Tatler* photographs of young ladies in riding-gear or ball-dresses. There were what appeared to be medical photographs of living growths and autopsies in progress. There were also a great many family snapshots. I thought, here surely, I shall encounter Destry-Scholes himself. A boy aged about ten with a fishing-net and a jam-jar of tiddlers suspended on string appeared to be a candidate. He had freckles, and a mop of pale hair, and a cheery expression and grey flannel knee-length shorts. (I assume they were grey. I read them as grey.) I looked at him, and at Vera Alphage. His face was unformed. There was no resemblance, and no absence of resemblance. Then I found a studio picture of a quite different ten-year-old boy, a lovely, raven-haired boy in profile with long lashes whose darkness at least resembled Vera Alphage's. But he was joined by a studious-looking boy with a satchel, rather plump, also dark, and by a very thin boy sitting on a rock at the seaside gripping his knees, with a messy forelock drooping between his eyes. There were several groups of young graduates, with no indication of when they were taken, or where was the lawn on which they posed. There were two quite different groups of military and service men, in khaki shorts and air force blue (how did I tell this from black-and-white images?). Any or none of all these might have been Destry-Scholes. I hate photographs. I have what amounts to a phobia as far as photographs are concerned. I do not permit photographs of myself to be taken. (There are not many people who would ever consider wishing to take any.) Roland Barthes was right, in his book on photography, to say that photographs are essentially involved in death. This creature was living, and will be dead, a photograph says, according to Barthes. His book is a secret elegy for his mother, the photograph he cares for (and doesn't reproduce) is one of her as a child, when she was there and he himself was not. That was before his lifetime. I believe this life ended, cut short by an errant laundry-van, before he could have seen the agonising and remorseless record, by a Danish photographer, of the photographer's mother's last days, from her wistful stare on arrival in her hospital bed, apprehensive and resigned (partly)—to her curled, foetal, skin-on-sharp-bones final leathery state. All writing about photographs, including this writing I am at present engaged in, has something decayed (decadent) and disgusting about it. People have not understood (except Barthes to a certain extent) the horror of these snatched imprints of light and shadow on jelly (Hiroshima gave us a way, a clichéd way quickly, of seeing what it was to leave your shadow etched by brilliance when you were evaporated). The horror of mirrors is nothing to the horror of photographs. It is partly, too, as primitive peoples believe, that the identity is chipped or sucked away by the black hole in the shutter. Snap. Shot. Jaws. Gun barrel. I hate photographs. Destry-Scholes had collected them, possibly at least because he too hated them. I found his collection gruesome. All the eyes were dead, like fish on slabs. But it is possible that I exaggerate, for my own reasons, which I have therefore tried to adumbrate. Adumbrate is a good word, in this context; it sprang to the pen. I notice that my writing is becoming perhaps too impassioned. But then, what sort of a piece of writing is it, for what purpose, for which reader? I may be passionate or dispassionate as I choose, since this document has no importance anyway.

I asked Vera Alphage if she thought any of the photographed faces might be Destry-Scholes. She said she didn't know, adding strangely that it wasn't the surface of faces that interested her. She was still holding the marbles up to the light, one after the other, like lenses. There was no longer much light. She said, without real enthusiasm, that she would poke about in the family photograph albums and see if she could find any matches, or hints. I asked then if I might be allowed to take away the index cards, to study them.

"I don't know you," she replied. "I don't know who you are, or why you want them. I can't let them out of the house, especially since you at least appear to attach some importance to them. But you are welcome to come as often as you wish, and study them here. I lead a quiet life; you wouldn't be disturbed. You have to come on my days off, which are, I'm afraid, irregular."

I asked, then, what she did. She replied that she worked in a hospital—St. Simeon's. She did not at that time enlarge upon what she did in the hospital. I couldn't tell whether she was a nurse, or a surgeon with delicate fingers, or an almoner, or an administrator. Or a psychiatrist, even? I am not, I have learned, good at human beings in the raw. I have no way of knowing who they are or what they want. We agreed that she would phone me on her next day off—"I am almost entirely at your disposal," I said wildly, "apart from two days a week in Puck's Girdle." I gave her that phone number too. She did not ask what Puck's Girdle was, any more than I had pursued the question of what she did in the hospital. We were, we are, tentative creatures, Vera Alphage and I. I formed the project of buying several packs of index cards identical in size to those Destry-Scholes had used. Photocopying was out of the question. I should have to rewrite his writings in my writing on my own cards. Fortunately our scripts, at least, are much the same size.

I have just written that I am not good at human beings in the raw. This was about to be proved in quite another context.

The Strange Customer returned once or twice to Puck's Girdle, never when Erik and Christophe were there. I put that down to the fact that his days off might coincide with mine. He always asked for Pim or Pym (I never found out which) and added a surname, Proctor (or Proktor, or Procter). On his third visit, it may have been, he handed me a card with his name on it—no address—Maurice Bossey—and waited for signs of recognition, which were not forthcoming, for I did not recognise it. He also instituted a curious habit of consuming very small meals, whilst sitting at the bible-shelf and consulting the chained books. These were nothing so vulgar as sandwiches or buns. He would produce from a small leather satchel a metal plate or dish (possibly silver, even) and an unfolding three-pronged silvery fork, not unlike the trident of a *retiarius*. There was also a kind of gentleman's flick-knife, with a fine, wicked blade. He would dissect a small quail, or cut paper-thin slices from a strip of bloody meat (fillet of beef, venison, veal? such things are outside my proficiency also). He would have a fresh roll and a little pat of butter in waxed paper, and this would be followed by fruit. He called me over once, to watch him dissect a ripe peach. I watched him insert his blade in the crease between the two rounds of the fruit, and then make a circle of overlapping half-moons round the kernel with fragments of pink flesh still adhering to it. He offered me a slice. I backed away. I did not want his fruit-flesh on a silver dish. On another occasion he called me over to watch him use yet another instrument—a long, fine corkscrew, a lacquered tube—to extract the cork from a half-bottle of Château Lacoste. He pushed it in with rhythmic screwing motions, and a smile on the corner of his mouth. He then produced two gilt-lined silver beakers, of a miniature kind, and poured me one. The wine was thick, rich, red and bubbled slightly. Again, it seemed important to refuse. I thought it was simply because I did not like him. He smelt vaguely of camphor, and beyond the camphor of a rather sickly incense, almost undetectable, but there. All this present writing of mine is making him sound rather suspicious, I know (I hope), but at the time all I felt was a vague unease, I think. We had a lot of eccentrics in Puck's Girdle. Backpackers and parsons, elderly ladies in stalwart stockings and brogues, sun-seeking skeletally thin girl-women in silky shifts, beefy mountaineers, beardy ecologists. Maurice Bossey was barely odder than the norm. And I was so anxious to do well, to live up to the hopes Erik and Christophe had of me, to further their imaginative vision of the pleasures of travel.

I was a failure as a semiotician, I do now see. I may be getting better at *writing,* now, when it is too late, but then I was slow, I did not read the signs.

After a week or so, Vera Alphage wrote to say that she had a free day, and I was welcome to come and study the photographs and cards. I went back to Willesden, where a space had been made for me at a little writing-bureau in what appeared to be the spare bedroom—sparsely furnished, with a single bed, some sort of floral curtains, a patchwork quilt. I took a sandwich and an apple—I didn't want Ms. Alphage to suppose she had to entertain me—but she brought up a bowl of watercress soup at lunchtime, a brown roll, and a piece of Brie. My initial feeling on confronting the cards, with so limited a time to read them in, was panic. I decided to read them all through, and to note—on paper—all the subjects of the "entries." Then I would look at the groupings (if any) and copy out what I myself found most striking. What other approach could I use? It was all peculiarly unsatisfactory. Nor do I think now that I can record here, in full, my "findings." It took me three visits to make a record of the contents of the box, which still appear to me so diverse and ramshackle that remembering them in any order or making any sense of them is no more than *botching.* I had the idea, which turned out to be hopelessly idealistic, that I should approach them with a completely open mind, a kind of researcher's version of the *tabula rasa,* in order to understand the whole of Destry-Scholes's purpose (if he had one) in accumulating the collection, and the subtleties (if any) of the ordering of the cards.

"To find, not to impose," as Wallace Stevens magnificently said. One of the reasons I had given up post-structuralist thought was the disagreeable amount of imposing that went on in it. You decided what you were looking for, and then duly found it—male hegemony, liberal-humanist *idées reçues*, etc. This was made worse by the fact that the deconstructionists and others paid lip-service to the idea that they must not impose—they even went so far as half-believing they must not find, either. And yet they discovered the same structures, the same velleities, the same evasions quite routinely in the most disparate texts. I wanted most seriously *not* to impose that sort of a reading, and, more primitively, not to impose my own hypotheses about who Destry-Scholes was, or what he was doing. This was not difficult, as my hypotheses were very ghostly, thin air, no more.

What shape do I give, in my mind, now, to that cubic mass of tiny writing?

The salient bits were where two or three consecutive cards appeared to be on the same subject. Here for instance, is a little sequence beginning with card no. 21 (I asked Vera Alphage's permission to number them—in pencil, lightly—and she agreed that I might).

Card no. 21

> The young man's name was Ludvig David. He dived from a second-floor window in a Roman apartment. He was unwell, suffering from a high fever, pouring with sweat and HI was of the opinion that he believed

that the wavering, liquefying surface he saw below him was the spumy surface of a cool, profound, refreshing sea. Like HI himself, the exiles all felt a perpetual longing for the tossing seas of the North. It is also possible that the young man meant to end, either his temporary but intolerable pain, or his life itself, for more settled reasons. Whatever the reasons for the leap, HI made it his business to be present at the autopsy. He wrote to B, Ludvig David's friend, with a precise description of the state of the corpse. "The skull was crushed at the apex, and the face was scraped, flayed in some sort, and bloodied. The arms and legs were intact, but the ribcage was crushed and the lungs ripped, which caused a great flow of blood." HI peered doubtless into the cavern of the skull. The scalp and the features were rolled back like the skin of an onion.

It is odd that he recorded all this in what appears to have been his first letter to B.

Card no. 22

"When I saw the stiff and lifeless body, the livid, pale and foam-flecked lips; when I thought of the loss of so old and excellent a friend and remembered the sleepless nights, the laborious days, the journeys, the midnight hours of exhausting study which had preceded his attainment of that learning in which he had no rival to fear—then I burst into tears. And when I foresaw that all this scholarship, which should have earned immortality for him and glory for his country, would perish with his death, then the love which I still felt for my friend commanded that the pledge we had once made—that the survivor would give to the world the observations of the other—must be honoured."

A. was drowned in a canal in Amsterdam on 27th September 1735 after a convivial evening with Seba. A few days earlier, he had read to CL all he had so far written of his book on ichthyology, keeping CL up almost all night—his usual habit was to go to the tavern from three to nine, to work from nine to three in the night, and to sleep from three till noon. CL wrote of their last, intense discussion:—"He kept me long, too long, unendurably long (which was unlike our usual practice) but had I known that it was to be our last talk together I would have wished it even longer." A. was only 29 when he drowned. CL described him as "the ornament and glory of his nation!" He wrote, "Thus too early did Fate pluck this unique genius! Thus did the most distinguished of ichthyologists perish in the waters, having devoted his life to the discovery of their inhabitants! . . ."

Card no. 23   [Thursday, April 14th 1840]
I went in a Steam Boat to Putney to see the Oxford and Cambridge rowing match. As we were returning, very fast and with the tide, through Battersea Bridge, we ran foul of the middle pier. I, who was behind the paddle-box, saw how we were going just before we struck, and caught tight hold of one of the paddle-box steps, expecting a general smash and determined to have a swim for it. Well, the body of the packet cleared, but

the paddle-box, behind which I was, came full crash against the sides of the arch. It split open just before me by the shock. I was thrown head foremost through the cleft, right amongst the paddle wheels, which were still going round, they not having touched the pier . . . Well, this regularly stunned me. Thank heavens my neck was not broken in the wheel. (Escape no. 1.) I was quite insensible, and how I cleared the bridge I have not the slightest conception. I must have been beaten down by the paddle wheels beneath the bottom of the boat—and fortunately enough, otherwise I must have been jammed between it and the pier and of course squashed. That makes Escape no. 2. Well, as I said, I was insensible, and when I knew where I was, I found myself under a large piece of wood which proved to be the outer side of the paddle-box . . . I of course gave myself up, but determined to have a regular push for life . . . I did not sink I daresay a foot below the surface, but I got entangled in some long bits of wood, which as I was all but spent nearly drowned me, and when I got to the surface they were too heavy to give me any real support, so I looked round, and saw the side of the paddle-box, which had before been so much in my way, floating down with the tide. I struck out and soon reached it—and I did feel happy. I climbed on to it and it was a perfect raft. (Escape no. 3.) On looking about me I found that the steamer was 300 yards or so in front and could not stir . . . Well, I was in the midst of the river, plenty of boats and watermen were at the shore, those nice dear fellows who when they see you struggling, look on, and never dream of rowing to you till you are either safe or dead—yes, and if safe, they swear they saved your life, march off to the Royal Humane Society and get a gold medal for their pains, with a long paragraph in *The Times* about "unparalleled bravery," and so forth. Well, after waving my hat, for I don't know how long, off some half-dozen came in a body. I was pulled into a boat and felt very seedy, I was dizzy and very sick. However, to put the captain out of his fright, I took an oar, declared nothing was the matter with me and pulled mechanically.

I was so dizzy that I scarce knew what I did. On getting to the packet everybody looked horrified, one or two ladies held up their handkerchiefs before their eyes. I couldn't make out what at, but on getting ashore and to an inn, with a looking-glass I found my face, ears and whiskers, shirt etc. all covered with blood. One nail had hooked me by the side of the nose, another had "carved" out my face and I had as many cuts on my ear as a Christmas pig. I got to bed, half dried clothes and walked to London. Now don't fancy I am ill. I took enough calomel and salts to do anything, and except a rather torn face and broken head, I really have *nothing* the matter with me . . . I have gained great glory by my splashes under water and it is a very good tale to tell—at least when the pain goes off. I now know something of what drowning is—I felt no pain, but rather dreamy—and I also know what my feeling will be when I am dying, as I firmly believed I was then.

Cards 24 and 25 were copied out (I supposed they were copied out. It was clear to me that 23 was copied from somewhere, and 22 was a mixture of copying and reporting) in a Scandinavian language I couldn't read. It could have been Swedish—Linnaeus—or Norwegian—Ibsen. The word Maelstrøm occurred, also the words Arcturus, Boreas, and Pisces. This caused me to suppose that these were quotations from Linnaeus—and they were, moreover, the first solid evidence I had had—*almost* solid evidence—that Destry-Scholes pursued his Scandinavian researches in the original languages. It is possible, of course that he copied the originals, as I copied his copies, with the intention of procuring translations. It occurred to me that Providence, or Fate, had presented me with a translator just when I needed one. I would send the cards to Fulla Biefeld for identification and translation. I would also send the description of the death of A (whom I soon identified as Petrus Artedi, Linnaeus's student friend, the originator of many of the classificatory systematics which Linnaeus used, or adapted).

Card no. 26

It has happened to me more than once to be nearly suffocated, and to have been surprised at the absence of that gasping desire for air that one feels when the breath is suddenly checked. A very little seems sufficient to divert attention from that desire, and to leave the sense only of being ill and on the point of swooning. My chief experiences may seem hardly credible; they were due to a fancy of mine to obtain distinct vision when diving. The convex eyeball stamps a concave lens in the water, whose effect has to be neutralised by a convex lens. This has to be very "strong," because the refractive power of a lens is greatly diminished by immersion in water. My first experiment was in a bath, using the two objectives of my opera-glass in combination, and with some success. I then had spectacles made for me, which I described at the British Association in 1865. With these I could read the print of a newspaper perfectly under water, when it was held at the exact distance of clear vision, but the range of clear vision was small. I amused myself very frequently with this new hobby, and being most interested in the act of reading, constantly forgot that I was nearly suffocating myself, and was recalled to the fact not by any gasping desire for breath, but purely by a sense of illness, that alarmed me. It disappeared immediately after raising the head out of water and inhaling two or three good whiffs of air.

Card no. 27

PEER: What a storm!

STRANGE PASSENGER: Yes! Beautiful!

PEER: Beautiful?

SP: The waves are running as high as houses.
It makes my mouth water. Think of the wrecks
There will be tonight. Think of the corpses
    drifting ashore.

PEER: God preserve us!

SP: Have you ever seen a man strangled?
Or hanged—or drowned?

PEER: What—

SP: They laugh; but their laughter is forced.
Most of them bite out their tongues.

PEER: Get away from me!

SP: Just one question. Suppose we, for example
Should strike on a rock, and sink in the darkness—

PEER: You think there is a danger—?

SP: I don't really know what I ought to say.
But suppose now, I should float and you should
sink—

PEER: Oh rubbish—!

SP: It's just a hypothesis.
But when a man stands with one foot in the grave
He sometimes tends to be generous—

PEER: [*Puts his hand in his pocket.*] Oh, money—

SP: No, no. But if you would be so kind
As to bequeath me your valuable body—

PEER: What!

SP: Only your corpse, you understand.
To help my researches—

PEER: Go away!

SP: But, my dear sir, consider. It's to your advantage.
I'll open you up and let in the light.
I want to discover the source of your dreams.
I want to find out how you're put together—

PEER: Away!

SP: But my dear sir! A drowned body—!

PEER: Blasphemous man!
You're provoking the storm. Are you out of your
mind?

Look at the sea! These waves are like mountains!
At any moment we may be killed.
And you're acting as though you can hardly wait
    for it.
SP: I see you're not in a mood for discussion.
But time, they say, changes everything.
We'll meet when you're sinking, if not before.
Perhaps you'll be more in the humour, then.
[*Goes into cabin.*]
PEER: Horrible fellows these scientists are!
You damned freethinker!

I am not quite sure in what order to recount the next few
parts of my tale, as I find that my memory for exact sequences
is faultier than I would wish. I feel a desire in myself—an
aesthetic desire—to punctuate my assimilation of Destry-
Scholes's shoeboxes (for I began to try to make sense of the
photographs as well as of the cards, with some success, as will
be seen) with my encounters with the Strange Customer. It
shows at least that I was now leading two lives—three, if you
count Ormerod Goode as separate from the card index. I had
not told him of my latest discovery. I was saving it up. Four, in
fact, if you count Fulla Biefeld, in Oxford. I cannot now
remember how often I went back to Willesden. A feeling of
panic—that I *must* get a record of the cards before Vera
Alphage grew bored or resentful—was replaced by a calm
rhythm of consecutive work, as I came to see that she enjoyed
my presence there, and even looked forward to my visits. At
around this time, Erik and Christophe took off for an explo-

ration of the northern islands of Japan. They left me in charge—I worked four, instead of two, days a week. This meant that my visits to Willesden took place in the evenings. Yes, that is how it was, at that time.

The Strange Customer asked me if I had favourite Web sites. I spoke of various useful travelling ones, hotel chains, art historical troves, etcetera. He said that was not what he meant. He said he would leave me a list of the ones he and Pym (or Pim) had found particularly helpful. I thanked him. He offered me a cigar. He had one of those curious little implements which nick a small hole in the top of a cigar. It had a very small, very sharp little pronging blade. I said I didn't smoke. Maurice Bossey said, levelly and expressionlessly, that I didn't do much, did I? I said I would try to help him if he would be a little more explicit about what he wanted. (Did I *really* say that? Yes, I did, I remember clearly, some memories ingrain themselves like light on photographic film.) He said he was glad that I intended to be helpful, or the reputation of Puck's Girdle might have been thought to be at stake. He smoked his fat cigar at me—burning cigar-tobacco has an element of *rot* in it, I find, an element of burning something already stale and decaying—and I asked him not to, as I am asthmatic. He referred to my "poor little lungs" and puffed more and closer, coils and clouds of dark, thick fume. (No, I am doing *too much writing* now. Cross that out? Leave it for the moment.) (Anyway, it *was* fume, and it was in coils.)

He opened his wallet and produced a very fine paper that contained nothing but a series of Web addresses.

"Try those," he said, "as a stimulus to a sluggish imagination. Your dear employers are altogether quicker, I'm sure . . ." He considered me.

"There's not very much of you, is there? Do they take you along with them, ever? Are you part of the crew, so to speak?"

"I mind the shop," I told him.

"Well, don't mind it with too tight lips," he said. "Allow a few things to get out or go in. A smile, a chuckle, a bit of information, a snippet of gossip from time to time."

I said I didn't know any gossip.

He said he was dreadfully afraid that might be true.

Cards 21–26 I called in my mind the "drowning and autopsy cluster." Fulla Biefeld wrote back very promptly in answer to my queries, and said that the cards I had sent her were related to Linnaeus. One described his theory that swallows spent the winters under water, under the ice in deep lakes (a theory, she told me, very widespread at the time). The other was a contemporary description of the death of Peter Artedi, who had wandered into an unfenced canal in Amsterdam in an inebriated state, and had been identified in the mortuary by Carolus Linné. Artedi, Fulla Biefeld said, was a person of much greater intelligence than Linnaeus himself, and his classification of the *umbelliferae*, published by Linnaeus after his death, had been a model for much of Linnaeus's own work. His system was also thought of, by our own contemporaries, despite having known nothing (of course) about evolution, as an ancestor of cladism, the classification of species by phylogeny, in which each named taxon should have a unique evolutionary history. He was more rigorous and less fanciful than

Linnaeus, said Fulla Biefeld. His death at twenty-nine was a long time ago. What exactly was I trying to find out? Scientists could not understand people like me who spent their time on past errors and culs-de-sac, however amusing. She enclosed an article on the effects of the blanket use of pesticides and weedkiller in certain Californian orchards. Such studies *should* be being carried out in East Anglia, in Bavaria, in Spain, and they were not. She was happy to give me any more help I needed.

My next definitive cluster—starting with card 42, but with some gaps this time, and some uncertainties of classification, might be called "hybrids and mixtures." It begins with the Hydra of Hamburg.

Card no. 42

The seven-headed hydra belonged to the Burgomaster of Hamburg. It had been looted by Count Königsmark in 1648, after the Battle of Prague, from the altar of a local church. Albert Seba, Artedi's patron, published a drawing of the hydra or seven-headed serpent in the first volume of his Thesaurus of Natural History. CL, taken by Kohl to see the creature, at once detected the fake. He found that the jaws and clawed feet were those of weasels, and that the body had been covered with snake-skins neatly joined and glued. That the creature had seven heads was in itself enough, in his opinion, to establish the fraud. "Good God," he cried, "who never put more than one clear thought [*tanke*] in any of Thy created bodies!" He presumed that the hydra had been manufactured by monks as a representation of an Apocalyptic beast, and makes no mention of Greek mythology.

The Burgomaster had for some time past been trying to sell his hydra and had at first asked an enormous sum for it. It was said that the King of Denmark had made an unsuccessful bid of 30,000 thalers; but latterly the price had been steadily dropping, and when L tactlessly made public his discovery, it fell to nothing at all. Fearing the vengeance of the Burgomaster he thought fit to leave Hamburg forthwith. On 16 May 1735 they went to Altona, from where they embarked in a small two-masted ship for Amsterdam (one ducat per head).

Card no. 43

When CL was visiting the Jussieu brothers in Paris in 1737 he accompanied them and their students on botanical hunts. One of the brothers constructed a spurious flower out of fragments of various other specimens, and asked him to name it. He, sharp of eye and quick of wit, was not at all deceived by what was, after all, a common enough student pleasantry. He answered urbanely that the student should consult Jussieu— "since only Jussieu or God could name the plant."

Cards 44 and 45 were both in Swedish. I sent copies of these, too, off to Fulla Biefeld. I give her answers now, since I am not writing to any strict consecutive chronology, and since they reinforce my decision to call this the "hybrid" cluster.

The first turned out to concern Linnaeus's experimental creation of the first fertile plant hybrid—*(Tragopogon pratensis x T. porrifolius)* and his description in *De Sexu Plantarum* (1760) of his manipulation of the flowers of *Mirabilis, Cannabis* and other species, by cutting off the stamens, binding paper round the pistils, etc. in order to confirm the basic principle of botany—that pollination—pollen on the stigma of the pistil—was necessary if the seeds were to ripen.

Fulla Biefeld added, on her own initiative, that many of the plant hybrids identified by Linnaeus were nothing of the kind. He believed, she told me, that both animals and plants consisted of two substances—pith (or marrow) and bark, *medulla* and *cortex,* of which the pith/marrow was inner, the bearer of vital and generative powers, whilst the bark stood for the "outer," primarily the nutritive faculty. The pith/marrow stood for the female in reproduction (the pistil in plants), the bark corresponded to the "male principle" (the stamens).

Fulla Biefeld was scornful (or perhaps simply dismissive) about these theories. Linnaeus had come, she said, to tell his disciples that the *will* resided in the female principle, the ability to expand and contract. In this context he cited the one-celled amoeba, the "lowest of all creatures" *(Volvox Chaos dicta),* which was "pure marrow" and hence could assume all conceivable shapes.

False analogy, said Fulla Biefeld, and the desire to construct a theory of everything from received ideas close at hand, were very dangerous. But you had to admire his inexhaustible ingenuity.

I wrote back—she tempted me into writing back—that in terms of false analogy I was, so to speak, metaphysically baffled by the bee orchid and the eyes on butterfly wings. I understood the argument (Darwinian) for the production of these solid living analogies, I *understood the argument* that a resemblance could be perfected over millennia by a flower, or the scales on a wing, by natural selection—but I couldn't really *believe* it. It still had a quality of designed poetry that left me baffled. I said I wasn't answering *her* point, I was adding one of my own.

Card 45, she told me, was Linnaeus's endorsement of Réaumur's account of the hatching of a chicken covered with hair, after the crossing of a rabbit and a hen.

Card no. 46

All the Darwin rabbit letters that have survived are those which *followed* the publication of Galton's paper "Experiments in Pangenesis by Breeding from Rabbits of a pure variety, into whose circulation blood taken from other varieties had previously been largely transfused." This was read at the Royal Society on March 30th 1871. These letters refer to a continuation of the experiments, also with negative conclusions . . . Those who read the letters below cannot doubt that Darwin knew the nature of the experiments, and knew that Galton was assuming that the "gemmules" circulated in the blood. The whole point was to determine whether the hereditary units of a breed A could be transfigured by transfusion of blood to members of a breed B and would "mongrelise" the offspring conceived later by B.

Was the "blood" indeed as supposed in folk-language all over the world a true bearer of hereditary characters?

Card no. 47

Dec. 11. 69. My dear Darwin, I wonder if you could help me. I want to make some peculiar experiments that have occurred to me in breeding animals and want to procure a few couples of rabbits of marked and assured breeds, viz: *Lop-ear* with as little tendency to Albinism as possible. *Common rabbits,* ditto. *Angora albinus*... Pray excuse my troubling you; the interest of the proposed experiment—for it is really a curious one—must be my justification...

March 15, 70.
My dear Darwin,

I shall hope in a week from now to give you some news and by Saturday week definite facts about the rabbits. One litter [?doe] has littered today and all looks well with her... I grieve to say that my most hopeful one was confined prematurely by 3 days having made no nest and all we knew of the matter was finding blood from the cage and the *head* of one of the litter. She was transfused from yellow and the buck also from yellow. Well the head was certainly much lighter than the head of another abortion I had seen, and was certainly *irregularly* coloured, being especially darker, about the muzzle, but I did not and do not care to build anything upon such vague facts and have not even kept the head. As soon as I know *anything* I will write instantly and first to you. For my part, I am quite sick with expected hope and doubt . . .

Card no. 48
Letter of Charles Darwin in *Nature,* April 27, 1871
"Pangenesis." In a paper, read March 30th 1871 before the Royal Society, and just published in the Proceedings, Mr. Galton gives the results of his interesting experiments on the inter-transfusion of the blood of distinct varieties of rabbits. These experiments were undertaken to test whether there was any truth in my provisional hypothesis of Pangenesis. Mr. Galton, in recapitulating "the cardinal points" says that the gemmules are supposed "to swarm in the blood." Now in the chapter on Pangenesis in my "Variation of Animals and Plants under Domestication," I have not said one word about the blood, or about any fluid proper to the circulating system. It is, indeed, obvious that the presence of gemmules in the blood can form no necessary part of my hypothesis; for I refer in illustration of it to the lowest animals, such as the Protozoa, which do not possess blood or any vessels; and I refer to plants in which the fluid, when present in the vessels, can not be considered as true blood . . . I have said that "the gemmules in each organism must be thoroughly diffused; nor does this seem improbable, considering their minuteness and the steady circulation of fluids through the body." But when I used these latter words and other similar ones, I presume that I was thinking of the diffusion of the gemmules through the tissues, or from

cell to cell, independently of the presence of vessels—as in the remarkable experiments by Dr. Bence Jones, in which the chemical elements absorbed by the stomach were detected in the course of some minutes in the crystalline lens of the eye; . . . Nor can it be objected that the gemmules could not pass through tissues or cell walls, for the contents of each pollen grain have to pass through the coats, both of the pollen tube and embryonic sac. I may add, with respect to the passage of fluids through membrane, that they pass from cell to cell in the absorbing hairs of the roots of living plants at a rate, as I have myself observed under the microscope, which is truly surprising.

When, therefore, Mr. Galton concludes, from the fact that rabbits of one variety, with a large proportion of the blood of another variety in their veins, do not produce mongrelised offspring, that the hypothesis of Pangenesis is false, it seems to me that his conclusion is a little hasty . . .

Card nos. 49–51
Letter of Francis Galton in *Nature,* May 4, 1871
"Pangenesis." It appears from Mr. Darwin's letter . . . that the views contradicted by my experiments . . . differ from those he entertains. Nevertheless, I think they are what his published account of Pangenesis are [*sic*] most likely to convey to the mind of a reader. The ambiguity is due to an inappropriate use of three separate words: "circulate," "freely" and "diffused." The proper meaning of circulation is evident enough—it is a re-entering movement. Nothing

can justly be said to circulate which does not return, after a time, to a former position. In a circulating library, books return and are re-issued. Coin is said to circulate, because it comes back into the same hands in the interchange of business. A story circulates, when a person hears it repeated over and over again in society. Blood has an undoubted claim to be called a circulating fluid, and when that phrase is used, blood is always meant . . .

Freely means "without retardation" as we might say that small fish can swim freely through the larger meshes of a net; now it is impossible to suppose gemmules to pass through solid tissue without *any* retardation . . .

I do not much complain of having been sent on a false quest by ambiguous language, for I know how conscientious Mr. Darwin is in all he writes, how difficult it is to put thoughts into accurate speech, and again, how words have conveyed false impressions on the simplest matters, from the earliest times. Nay, even in that idyllic scene which Mr. Darwin has sketched of the first invention of language, awkward blunders must of necessity have often occurred. I refer to the passage in which he supposes some unusually wise ape-like animal to have first thought of imitating the growl of a beast of prey so as to indicate to his fellow-monkeys the nature of the expected danger. For my part, I feel as if I had just been assisting at such a scene. As if, having heard my trusted leader utter a cry, not particularly well articulated, but to my ears more like that of a hyena than any other animal, and seeing none of my companions stir a step, I had, like a loyal member of the flock, dashed down a path of which I had happily caught sight, into the plain below, followed by the approving nods and kindly grunts of my wise and most respected chief. And I now feel, after returning from my hard expedition, full of information that the suspected danger was a mistake, for there was no sign of a hyena anywhere in the neighbourhood, I am given to understand for the first time that my leader's cry had no reference to a hyena down in the plain, but to a leopard somewhere up in the trees; his throat had been a little out of order, that was all. Well, my labour has not been in vain; it is something to have established the fact that there are no hyenas in the plain, and I think I see my way to a good position for a lookout for leopards among the branches of the trees. In the meantime, Vive Pangenesis! Francis Galton."

Card no. 52

In view of the previous correspondence lasting for nearly two years—referred to only in words which Darwin alone could appreciate: "followed by the approving nods and kindly grunts of my wise and most respected chief"—I think this letter of Galton's in *Nature* is one of the finest things he ever wrote in his life; it is few men who have such a great opportunity and use it so bravely. Vive Pangenesis!

Card no. 53

It is a biographer's duty to illustrate the real strength of his subject's character, not merely to call it great. I know of no case in which a disciple's reverence for his master has exceeded that shown by Galton for Darwin in this matter. I doubt if any natures the least smaller than those of Darwin and Galton would have sustained their friendship unbroken, even for a day, after April 24th 1871. I feel that the self-effacement of Galton in this instance is one of the most characteristic actions of his life; but it is not one that a biographer can disregard, however great his reverence for Darwin.

I (Phineas G. Nanson, that is, the ur-I of this document) feel I should intermit here the transcription of the Hybrids and Cluster—*my* hybrids and cluster—to comment more particularly on card 53, which, as will not have escaped an attentive reader, is not about hybrids or mixtures, but very clearly about biography, about the relation of biographer to subject. I have to admit that I was moved by Galton's eloquence, by his linguistic indignation, by his beautifully sustained and nuanced linguistic/evolutionary metaphor for what amounted to Darwin's betrayal of his friend and cousin. I hoped, and briefly I believed, that the first-person biographer, who here suddenly and surprisingly makes a statement of faith, was no other than Scholes Destry-Scholes himself. After all, he had written at least part of a biography of Galton, in his vivid description of Galton's journeys through Ovampoland to Lake Ngami and his visionary experiences there. It was Galton the explorer, in some sense, who had played with the laugh of a hyena, the cough of a leopard and the kindly grunts of Charles Darwin. I liked to think that he had stopped to record his admiration for his subject and to state his sense of "a biographer's duty." It was, however, my duty as his biographer, to check the sources, and on my next visit to the British Library I rapidly discovered that the words I had taken to be those of Scholes Destry-Scholes were in fact the measured tones of Karl Pearson, Galton's first biographer, author of *The Grammar of Science,* whose activities at University College London were inspired and financed by Galton. (The Biometric Laboratory, the Eugenics Laboratory, the Galton Professorship of National Eugenics [later Human Genetics], the Chair of Statistics, the *Annals of Eugenics, Biometrika* . . .) When I found this out—the discussion of the rabbit episode is in Volume II of Pearson's very weighty four-volume work—I assumed for some time that Destry-Scholes had copied it out so carefully because he approved of it, shared its emotion and its definition of the relations between biographer and biographee. Then, as I read further in Pearson, at once entranced and slightly repelled by the apostolic fervour of his devotion to Galton, I began to wonder. Respected modern biographers after all are not remarkable for their reverence for their subjects, or for their subjects' beliefs. Pearson's belief in Eugenics I discovered to have been fervent. He states (Vol. IIIA, p. 435—I cannot bring myself to imitate Destry-Scholes's insouciant lack of reference) that Galton's "life-aim" had been "to study racial mass-changes in many fields, with the view of controlling the evolution of man, as man controls that of many living forms." This was of course written in innocent ignorance of the uses to which such ideas were to be put, and our present nervous horror of such declarations would no doubt have surprised those idealistic late Victorians. Pearson goes on to believe that Galton will have a place in the history of civilisation equal to that of Darwin in science:

Galton taught a new morality, an unwonted doctrine of altruism—like all new creeds, difficult to accept and easy to pour scorn on: *"Help the strong rather than the weak; aid the man of tomorrow rather than the man of today; let knowledge and foresight control the blind emotions and impetuous instincts wherewith Nature, red-clawed, drives man, mindless and stupefied, down her own evolutionary paths."* "Awake my people," was Galton's cry, like that of a religious prophet of the older time. He was an agnostic, in that he saw the weakness of the creeds so far proclaimed by man, suffice, as they may, for many less deeply-probing minds; yet as his niece said to the biographer, he was a *religious* agnostic; the term seems to me an apt one.

Here we have, in the passage in quotation marks, a mundane version of a tendency which I was beginning to suspect has been (possibly deliberately) *extravagantly* elaborated by Destry-Scholes. The prophetic utterances and adjurations ascribed by Pearson to Galton are Pearson's own, and I believe—having now read much further in Galton, whose style is *intellectually* agnostic and questing and always open—a trait which enabled him to accept Darwin's *volte-face* with wit and equilibrium—that stylistic analysis would show that Galton could not have written that sentence. However, this rhetorical device is neither here nor there beside the indisputable fact that *Galton never reached Lake Ngami* (any more than Linnaeus ever sailed to the Maelstrøm, or travelled to Torneå). In the case of Linnaeus what we may charitably call the *distortions of fact* were his own, and are thus in themselves biographical facts. (I am becoming infected by the Victorian sonorous reasoning of Pearson. Just when I had come to believe that I was finding a style *of my own,* entirely freed from post-post-structuralist clutter.) *But Galton never claimed to have reached Lake Ngami, and even denied—to his companions' annoyance—that his intention had been to reach Lake Ngami.* Nor have I ever found any source for the visions Destry-Scholes ascribes to him on the shores of that lake, though it is only fair to record scrupulously that many of the elements—for instance, Galton's vision of the hanging body of the wretch crucified by Roman soldiery—can be found in his autobiographical memoirs, or his *Inquiries into Human Faculty and Its Development.* He states that his vision of the crucified body came without religious overtones, simply a body.

What was Destry-Scholes up to? There's the question, my question. I formed a tentative hypothesis, after reading Pearson, that he was conducting an experiment in the nature of biographical narrative. There is a difference between the kind of biography Pearson wrote, the kind Destry-Scholes wrote of Elmer Bole, and the modern critical, or psychoanalytical, biography. The modern way of characterising Pearson is as a "hagiography" (would he, would Galton, have smiled or frowned at the religious connotations of this?). It could be compared to John Cross's biography of his wife, George Eliot, with its full, but tendentious and bowdlerised quotations. But there is a sense in which what may appear to be the redundant *fullness* of quotation, of illustration, saves such hagiographical words from bias. For Galton's voice speaks beside his disciple's, and in a different style. And what modern readers, eager for a thesis, a hypothesis, would find redundant, appear to readers on a quest like mine to be *facts,* to be even *things,* to be nuggets of pure quiddity. And if you have an ear, the sound of truth, the fall of a sentence, the inspissated muddle of a real controversy of which the end is not known, is there for both instruction and delectation. Pearson did not know (even) about genes. He and Galton did know about Mendel.

I find I need to record—because I appear to be, because I am, unsympathetic to Pearson—his reaction to Galton's burial, which he confines to a footnote (IIIA, 435):

> †Francis Galton's remains were placed in the family vault constructed in the churchyard by his father. He lies by his parents, Samuel Tertius and Violetta (Darwin) Galton . . . Galton no doubt expressed a wish to lie there, and a simpler village churchyard, more remote and peaceful, could scarcely be found. Yet cremation, as in the case of Herbert Spencer, or of Galton's own brother, Erasmus Galton, would have seemed to his biographer a more fitting end for what must one day perish. It is with pain that I think even to-day of Francis Galton's mortal remains coffined in a vault.

What a strange, what a moving thing this footnote is. How full of curious, precise, local feeling. Here is a man fully aware of the emotions that are aroused by the idea of "a simple village church-yard, remote and peaceful." A man, moreover, obsessed with genealogy and ancestry, who records and respects his subject's desire to be buried (I avoid, as he did, the anthropomorphism, "to rest") where his parents are buried. Yet this man's own emotions are also powerful. He has a "religious agnostic" belief that cremation is purer, more appropriate, symbolically and in fact. He leaves his reader with the merest frisson of a suspicion that his love of the dead man finds the idea of his bodily deliquescence revolting, that the disintegrating corpse haunts his imagination. I do not really know whether this feeling can legitimately be read into his phrase "It is with pain that I think even to-day . . ." I only know that I did myself so read it, before I was checked by wondering whether I was *reading into* it. And then, there is his use of the word "biographer." All he can now be to his friend, he seems to say, is *his biographer.* At the same time, he claims for that rôle the right to pronounce on what would seem to be—in the context of his and his subject's beliefs and principles (despite his subject's *expressed wish,* we note, but note also that it is from him, the biographer, that we have our information about this wish)—what would seem to be the appropriate ceremony with which to take leave of "what must one day perish."

What did Destry-Scholes think the rôle of a biographer was? Why did he tell lies and write parodies? I was finding it increasingly difficult to disentangle his ideas about his three Personages—and the threads ran out all the time, from Linnaeus to Artedi, from Galton to Darwin and Pearson—from my own quest for a way to look at the world, for some kind of direct collision on my part with *things.* All right, also with *facts.* Looking back on my own times, what most strikes me is that we have developed endlessly subtle styles and techniques to reveal the secret meaning behind the apparent meaning, to open up the desires and assumptions behind what people say and explain about what they feel and believe. And all that can really be read into what we write is our own desire to translate everything, everyone, all reasoning, all irrational hope and fear, into our own Procrustean grid of priorities. The world is very old, and modern theories of the mind and its politics are very recent and very local. They have not stood the test of time (beware cliché, PGN) as Plato's metaphors of the Cave or Empedocles' account of the atomic universe have.

In the end, all I can do, is read the biographer's paragraph on his subject's dead body and make an *imaginative stab at* the penumbra of his words. My own ideas of the duties of a "biographer," of "thinking with pain," "of mortal remains," of "a fitting end for what must one day perish" confer life, but not necessarily more truth, on what Pearson had, in his own terms, *quite adequately expressed.*

But no string has an end. Like spider-silk unreeling.

I have managed to trap myself in digressions, if there can be digressions in a project that appears alternately to have too little and too much form. I start too many hares. (What *does* that mean? I have never seen a hare run. I am an urban animal. Ah, but in the mind's eye . . . And whose voice is *that,* with its plangent Ah, but . . . ?) I shall go back to my list of what was, before I or Destry-Scholes interrupted it, a reasonably coherent "hybrids and mixtures" cluster.

Card no. 54
    June 5th 1888,
        The sea's magnetic power. The longing for the
    sea. Human beings akin to the sea. Bound by the sea.

Dependent on the sea. Must return to it. One species of fish is a vital link in the chain of evolution. Do rudiments of it still reside in the human mind? In the minds of certain people.

Images of the teeming life of the sea and of "what is lost forever." The sea operates a power over one's moods, it works like a will. The sea can hypnotise. Nature in general can . . . She has come from the sea. Became secretly engaged to the Strange Passenger . . . At heart, in her instincts—he is the one with whom she is living in marriage . . .

Card no. 55

PROFESSOR RUBEK: All the same, I can assure you they're not simply portrait-busts.

MAIA: What else are they then?

PR: There's something subtle and equivocal lurking below the surface of all those portraits . . . a secret something that the mob can't see.

MAIA: Oh?

PR: Only I can see it—and how it makes me laugh! On the surface, there's the "striking likeness" as they call it, that they all stand and gape with wonder at. But deep down underneath, there's the pompous self-righteous face of a horse, the obstinate muzzle of a mule, the lop-eared, shallow-pated head of a dog, a greasy hog's-snout . . . and sometimes the gross brutal mask of a bull!

MAIA: (*indifferently*) All the dear old farmyard, in fact.

PR: Just the dear old farmyard, Maia. All the animals

that man has perverted for his own ends, and who
in their turn have perverted man.

Card no. 56

Besides, the lad has no obvious defects,
And seems well-built. True, he's only got one head,
But my daughter is no better off in that respect.
Three-headed trolls are going right out of fashion.
Even two heads are rare nowadays,
And they are not what they used to be.

Card no. 57

Well, well, my son, we must give you some
  treatment
To cure this human nature of yours.
PEER: What will you do?
OLD MAN OF THE MOUNTAINS: In your left eye
I'll make a little cut, so that you'll see awry
But all you see will seem bright and fair.
Then I'll nip out your right window-pane—
PEER: Are you drunk?
OLD MAN: [*Lays several sharp instruments on the
table.*]
Here you see the glazier's tools.
We'll blinker you, like a surly bull.
Then you'll see your bride is beautiful.
And there'll be an end to these illusions
Of dancing sows, and cows playing harps—

The last card may be thought to be more appropriately
a part of my next cluster, which I have tentatively called

"(Composite) portrait photography." Or possibly "Composite portrait (photography)." It was easy enough to identify the quotations from *Peer Gynt* and *When We Dead Awaken.* The fish/sea card, which might also go into my "drowning" cluster, is part of Ibsen's notes for *The Lady from the Sea.* Writing down the reference to the Strange Passenger reminds me of my own Strange Customer, Mr. Maurice Bossey.

I looked at some of the Web sites he had listed. They were, as I believe I had always suspected, sites of a pornographic nature. They showed pictures—both still and moving—of . . . I don't have to write down what they were of. I could find a string of little, cold, categorising words. Pederasty. Paedophilia. Sado-masochism. Sadism. Some of the collars and claws and forks and chains and things were quite funny. Some of the flesh was, too. Like rubber balloons. Some of the photographs were better than others, you got convincing gouts of blood (well, they were real, in some place, at some time, I imagine, I suppose). There are other words. Pain. Hurt. Damage. I suddenly saw the *point,* so to speak, of the semiotic thrust of all Maurice Bossey's little implements, his knife, his screw, his piercer-and-cutter. All these photographs were intermingled (from site to site) with idyllic or Edenic holiday "suggestions." The photography for some of these was very lovely. Gold-skinned pre-pubertal boys ran across white sands under waving palm-trees, and rolled, open-legged, in the softly curling edges of the surf. Next to them, naked babies played in pools, patting liquescent sand-towers with sharp spades.

I had never liked Maurice Bossey. Now the thought of him made me feel sick. (That is the way *I* am. It is no good pretending to a breadth of sympathy I don't have. And don't want to have. I know a victim when I see one, however sweetly he smiles.)

The real problem was that the sickness I felt spread over into my feelings about my absent employers, so gently, so variously hedonistic, so comprehensive in their provision of pleasure for everyone. Had they left me alone with Bossey as a *test*? Or did they not know about Bossey, was he a contact of the absent Pim or Pym whom they had never once mentioned? The images of the unpolluted beaches on Pacific atolls which were part of Puck's Girdle's furniture of human dreams merged in my mind with these sweet images of terror and pain, and would not be separated again, as though sun and sand were filmed over with the sickly scent of blood. (A mixed metaphor. Let it lie.)

I had no one to talk to about any of all this. I intended to present Ormerod Goode with my selective and *arranged* account of the card-box, when it was done. That left Vera Alphage, who appeared to wish to keep a pleasant distance. She did not, for instance, ask me how I was getting on, though she continued to provide tasty little snacks. Then one day, as I was leaving, she called me into her little sitting-room. She had set up a green-felted card-table—there was a bizarre moment when I expected her, like Miss Havisham, to require me to "play." I first thought she was playing some intricate and unusually numerous kind of solitaire against herself. I then recognised Destry-Scholes's marble collection, deployed across the green field in little clusters and lines, of varying colours and sizes. She said,

"I had the idea, in an idle moment, of seeing whether I

could fit Uncle's names to his marbles, so to speak. You know—he's got this list of names, and then the lists of the clans and cohorts and so on of the army—if it is an army and not a hierarchical society, or an imaginary kingdom, or whatever. Then I got rather annoyed—you find you've got six possible marbles to one name, and six possible names to one marble, and others that are just *baffling*. I decided to start by dividing them into colours. Blue, green, brown, purple, white and clear, red, pink, and so on. I got out the table because I had to put what I call the *overlaps* or *links*—ones that are equally blue and green, or yellow and brown—between the major groups. The ones that are merely flecked with one colour, but predominantly another, I've put with the colour.

"Then I've divided the colours into opaque and transparent. Then I've got oddities, like turquoise, and fawn. And a couple of iridescent ones. Like opals. There's a whole group of names which are merely precious stones—Jade, Jasper, Chrysolite—though *not* Opal—and some, like Sapphira that are *almost* stones, or Smaragdine, which turns out to be an old word for emerald, and Sardonyx. And Topaz. The only one that looks much like a topaz is also the perfect candidate for Tiger's Eye."

I was interested in her little circles of spheres—perhaps even more so because I felt a pointless but aesthetically interesting affinity with my own clusters of cards. I said,

"The cards in the card index are falling into related clusters. Like the sea, as a theme. Or *composites*."

"I thought some of those old photos looked rather like Galton's composites," she said, revealing knowledge I hadn't known she had.

"You know about Galton?"

"Not really. But I know quite a lot about photography, one way and another. I thought one of the marble-armies might be, so to speak, *marine*. I've got Bladderwrack, Wrasse, Tsunami, Maelstrøm, Crest, Chronofoam (whatever that is— it could be a kind of shaving cream). I've got Atoll, Sea-green Ink, Painted Ocean, Wake—which could mean all sorts of things, but there's one or two with trails of bubbles that look just like wakes—"

I said that "sea-green ink" might be an abbreviation of "sea-green incorruptible" and refer to Robespierre. She said that there were the names Thermidor and Fructidor and one called Pimpernel, which might be to do with *The Scarlet Pimpernel*. Then, she said, there were the names of body parts. Thorax and Omoplat, Cervicle, Bum, Lung and Cocky, though that went with all sorts of other groupings, poultry and human attributes like Sultry and Snazzy . . .

I said it seemed impossible to reconstitute such an arbitrary system.

She said it was *not* arbitrary, each marble had been carefully and uniquely *named*.

She said she loved the little glass balls absolutely in themselves, they were magical. She held up several to the light, and we peered through them. White worms or ribbons twisted wildly through emerald and amethyst caverns. A spiral danced round itself, pink and gold, in clear glass with a blueish cast. Vera Alphage handed me two particular ones.

"I thought *Bum* couldn't be hard to identify. I thought one of these must be Bum."

One had two white hemispheres in transparent toffee, like

the summits of hard-boiled eggs. One had a scarlet opaque object, with a startling resemblance to the male organ of generation, inside a transparent turquoise veiling. She said, "I don't know what sort of age he was when he started naming them. *Little* boys call the whole system indifferently, "Bum." Later they differentiate."

I pointed out that this system was not constructed by a *little* boy. Little boys don't know words like Smaragdine and Omoplat. Vera Alphage said that she had the feeling that the collection had accumulated over a very long period, that he had started with maybe half-a-dozen cherished marbles—and had added, and added, "as one does." Her empty little room showed no sign of a collector's passion. I said this was an interesting theory, but where was her evidence? She said that the little notebooks showed a development in the handwriting—some was quite infantile, and the lists in this handwriting were short.

She said, "There is a possible grouping of atomic energy names. There is Fusion, and Fission, and Neutrino and Cloud Mushroom. And in that case Atoll would go with Mushroom Cloud, of course. But then Cloud Mushroom might go with Seaweed, and Bonsai, and Chrysanthemum and Miso, a kind of Japanesey group."

I said surely the lists themselves, the order in which they were presented, gave some clue. I thought of my painstaking numbering of the cards. She said, "But the same names appear in different orders in several of the lists. They obviously changed allegiances, that is to say, categories." She said, "Often, he doesn't name the lists, themselves. Just little *signs,* like hieroglyphs, or picture-writing."

I said that was just like his not-quite-system in the boxes.

She held up a very large rose and emerald and cobalt whirl. "Do you think this is Aurora Borealis? Or"—she held up one with a gold rim and a flare of transparent crimson like a dancer's skirt—"this?"

I said I wasn't quite sure what she hoped to achieve.

She said she had no hope of ever understanding the system. But by process of elimination, she wondered whether it would be possible to fix a name to each marble. She did believe each had had one name and one only.

She looked at me defensively. She said, "It's a silly idea." She put out her arms to roll all her groups into an indiscriminate cluster. I put my hand on hers, instinctively, to stop her. I took hold of her wrist. I felt the blood pulse under my fingers and saw it jump blue under her white skin. (There was a marble called Azurevein, somewhere.) I said, holding on to her wrist, that it wasn't a silly idea, no more silly than what I was doing myself. We were both mapping the mind of Scholes Destry-Scholes.

There was a blue flicker of electricity in the blue veins and my own fingertips.

I let go. What else was I to do?

I see the next cluster, the photography cluster beginning with card no. 75, as the (composite) portrait photography, or composite portrait (photography) cluster. And what came in between, my non-existent reader may well ask. All sorts. A description of an overcoat. A list of high and low tides (I don't know where). A few bits of poetry on subjects I can't track down (time passing, in various languages, roots and flowers, ditto). None of these are *obviously* connected to the three personages, though a reasonable guess would be that they might be, must be. Anyway, here are some of the photos.

Card no. 75

My first idea of composite portraiture arose through a request by Sir Edmund du Cane, then H.M. Inspector of Prisons, to examine the photographs of criminals in order to discover and to define the types of features, if there be any, that are associated with different kinds of criminality. The popular ideas were known to be very inaccurate, and he thought the subject worthy of scientific study. I gladly offered to do what I could, and he gave me full opportunity of seeing prisons and of studying a large number of photographs of criminals, which were of course to be used confidentially.

At first, for obtaining pictorial averages, I combined pairs of portraits with a stereoscope, with more or less success. Then I recollected an often observed effect with magic lanthorns, when two lanthorns converge on the same screen, and while the one is throwing its image, the operator slowly withdraws the light from it and throws it on the next one. The first image yields slowly to the second, with little sense of discordance in the parts that at all resemble one another. It was obviously possible to photograph superimposed images on a screen by the simultaneous use of two or more lanthorns. What was common to all of the images would then appear vigorous, while individual differences would be too faint for notice. Then the idea occurred to me that the pictures themselves might be severally adjusted in the same place, and be photographed successively on the same plate, allowing a fractional part of the total time of exposure to each portrait.

Card no. 76 18 May 1871, Dresden

I have often thought about what you once wrote, that I had not taken up the standpoint of modern scientific knowledge. How could I overcome this failing? But is not each generation born with the prejudices of its time? Have you ever noticed in a painting of a group from some previous century a curious kind of family likeness between people of the same period? So it is in the field of intellect too. What we profane creatures lack in knowledge I think we possess, to a certain degree in intuition or instinct. And a writer's task is essentially to see, not to mirror; I am conscious of a peculiar danger to myself in indulging the latter tendency.

Card no. 77

I have successfully made many composites both of races and of families. The composites are always more refined and ideal-looking than any one of their components, but I found that persons did not like being mixed up with their brothers and sisters in a common portrait. It seems a curious and rather silly feeling, but there can be no doubt of its existence. I see no other reason why composite portraiture should not be much employed for obtaining family types. Composites might be made of brother and sisters, parents and grandparents, together with a composite of the race, each in their due proportions, according to the Ancestral Law (see chapter on Heredity). The result would be very instructive, but the difficulty of obtaining the material is now overwhelming. Male and female portraits blend well together with an epicene result.

Card no. 78

Stephen Sinding on modelling statue for theatre. "I worked and worked and couldn't get it right. I discarded one effort after another. While I was working on the sixth it occurred to me to ask Ibsen to take his spectacles off. He laid them aside and looked at me. I have never seen two eyes like those. One was large, I might almost say horrible—so it seemed to me—and deeply mystical; the other much smaller, rather pinched up, cold and clear and calmly probing. I stood speechless for a few seconds and stared at those eyes, and spoke the thought that flashed into my mind: 'I wouldn't like to have you as an enemy!' Then his eyes and his whole body seemed to blaze, and I thought instinctively of the troll in the fairy tale who pops out of his hole and roars: 'Who's chopping trees in *my* forest?' "

Card no. 79

THIN PERSON: There are two ways in which a man
                can be himself.
            A right way and a wrong way.

You may know that a man in Paris
Has discovered a way of taking portraits
With the help of the sun. Either one can produce
A direct picture, or else what they call a negative.
In the latter, light and dark are reversed;
And the result, to the ordinary eye, is ugly.
But the image of the original is there.
All that's required is to develop it.
Now if a human soul, in the course of its life,
Has created one of those negative portraits,
The plate is not destroyed. They send it to me.
I give it treatment, and by suitable means
Effect a metamorphosis. I develop it.
I steam it and dip it, I burn it and cleanse it
With sulphur and similar ingredients
Till the picture appears which the plate was
    intended to give.
I mean, the one known as the positive.
But when a soul like yourself has smudged himself
    out
Even sulphur and potash can achieve nothing.
PEER: Then one must come to you as black as a raven
To be sent back as white as a dove?

These cards, as may be imagined, took me back to the
shoebox full of photographs. As I said, some of these were in
fact faded cuttings from newspapers, carefully pasted to postcards. There were photographs of General de Gaulle, Stalin,
an African ruler in leopardskin ceremonial costume, two
wartime weddings, the Princesses Elizabeth and Margaret
Rose as little girls. There were picturesque ancient peasant

women, their faces furrowed with taut wrinkles, their eyes lost black dots. There were workmen in Sunday best, or brawnily stoking furnaces in picturesque clouds of steam. There were also cadavers on mortuary slabs and black-and-white reproductions of Mantegna's foreshortened dead Christ and Holbein's rigid horizontal one—both, it appeared, cut from illustrations in books. There were a great many babies, hairless and tufted, scowling and simpering. There were also several portraits of the dead, laid out before burial, amongst whom I was able to identify Galton and Ibsen. I have written that photographs partake of death. There were several postcards of Julia Margaret Cameron's posed women, with heavy tresses and heavy arms and heavy breasts, representing Persephone, Pomona, Maia, ripeness. These were impressions on the photographic plate of living, breathing flesh, and warm hair, shadows of where sunlight had fallen on the lump of bosom or the hollow of collarbone or the red lips which appeared heavily black. Great bunches of roses and lilies, romantic tangles of ivy, domes of eyelids, all imitating the stillness of death for the long attention of the lady under the velvet pall, all now bones and dust, having passed through wrinkles and swollen ankles, unless they were taken early, as many were—all consigned, like Galton, to peaceful churchyards, under stone angels, of which there were also photographs in the shoebox, drooping or staring upwards. The photographs of the truly dead are not shocking as the photographs of the living are shocking. For one thing, their eyes are decently closed, and not dead paper spaces.

Galton and Ibsen resembled each other in death, as they did not, much, in life, except in that sense Ibsen himself accurately remarked on, in which all people of a certain period resemble each other, like family portraits. Galton was a large man and Ibsen was tiny, but in these photographs Ibsen, in his frock coat as far as the taut white sheet across his stomach, is more imposing than Galton in a soft nest of white cloth, like snow against a grey sky. Both men—in life as in death—had lipless mouths, Ibsen possibly because he tightened his face perpetually in a rictus of bad temper, Galton because, it is clear, he was born that way, with a long, mild, slit of a mouth. Both faces, in death, have floating remnants of silver-white hair. Ibsen's is a little tousled, which is touching, and the ghost of his immense mutton-chop whiskers floats above his collar. Both have the sharp noses of the dead—Galton's is cavernous—and *can be seen not to be breathing.* How? Both have what I will call "the same" expression, which is one of complete (completed) exhaustion, so that those who look at the photograph are glad that it is all over, whatever it was. That is, those who look are glad that the dead man is now dead. I do not, as Karl Pearson did not, use the words "at peace" or "at rest." Who knows? But they are not bad to look at, these death's heads, and they resemble each other. In life, photographs of Galton show someone mildly vacuous, withdrawn a long way behind the chalky patient face. Ibsen is always combative, always *cross,* even in the photograph taken when he was paralysed, propped in his chair, in 1905. A composite of these two would approximate an elderly stone angel.

None of the photographs in the box had any markings to suggest that it represented—had snapped—Scholes Destry-Scholes.

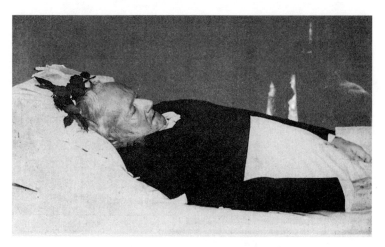

Henrik Ibsen on his death bed, May 1906

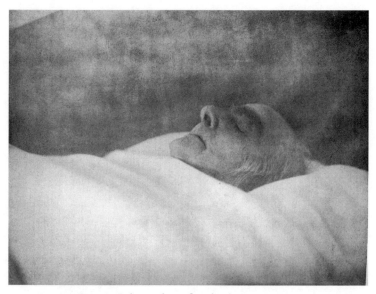

Francis Galton taken after death, January 1911

There were, however, clearly also snipped from books, some of Galton's famous composites.

"Composite made from Portraits of Criminals convicted of Murder, Manslaughter, or Crimes of Violence." The plate has eight blurred images of what may on the whole be described as dignified, resigned and, perhaps to a lesser extent, *apprehensive* male figures. These are said to be made up of 3, 8, 7, 9 and 5 components each. Their faint imprecision makes them ghostly, more than ghastly. Galton noted that in his criminal composites "the special villainous irregularities have disappeared and the common humanity that underlies them has prevailed." Destry-Scholes had also acquired a copy of Galton's Plate showing the composite images of officers and men of the Royal Engineers (5 officers, 12 officers, 11 privates, 30 privates), but not one of what Pearson considered his greatest achievement, the "Jewish Type." There were three of the composites Galton had made of coins and medals, the images of Alexander I, Napoleon and Cleopatra, taken from coins and medals. Galton had photographed the collected individual coins—in Alexander's case, dividing them into "Indian" and "Greek" collections, and had added his own composites in the centre. He commented that in each case the composite image was more lifelike and more handsome and ideally beautiful than any of the individual ones—adding that Cleopatra (hook-nosed, sharp-jawed) would be found hideous by any modern standards of beauty. It is hard not to agree with him that his superimpositions—possibly partly because of a stereoscopic effect, and a sense, to a modern eye, that the subject has moved at the crucial moment of the opening of the camera shutter—*do* have more liveliness and are better proportioned than their component images. (Though something is lost of the stylised horned and serpentine-curled heads of the Indian Alexanders.) Destry-Scholes also had two of Galton's composite family images, one of three sisters, each taken full-face and in profile, then amalgamated to make what did look like a fourth sister, the Family Face, and one of a whole family, several generations, men and women, grandparents and children, uncles, nieces, amalgamated ingeniously into not one but several composites—"men," "women," "children," "men and women together." It was possible, I thought, to see why the subjects of these images resented them. Something had been taken away by being added.

There was also a plate with photographs of eighteenth-century portraits of five women, all with the same long, oval face, composed mouth and elaborate high powdered hairstyle, except for one, who wore a sort of floppy bonnet with a rose at the apex of her brow. The composite, in the centre, was more animated than any of the single ladies. I came across them, much later, in my researches. They were Linnaeus's wife Sara Lisa, and his daughters Lisa Stina, Louisa, Sara Stina and Sophia (his darling, the books say, the beauty of the family they say, too, though I prefer the severe carved look of the others). I have been unable to find any reference, anywhere, to Galton making a composite of Linnaeus's daughters. Perhaps, nevertheless, he did. They are an excellent subject for one. The resemblances are striking, the differences subtle. Perhaps Destry-Scholes made the composite, for his own amusement, having collected the others. There is no evidence, no

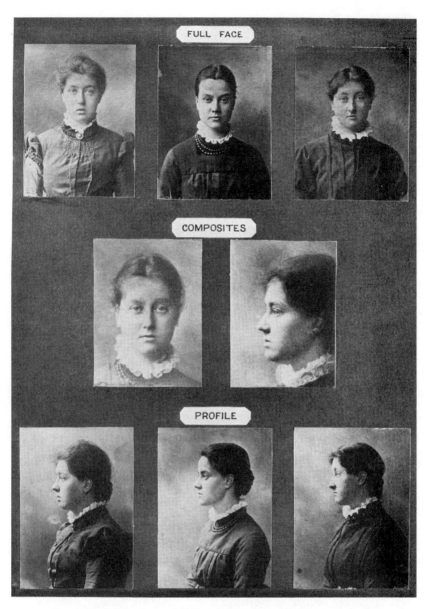

Portraits of three sisters, full face and profile, with the corresponding composites

evidence at all, that any of the photographs are his work, or represent anyone associated with him.

I did, of course, ask Vera Alphage to look through the photograph collection for anyone she recognised.

She did this, she told me, very carefully, and had found no one. She held up one blurred beach photograph, taken by a beach photographer at Scarborough (the address was on the back), of a huge poised family in front of a beach tent, the grandparents in deckchairs, the parents standing behind the chairs, the babies (two) in arms, the small children in swimming costumes squatting in the sand, brandishing buckets and spades. That family face rippled across grandparental wrinkles into weary maternal half-smiles into adolescent pouts, and infant grins. Dark, hooded eyes, curved lips.

"I recognise that child," said Vera Alphage, "including her swimming costume with butterflies on, *because it is me.* Except that I don't recognise anyone else at all in the picture. But I dug out a picture of me—not in Scarborough, but in that swimming costume—I do think frills look *silly* round little girls' bottoms—so you could see I wasn't fantasising."

The little girl—aged maybe eight—clung to the leg of a tall, slender woman in a white halter-necked sundress. (If it was white. All the photographs were black and white. Vera told me the swimming costume with the butterflies was in fact yellow, with pink and blue insects, and viridian—she said specifically viridian—bindings to the neck and the frills. Grey on grey, in the picture.) The woman in the sundress bore a startling resemblance to Vera Alphage as she is now. I realised that I was seeing something of the face of Scholes Destry-Scholes. But it was blurred, in three-quarters profile, a bit beaky, with the wind wrapping long dark hair partly round it; how did it resemble him, how did it differ? Vera Alphage's mother had wonderfully sexy legs. Poised on high-heeled sandals. A tall woman. The child was indeed, as far as I could see, *the same child.*

I said I saw what she meant. I did not want to ask if she had any more photographs of her mother. In some curious way this study of the two photographs of the little girls was an intimate moment.

Vera said, "Of course, I don't remember that photo being taken. I don't remember what holiday it was on, or what it felt like to be me looking out of those eyes. I was given the photograph to remember my mother by, when she died. It was one my father liked. I expect he took it. I remember the swimming costume because I thought it was silly. But how did it—how did I—get into the *other* picture? We use snaps to remember who we were, but that causes us to remember *only* those snaps. I don't remember how I looked to myself in the mirror at that age, if I looked in the mirror. It's a memorial of me, as well as her."

She looked down again at the photographs we had taken out of the box. In a corner of one of Galton's composites is a tiny image of his attempt to make a composite skull. It is very blurry and its neck and vertebrae appear disproportionately elongated.

Vera Alphage said, "Would you like to see my work? I told you I made photographs." She said, "I keep them in the bedroom. They're not to everybody's taste."

So I followed her, feeling rather worried, into her bedroom, which had a secluded view of the small, square back garden. She went across and drew the curtains, white musliny stuff, lined.

"Better in artificial light," she said, and put on one or two strategically placed, diffused lights, so that the room became a box of soft violet-blue light. The walls were covered with largish photographs framed in steel. They were essentially black-and-white photographs, but the grounds were blues and greens, submarine, ultra-violet. They were photographs of bones. With a haze of other organs hanging between them, curtains of translucent tissue. Vertebrae, jaws, pelvis and femur, collarbone and shoulder blade, fingers and toes. They were extremely beautiful, partly because of their symmetries, partly because of the veiling of the shadows, the depths of three-dimensional space shown by the searching X-ray, partly because she had so arranged them that there were waves and ripples of curves and links of joints and junctions, all round the room.

"I am a radiographer," said Vera Alphage. "By profession. Most people think my pictures are morbid. I don't see why. They're pictures of the living, not the dead. Some of them are worn or damaged, but they're all alive, they're pictures of our inner life, so to speak."

I didn't know what to say. I turned to look at her. In this blue half-light she was extraordinarily beautiful. She had her mother's sexy legs, whose wonderful tendons were discovered and illuminated. I stared. She smiled. I said, I seem to remember, "Beautiful," meaning both the photographs and the woman. There was nothing in the room but a white bed and a white chest of drawers. We got into the bed. I was going to write we *fell* into the bed, but we didn't. And I am not going to describe what happened, though I am going to record that it *did* happen, because I am not that sort of writer. I think. It's becoming more difficult to know what sort of writer I *am*. Also, afterwards, I was not the same person.

I had decided to keep mum about Maurice Bossey's Web sites. I had decided to put a new punctilious formality into my dealings with him, I seem to remember. I got to thinking of him in cultural clichés, the vampire with the swirling cloak and opera hat, neither of which he had, though I think perhaps the image haunted and pleased Bossey himself. Or perhaps not. When he next came into the shop, he appeared to be agitated. I was talking to another customer—a young woman who was booking a mosaic-making holiday in Ravenna. I was telling her what Destry-Scholes had said about the angles of the tesserae in the shining haloes of the angels. Bossey lurked in the doorway. It is difficult to lurk in a small well-lit shop. When my customer had taken her train-tickets and hotel reservations, and the references to Destry-Scholes, and turned to say goodbye in the doorway, herself, Bossey could be said (figuratively) to be foaming at the mouth. He advanced on me. He said,

"You spun all that out an unnecessarily long time."

"Good afternoon," I said, pursuing my policy. "Is there anything in particular I can help you with?"

"Of course there is, damn you, and I think you know very well what it is. I don't really believe the solicitous Erik and Christophe went off without giving you at least a *hint*. I suspect time's running out, I suspect I should be on my way. *Would you care for some snuff?*"

He pushed an enamel snuff-box across the counter. Aggressively. It had a naked pink cherub (male) on it, in a sea of what might have been blood, or fire.

I said I didn't take snuff, and pushed it back.

As I have said before in this document, I am not very good at codes in real life, or even any glaring semiotic system.

He said I was a very stupid young man, and he was sure Erik and Christophe had told me that snuff was amongst the pleasures I needed to know about, in that job.

"They provide what they provide. The full service. Even including snuff. *You know that,*" he said. His brow was damp.

"I think you will have to ask elsewhere," I said, "for the sort of services you require."

"Don't be an idiot. I've paid. Through the nose and every other part of my anatomy. Very considerable sums. They pocket the sums, you deliver the tickets and the contacts. The *dogsbody delivers,* that's the arrangement. I shall miss the event. I'm quite sure there's a code somewhere in your documents. There has to be."

I said, naturally I would do my best. But I didn't think so. I said I was by no means sure that Erik and Christophe knew what he was talking about. I said I didn't.

"One of Christophe's favourite sayings," said Maurice Bossey, "is that *schadenfreude* is a human universal. Isn't that so?"

It was. I nodded.

"I am only after my own form of pleasure. It's ancient and universal. You shouldn't be working here, if you don't understand that."

"Please," I said, "go away."

"*Have you any idea how much I've paid out?*" he said then. "Look into it, dogsbody."

He went.

Leaving in my anxious mind the insinuation that "dogs-body" too was part of a code, like peaches and snuff, knives and screws.

I had been happy in my work.

I do not know very much about what I believe are generally known as "snuff movies." I had met them in contemporary cultural lists of urban myths, like alligators in the sewers, and the grandmother on the luggage rack. But alarming news about recent events in Belgium had led me to suppose they were real enough. Maurice Bossey was complaining about having missed the recent events in Belgium. There may have been no connection, but I thought there was. No literary person who has read about Roman bread and circuses, or Japanese tortures, or Turkish imperial households or the Holocaust, or for that matter what went on in the Tower under the Tudor queens, can suppose that such things are impossible. You just do not expect to come across them, let alone to be asked, over the counter, to provide them. I see, looking back, that there were many sensible, practical things I could, or might have done. But like a bullied little boy in a school playground (and I was, *of course,* a bullied little boy in a school playground) I kept mum, and panicked, and suffered. I wonder what the origin of the phrase "kept mum" is? It is a nice paradox that a bullied child might want to squeal to mum, but must keep mum. I see as I write that of course there is another circle to this spiral. There are schoolyards which contain prototype snuffers, snuff directors, snuff audiences, infant Bosseys, who may be, as I was, at that stage the victim. Bossey's excitement caused me, I now see, somehow to see *myself* as the little candle to be snuffed. And in my sleep he and Erik and Christophe were the Big Boys with the bicycle chains and the penknives and the matches, and that certain smile.

Anyway, there was no mum to squeal to. Ormerod Goode had nothing to do with any of this. It is true that I was now regularly making love to Vera Alphage in her crisp white sheets, but this does not mean that we had become—*conversationally*, so to speak—intimate. She was a tentative and a delicate lover—it is probably clear that I don't have much to compare her with, but I don't think that kind of gentleness and attention can be faked or misinterpreted. But it was all largely in silence. She is, I think, naturally very reserved. She does not talk about her personal history, her family, or how she came to choose her profession. She does sometimes, under stress, relate incidents that have happened at the hospital, patients whose agony has distressed her, dangerous procedures that have turned out well, or badly, deaths of accident victims, or victims of domestic violence. She never gossips about colleagues, or complains about organisational problems. It took some time for me to see that this was so. I never talked to her about the university (I didn't really go there anymore) and because of my distress, I didn't even mention Erik and Christophe. I am not the sort of writer, and this is not the sort of writing, to make the most of the undoubtedly fantastic elements of my situation at that time. There I lay, in the bed of the niece of the man whose biography—whose *life-writing*—I was vainly trying to piece together, surrounded by anonymous photographs of living skeletons, of heart muscles and lung tissue and the roots of teeth. I began to think in a mad way that a biography was a kind of snuff movie, that there was an element of *schadenfreude* in piecing together long-dead pleasures and pains. I had a dream—once or twice—in that bed, of that kind which fuses many images into one image, and thus strikes the watching mind as a kind of indisputable vision of the truth, although all it is, is a stirring and cooking together of disparate things by the unconscious (the sleeping) mind. I dreamed I was watching Destry-Scholes pouring head-first into the Maelstrøm, which, although immense, dark and boiling, was also the beautiful formal spiral of Erik's origami Maelstrøm in the window, which was also a spiral blade, made of Maurice Bossey's corkscrew and penknives on an immense scale. And I was swimming in the inky water, trying to get safely nearer, to see the unseen face, to see *who he was,* and my limbs were not under my control, I was being swept towards the funnel of blades and water . . .

I would wake, and shake myself, and say to Vera that I'd been dreaming. And Vera would not ask what about, and I wouldn't say. We resembled each other in that.

So what did we talk about? She had become wholly engrossed in the problem of the marble connection. She would report minor triumphs—she had identified Cyanea as the "Lion's-mane" organism in the short story by Conan Doyle in which a man is killed by something that leaves a network of burning weals on his back. She had attributed the name, tentatively, to a sea-green marble containing a fine tentacular swirl of reddish hairs. She marched columns across her table—plant-names, insect-names, sea-creatures—and always found that she had two marbles, or three, to one name, or two or three names to one marble. I think she was beginning to know them almost as well as their original collector, a difficult feat, with several hundred small glass spheres and no fixed taxonomy. She would get out particular choice ones in the evening for my delectation, bright primary colours one night, subtly shaded all-greens another. We developed a ritual of holding them up and staring into them, like many-coloured crystal balls with a variety of fantastic features.

I was still, doggedly, pursuing my own task of cataloguing Destry-Scholes's wayward card collection. Possibly under the influence of the marble taxonomy I thought I detected a subset of cards on taxonomic collections. The prize exhibit in this was Pearson's account of Galton's specimens of glass eyes and hair.

Card no. 90

In the test of the *Eye and Hair Colours* Galton used artificial glass eyes respectively dark blue, blue, grey, dark grey, brown grey (green, light hazel), brown, dark brown, black. He also used standard samples of hair: flaxen, light brown, dark brown, black and 3 shades of red: fair red (golden), red, dark red (chestnut auburn). He was certainly the first to introduce standard scales of this kind, and, what is more, to realise the difficulty of reproducing them. Such eye and hair scales are common enough now, but were by no means so in 1882, yet the difficulty remains of reproducing them accurately even when manufactured by one firm. The glass eyes of the two standard scales are found not to have the same types of pigments in them, and the spunglass silk used for standard hair scales not always the same amount of dye.

Galton felt keenly the need for a standard and permanent set of colours, and made a suggestion on this point of great value. In 1869 he had been struck by the great variety of permanent colours which are produced for mosaic work. He had been over the *Fabbrica* of mosaics attached to the Vatican and seen their 25,000 numbered trays or bins of coloured mosaic. He realised at once the opportunity thus afforded not only for the establishment of a general colour scale in this country, but, as the mosaics were manufactured for the representation of human figures among other things, for skin, hair and eye-colour scales for anthropometric purposes.

Card no. 91   Feb. 3. 1870. Letter to Science and
Art Department, South Kensington, from FG

I beg to propose that the authorities of the South Kensington Art Department should make application to the Pope for mosaic tablets containing in order specimens of each of their 25,000 bins to be suspended in the Museum for the purpose of reference as a standard of colour . . .

It might be disposed as a frieze running along the

wall at a height convenient for reference, the bits of mosaic perhaps arranged in tablets of 100 containing ten ranks and ten files, with dark lines at the 5th division each way for convenience of immediately ascertaining the number appertaining to each several bit . . .

It might well be a subject for the subsequent consideration of the authorities of South Kensington whether they should not select by means of the large amount of skill and science at their disposal say one tenth of the Vatican series to create what might be called a South Kensington scale of colours, and distribute identical copies of it in mosaic, which would occupy a space according to the above calculation of less than 10 feet × 8 feet among the art schools of the United Kingdom.

Card no. 92

Sixteen years later (1886) Galton returned to his suggestion impressed by the fading of the original paintings of Broca for skin tints, and by a further brief stay in Rome where he had again visited the Vatican factory . . . He now found that there were 40,000 bins of mosaics, and of these 10,762 were classified; they occupied 24 cases in each of which were 16 rows of 28 samples. The flesh tints appropriate to European nations were about 500 in number, so that the Vatican factory provided ample material for the selection of a series of tints such as anthropologists desired . . .

Mr. Odo Russell—later Lord Ampthill—our semi-official representative at the Vatican (till 1870) was ultimately asked to inquire as to the feasibility of carrying out the scheme, "but the price asked by the Papal government was altogether excessive, and so the matter dropped."

Card no. 93

Among matters which concern us in this chapter are standards for hair and eye colours. Here Galton directly suggests "glass spun by a glass blower for comparison with hair." Thus before 1886 he had proposed sets of standard glass eyes, mosaics for skin colour and spun glass for hair; all 3 of these suggestions have been carried out in this century—by Germans—in the well-known eye-scale of Professor R. Martin, in Professor von Luschau's skin-scale and Professor G. Fischer's glass-silk hair scale. Thus the best of what we can do *now,* was suggested by Galton twenty to thirty years earlier.

A list of Ibsen's medals and honours might make up part of this cluster on collections. Otherwise, why did Destry-Scholes bother to make a card of it? (It was not adjacent to any of the other items in this cluster. It was between the drafts made by Francis Galton of Erasmus Darwin's tombstone, and a list of school exam results I haven't identified—chemistry B+, religion C, pure maths B−, applied maths B+—maybe Destry-Scholes's own, maybe not, there is no way of knowing. No date, either.

Card no. 132

Vasa Order. Medjidjie Order (Turkish) Commander Third Class, Danebrog, Order of St. Olaf, Knight, Saxe

Ernestine Order, Knight First Class, honorary doctorate Uppsala, Order of St. Olaf Commander First Class, Great Cross of St. Olaf, Great Cross of Dannebrog Order, Great Cross of North Star.

Card no. 115

Voice from the grave to her who was my dear wife.

1 *The two herbaria in the Museum.* Let neither rats nor moths damage them. Let no naturalist steal a single plant. Take great care who is shown them. Valuable though they already are, they will be worth more as time goes on. They are the greatest collection the world has ever seen. Do not sell them for less than a thousand ducats. My son is not to have them because he never helped me in botany and does not love the subject; keep them for some son-in-law who may prove to be a botanist.

2 *The shell cabinet* is worth at least 12,000 dalers.

3 *The insect cabinet* cannot be kept for long, because of moth.

4 *The mineral cabinet* contains things of great value.

5 *The library in my museums* with all my books, is worth at least 3,000 copper dalers. Do not sell it, but give it to the Uppsala library. But my son may have my library in Uppsala at a valuation.

CL

Another passage, which I sent to be translated by Fulla Biefeld, turned out to be a description of Linnaeus's workroom.

Card no. 117

You would have admired, enjoyed,—yes, quite fallen in love with his museum, to which all his students had access.

On one wall was his Lapp dress and other curiosities; on another side were big objects of the vegetable kingdom and a collection of mussels, and on the remaining two, his medical books, his scientific instruments, and his minerals. In a corner of the room, which was a high one, were the branches of a tree in which lived about thirty different kinds of tame birds, and in the window recesses stood great pots, filled with earth, for growing rare plants. It was a joy, too, to look at his collection of pressed plants, all gummed on sheets of paper; there were more than three thousand Swedish plants, both wild and cultivated, as well as many rarities from Lapland. Further, there were a thousand species of Swedish insects and about the same number of Swedish stones, tastefully displayed in spacious boxes and arranged according to the entirely new system founded on his own observations.

Fulla Biefeld attached a note to this translation, asking if I was getting anywhere, and informing me that Linnaeus's geological collection had been dispersed when the collections were sold by Fru Linnaea to James Edward Smith in 1784, to the great distress of the Swedish universities and government. Smith (aged twenty-four at the time) became the first President of the Linnean Society, which purchased what remained of the collections. Fulla Biefeld hoped to be back in

London at some point for further study of some of Linnaeus's type specimens. She would look me up. She was curious to see the results of my researches.

This explained a rather dry card (no. 128), which I append.

James Edward Smith. 26 large chests. 19,000 sheets of pressed plants. 3,200 insects. 1,500 shells. 700–800 pieces of coral. 2,500 mineral specimens. 2,500 books. 3,000 letters (to and from). various mss.

Card no. 129

Instruments designed by FG. Anthropometric, psycho-metric, meteorological et al. Many unidentified devices, and drawings of devices, whose purpose may now only be divined are collectively known in the Anthropometric Laboratory as Galton's Toys.

Drill pantograph. Weather balloon. A lock. A lamp. A balance. A printing telegraph. A device for compounding six objects. A hyperscope. A wave engine. A heliostat. A "Tactor" machine. A machine for optical combination of images. An Iceland spar compounder. A measurement of resemblance machine. An instantaneous attitude snapper. Spectacles for divers. Whistles for high notes. A Pocket registrator. An instrument for testing the perception of tint differences. An instrument for measuring the movement of a limb.

Card no. 130   *Substitutes*

The substitutes for thread, string and cord are as follows:—Thongs cut spirally, like a watch spring out of a piece of leather or hide, and made pliant by working them round a stick; sinew and catgut; inner bark of trees—this is easily separated by long steeping in water, but chewing it is better; roots of trees, as the spruce-fir, split to the proper size; woodbines, runners, or pliant twigs twisted together. Some seaweeds—the only English one of which I have heard is the common olive-green weed called *Chorda filum;* it looks like a whip-thong, and sometimes grows to a length of thirty or forty feet; when half-dried, the skin is taken off and twisted into fishing-lines etc. Hay-bands; horsehair ropes, or even a few twisted hairs from the tail of a horse; the stems of numerous plants afford fibres that are more or less effective substitutes for hemp, those that are used by the natives of the country visited should be noticed; "Indian grass" is an animal substance attached to the ovaries of small sharks and some other fish of the same class.

In lashing things together with twigs, hay-bands, and the like, the way of securing the loose ends is *not* by means of a knot, which usually causes them to break, but by twisting the ends together until they "kink." All faggots and trusses are secured in this way.

Vera remarked that *Chorda filum* was among the marble-taxonomy, as were mare's tail and horsetail. I tracked this quotation down without much trouble to Galton's *Art of Travel,* a wildly concrete book for the armchair voyager, which in happier days I had felt should be on sale in Puck's Girdle (there is a David & Charles reprint currently available). There were other quotations from this work in the shoebox, including Galton's belief that women make good bearers because they like carrying weights. Women, Galton said, became "the helpless dolls they were considered to be" by doing needlework in the boudoirs of baronial castles ("herded together like pigs"). "It is in the nature of woman to be fond of carrying weights; you may see them in omnibuses and carriages, always preferring to hold their baskets or their babies on their knees, to setting them down on the seats by their sides. A woman, whose modern dress includes I know not how many cubic feet of space, has hardly ever pockets of sufficient size to carry small articles; for she prefers to load her hands with a bag or other weighty object."

Vera said much damage was done to women by carrying badly distributed weights. She had seen injuries and distortions directly due to manoeuvring pushchairs and heavy bags. She said Destry-Scholes and the personages appeared not to be much interested in women. I said Ibsen certainly had been—at least in young girls, he had *collected* young girls to flirt with. There were, however, no cards about that aspect of his life. Our discussion of Ibsen's penchant for young girls called up obscurely my Strange Customer and his apparently desperate need. I said nothing to Vera about him, however. It wasn't appropriate.

Card no. 193

Samuel John Galton (1753–1832) was very fond of animals. He kept many blood hounds; he loved birds, and wrote an unpretentious little book about them in 3 small volumes, with illustrations. He had a decidedly statistical bent, loving to arrange all kinds of data in parallel lines of corresponding lengths, and frequently using colour for distinction. My father, and others of Samuel Galton's children, inherited this taste in a greater or lesser degree; it rose to an unreasoning instinct in one of his daughters. She must have been an acceptable customer to her bookbinder on that account, as the number of expensively bound volumes that she ordered from time to time, each neatly ruled in red, and stamped and assigned to some particular subject or year, is hardly credible. I begged for a bagful of them after her death, to keep as a psychological curiosity, and must have it still; the rest were destroyed. She must have collected these costly books to satisfy a pure instinct, for she turned them to no useful account, and rarely filled more than a single page, often not so much of each of them. She habitually used a treble inkstand, with black, red and blue inks, employing the distinctive colours with little reason, but rather with regard to their pictorial effect. She was perhaps not over-wise, yet she was by no means imbecile, and had many qualities that endeared her to her nephews and nieces.

Waiting for the return of Erik and Christophe became increasingly tense and painful. Their return was in a sense worse than anything I had feared—partly at least because of the over-excitement the waiting had induced in me, myself. I tried, of course, to be sensible and rational, worked harder and harder both on the photographs and the quotations, and on my work at Puck's Girdle. I found several of Galton's collections of fingerprints in the photograph box, including those of himself, various axe murderers and poisoners, and a gorilla from the London Zoo. There was obviously a way of cross-referring the photographs and the quotations, but where was it getting me? There was also a photograph of Galton, taken "as a criminal" by the police, as a sample, looking distinctly shifty and threatening. At Puck's Girdle I was in a state of continuous terror—I am not a brave man—about the imminent return of Maurice Bossey. I sold some holidays in South Africa and in Cairo which made me think of Galton's sojourns in those places, a gorilla-watching holiday in Rwanda, and some rather dubious sunbathing days in a club for under-thirties on Copacabana beach. I tried, in the interim, in a clumsy way, to reorganise my files on my computer there—*id est,* to remove *all traces* of any search made at the suggestion of Maurice Bossey, and moreover, any site he had shown an interest in, however innocent it appeared ("the Lost Kouroi of Hellas," "In search of Youth Culture in Kuala Lumpur"). This had, since I am computationally inept, the effect of losing, temporarily or permanently, all sorts of other parts of what had been an orderly data-bank, of amalgamating fields and lists of clients, of inserting, shall we say the Lofoten Islands cruise into the tropical jungle (diminishing) in Belize and Guatemala. I tried, I seem to remember, *not to think* about resigning my job. But the job was so delightful because of the openness and insouciance of Erik and Christophe.

In the day I was trembling, calm and collected. At night I inhabited a phantasmagoria. (Whether I was in Vera's bed or my own. Our encounters were decorously separated. A kind of cool distance was essential to both our pleasures.) (I think.)

Erik and Christophe stalked through my dreams, in many guises, all appalling. Erik was a golden berserker in a horned helmet and very little else, howling a battle-cry, his beautiful skin running with blood (not his own). Christophe was a surgeon, naked under his white coat, dissecting a small boy who was and was not Phineas G. Nanson. They pranced across veldt in leopard-skins and feathers, they crawled out of the jungle in enormous penis-gourds carrying pathetic shrinking, decomposing heads. I dreamed of impalings and freezers with meat-hooks, of bull-headed men, and bleeding seals harpooned in water-holes with human faces. One of my most bizarre creations was a room full of lively pink worms (rather beautiful, transparent, slender pink worms) on which Christophe was stamping nonchalantly and remorselessly in specially-designed tennis-shoes with blades. Phrases rose to my mind. *Trollaukin*—humans with something of the troll in them. Once I saw the crucified man Galton had seen—that is, I saw his vision, of a completely identifiable hanging figure in agony (somewhat burly and greying, thick lips pulled back over yellow teeth, flies clustering on his eyes). And the phrase came into my mind "butchered to make a Roman holiday." As it did into his.

It was of course, *my* mind, the mind of Phineas G. Nanson, that was doing all this work of redesign and recombination.

It wasn't nice.

They came back on a day when I wasn't in Puck's Girdle. I thought I'd got the files back in order, but wasn't sure. By the time I went in again, I had managed to transfer some of my excessive anxiety to the question of what I had possibly lost along with Maurice Bossey's favoured sites. When I came in that morning, Erik and Christophe were in what I should describe as a frisky and expansive mood. They had stopped off in San Francisco, and had a gay time. They had made friends, through Christophe, with an ex–tennis star who was offering sports holidays with a difference in exclusive resorts. They were full of laughter and, for them, unusually full of camp movements and jokes. They chattered with a mixture of affection and malice about new acquaintances and new "scenes" in a way they didn't, usually. It is true that during my time at Puck's Girdle I had envied them their world of endlessly interconnected friends and acquaintances. It is also true that I had even more admired their grave and settled affection—love— for each other. On that day, this love was unusually showing the form of playing at being queers. It made me edgy, right away.

They had brought me presents. A Japanese netsuke with a tiny gnome-like person with an enormous phallus. A beautiful silver paperknife with a handle in the form of a naked Janus-figure, young and nubile, male one side, female the other. A prize they had won in an Easter raffle in San Francisco. "We didn't know what to do with it, so we thought, why not take it home for our dear dogsbody." It was an Easter basket full of tiny chocolate eggs, each wrapped in a different colour of silver paper. There were two white fluffy Easter Bunnies sitting amongst the eggs, and chained by tiny silver handcuffs and chains to the handle of the basket. They wore S and M leather masks and panties. They had little cat-'o-nine tails and truncheons, and various other miniature instruments in amongst the eggs. I sat and stared at it.

234

"He doesn't like it," said Erik. "He doesn't find it funny. Never mind, dear. Throw it away."

I sat and stared.

Christophe was fiddling with the computer.

"I can't find—" he said. "This is all a bit odd. Where's all my tennis-stuff? And all the stuff on the starvation-and-get-fit-and-beat-your-friends-at-something even if it's only mini-golf? Rolf agrees with me about beating people, or watching them lose. An essential pleasure. *Schadenfreude's* a human universal . . ."

He said, "Phineas, you have been being *naughty.* I didn't know you were into all this hard-core stuff. I'm surprised at you. It's all got stuffed into my innocent tennis. What have you been up to?"

The next few minutes were horrible. I do not remember them clearly. I do remember throwing the Easter eggs with some violence at both of them. I remember hearing my own voice screaming incoherently about dogsbodies, *schadenfreude,* Pym or Pim, semiotics, disgust, *limits after all,* everything *doesn't* go; I remember screaming and growling and howling—yes, and weeping—in complete sentences. I remember mentioning—rather late—Maurice Bossey and snuff and Belgium. At some point—*that* point—Erik and Christophe began to shout too, and so to speak *advanced upon me.* I was tearing things up, letters I'd written, bookings I'd made. I was shrieking words I'd never used and didn't exactly know the import of.

I remember crouching on the counter like an angry monkey—gibbering—and stabbing the silver paperknife into the flesh of both Erik and Christophe. Their faces were no longer smiling but distorted with fury. They went for me with four hands, one of which (Erik's right) was bleeding from a slash I had given it. Blood dripped on the counter. At which point, the door opened (did I say it was announced by a delicate silvery bell?) and I saw a blazing halo, a crown of golden fire, advancing to my salvation.

"What *is* going on here?" said Fulla Biefeld.

I had cut Christophe's cheek too. His shirt was soaking up blood. My own hands were smeared with it, and my own face, where I'd pushed back my hair. Fulla said to me, "Phineas, are you hurt?"

Erik and Christophe sat down on the beautiful chairs, took beautiful duck-egg blue handkerchiefs out of their pockets, and began very gently to wipe away the blood from each other's wounds. Erik kissed Christophe's cheek. Christophe bent his face over Erik's hand. Fulla Biefeld held out a steady hand and helped me off the counter.

"Of course the little shit isn't hurt," said Erik. "You ought to take his weapon away. He went for us. With a nice knife we'd just given him. He's fired."

I said I didn't want to stay. I said there were limits. I said I hadn't known about Maurice Bossey. They had no right to expect me to deal with Maurice Bossey.

Fulla was picking up chocolate eggs from the floor.

Erik said I was sacked because I had been able to think even for a moment that they had dealings with Maurice Bossey.

Christophe said, "We sacked Pym Purchase the moment we found out what he was up to."

Erik said, "How could you think, even for one moment, we would go in for that sort of thing?"

Fulla, rummaging around the counter for a receptacle for the eggs, found the basket with the chained fluffy rabbits, the little whips, the cuffs. She put it on the counter and heaped in the eggs.

"He quoted Christophe on *schadenfreude*," I said. "He said the dogsbody fixed his kind of holiday. He said he'd paid through his—"

"*What* kind of holiday?" said Fulla Biefeld.

Erik told her to shut up and keep out of it. He said, "Anyway, that's that, you're fired, piss off."

Fulla said, "That's no way to behave." Her voice had a Swedish sing-song.

Erik said, "I told you, *shut up.*"

Christophe was bandaging Erik's hand, very gently. He said, "I can see how some of the things we say—our style—might lead him to construe—"

Fulla Biefeld brandished the chained bunnies.

"I came here with what I thought was an interesting idea," she said. "For combining my research—which might yet be needed to save your food crops—or your children's—"

"We shan't *have any* children, dear," said Christophe. "Or maybe a few anonymous test-tube ones."

"Well," said Fulla, imperturbably, "Phineas's children, then. Somebody has to care. You'd think the fate of the earth would impinge even on fairy hedonists."

"Fairy's not a nice word," said Erik.

"Well, whatever a *Puck* is then, hedonists," said Fulla. "You send people out there into fantasy worlds, and they choke in real forest fires in Indonesia, in palls of smoke from burning forests that aren't in your pretty cutouts. The Danube is full of asphyxiated and radioactive fish corpses after the bombing in Kosovo; there has been a huge tidal wave of *human sewage* on Copacabana Beach in Rio de Janeiro; you send out physically *unfit* teachers and clerks to disturb the gorillas in Rwanda and they in turn get slaughtered by Hutu guerrillas, or to look at ever-so-romantic mediaeval fortresses in the Yemen and they get in the crossfire in a religious war. You can't fly round and round on your pretty invisible girdle without impinging and being impinged on. The Mediterranean's a *dead sea,* owing to the Aswan dam and international deluges of tourist shit and preservatives and herbicides and pesticides . . . but just the shit would do for it. We are an animal that needs to use its intelligence to mitigate the effects of its intelligence on the other creatures. And the air, and the earth, and the water. But we don't, do we? We use chlorine bleach to make nice fluffy white bunnies and we tie them up in little bits of real leather off some other poor beast's back, and that's what we think the creatures are, fluff and glass eyes and pretty chains."

"Bravo," said Christophe, whether ironically or otherwise was not clear.

"Fuck off," said Erik, who was much crosser, and whose wound was nastier. He was crosser because he was bigger and stronger than Christophe, and actually kinder. Something in Christophe acknowledged the existence of Maurice Bossey—and therefore of my own distress—whereas Erik, a Scandinavian moralist at heart like Fulla, his opponent, was simply enraged. "If you've finished talking," he told her, pompous and absurd, "just go away. Even if you haven't."

"I will," she said. "Come on, Phineas."

I don't know how it would have ended if Fulla hadn't swept in like a Valkyrie. I might have injured one, or both of my employers seriously. Or we might—so to speak—have kissed and made up. Seen the absurdity of it. As it was, I followed Fulla out of the shop, with Erik behind me reiterating that I was fired, fired, fired. And that Fulla had no sense of humour. This annoyed her. "I do," she said to me, as we went into the street. "But it doesn't have to be uppermost all the time. There's a proper time for everything. Even humour. Though the British don't think so." I said Erik and Christophe were not British. She said she knew that, she wasn't a complete idiot. She stopped in her tracks.

"You don't *mind* me shouting at them, Phineas?" she said, doubtfully. "They were being horribly aggressive and irrational."

I said of course I didn't mind. I was in fact touched by her championship. It was the first time, I think, anyone had ever tried to defend me. From bullying or from anything else. I hadn't thought we knew each other well enough—she called me "Phineas" as though we were old and close friends. I found myself—despite her exaggerated personality, despite her extreme beliefs—hoping that we were indeed friends. She might have lost me my job. (I might have lost it myself.) I said, "Thank you, Fulla."

She took out a large, clean, gold-and-white checked handkerchief. "Come here," she said. She pulled me towards her. She wiped the blood, which was not my own, from my face. She put out a sharp little tongue and damped a corner of the handkerchief, rubbing at the corner of my eyebrow. The transferred touch of her damp made me weak at the knees. I

239

was overcome with a memory of my return to consciousness under her skirts. As she lifted her arm, I smelled her sweat, salt and pungent. I put out a hand to steady myself on her shoulder. I swayed towards her, and converted the fall to a brief, darting, respectful kiss of gratitude on her cheekbone.

"Now what?" I said, with uncharacteristic insouciance. "I've just lost a job, and have nothing to do with the rest of the day. What shall we do now?"

What would she say? I needed to stop feeling drunk.

"We shall go to Richmond Park," she said. "I have something I wish to show you."

"We shall buy a picnic," she said, and led me into Fortnum & Mason's, where she bought wholemeal baps, and sheeps' cheese, and endives, and tomatoes, and large crisp apples, and yogurt, and honey, and bitter chocolate, and bottles of water. All this she stowed in a kind of knapsack she always carried. We made our way to Richmond by tube, bus and then foot. It was a very bright late-spring early-summer day. In central London the tube was crowded, and I stood with my nose in Fulla Biefeld's huge spangling wing of hair. I breathed its scales, the pulse of the scalp under it. I offered to carry her knapsack-thing, but she refused me, saying that she had carried it through forests and deserts, and would feel *amputated* without it. So there I was, empty-handed, with my nose in her hair.

It was midweek, and Richmond Park, once we got off the roads and the beaten track, was unpeopled. Deer grazed among the bracken, butterflies hovered over dandelions and thistles, twisted hawthorns were in full bloom, and the air was full of many kinds of pollen. Fulla strode along steadily—she knew where she was going. There were flocks of jackdaws, and a woodpecker tapped, invisible. There were rabbits, squatting and scattering unconcernedly. Fulla was looking at smaller things than these. She strode along—she was wearing a kind of full-length shirt, and trainers. I kept up. We passed huge ponds with sailing swans and coots and geese and variegated ducks. I felt like a little boy on a magical walk, except that I felt very aware of being male, beside this almost *violently* female creature. I had never been to Richmond Park before. Our school "nature walks" took us to a local children's zoo, with guinea pigs in cages and a few tattered, cross goats.

Fulla was heading for a kind of oaky glade, where centenarian trees stood amongst the rotting stumps of their fellows. "They understand—the verderers—that you need to leave rotten wood *lying around,*" said Fulla, with satisfaction. "This is what I brought you to see." She examined the stumps with satisfaction, finding signs of burrowing and drilling which she didn't explain. "Wait," she said. "They'll come. Have some bread and cheese." We sat side by side on the edge of the clearing, our backs against a stump, and munched. Fulla—not a *graceful* woman—stuck her legs straight out in front of her. They were shining with golden hairs, which caught the light. After a time, creatures began to impinge. A tiny spider let itself down on a long thread and scurried away into her hair. A twiggy olive-coloured caterpillar of the kind that hoops itself, stretches, and peers, found its way on to her knees and negotiated them. Other caterpillars arrived on sailing threads and fell on to the hair, or the breast-pockets of her shift. She made no move to brush anything off. A hoverfly darted about her moving lips, as she ate. Bees hummed past, or tunnelled into the light earth round the roots. She identified them obligingly. Solitary bumble-bees, carder bees, male and female, a cuckoo bee, *Nomada flava,* on a dandelion. Another cuckoo bee, *Psithyrus bohemicus,* which Fulla said laid its eggs in the bumble-bees' nest *(Bombus lucorum).* It hides amongst the moss in the nest until it smells of the nest, Fulla said, and then creeps out and eats the eggs of the bumble-bee queen, leaving its own in their place. Cuckoo bees have thick cuticles, to resist stinging, and tend to be bright and to produce many more eggs than their hosts. The male *Nomada* imitates the smell of its host, *Andrena,* and patrols its nest to attract females of its own species. Their larvae often start with huge sickle-shaped jaws—like the egg-heaving hump on the cuckoo-bird fledgling—to enable them to destroy their host's eggs and larvae. "Not much was known until recently about male bees," said Fulla Biefeld. "Studies concentrated on the social life and the pollen-gathering, which is female. But the males are very interesting. Bumble-bees for instance—the males congregate in a kind of *run*—on an open hedge—and invite the females to run the gauntlet with a kind of dancing display. Or there's this carder bee, which specialises in making nests from the down on salvias and lambs' ears. The male is (unusually) bigger than the female, and very territorially aggressive. It fights and kills all intruders—including much larger bees." I asked how. I said I thought male bees didn't sting. They don't, she said. They have an armoury of spikes on their bellies which they curl round enemies, to pierce them. The females of that species—

unlike most—mate more than once. "Most females—we think—put out a hormonal signal after they've mated. They don't want to be pestered and lose breeding energy to pestering males. They only live six days."

I asked, had we come to look at aggressive male bees? No, she said. Here they come. I'll show you what we've come to see.

They came in, flying like tiny demons from some fresco of the Last Judgement, horned and ponderous. Their flight was ungainly, the sound of it burring and clicketing. They are heavily armoured, and yet seem hugely vulnerable, huge in the insect world, eminently crushable in the human. Fulla said, "Southwest London, you know, is the only place they are known to breed in the British Isles. They lay their eggs precisely in rotting oak-stumps. A male will hold a territory—a stump—and fight off the others. Watch, Phineas, the jousting is beginning."

They do, precisely, joust. A large, shining male sat on a stump, and Fulla pointed out the female waiting in the shade of some dead leaves. She produced from her knapsack a magnifying glass, which we passed from one to the other. The male beetle was a very dark chestnut brown with a (Norman) shield-shaped wing-case and huge jaws, resembling both the indented claws of lobsters and crabs, and the antlers of stags. Behind these was a pair of long feelers with agitated combs on the end, at a right angle. His head too had a carved look, with a wide brow and curving case with bright little gold eyes on the side of it. He had six arms or legs with feathery ends. The female was smaller, and blacker, with discreet pincers in place of the extravagant antlers. He stood on his log, his rival flew

243

in, and battle began. It did indeed, resemble the head-to-head bellowing engagements of true stags, which must also take place in these ancient clearings. They ran at each other, almost prancing, and locked their jaws, twisting and wrestling, the aim being to dislodge the opponent or, it seemed, to overturn him. In the event the challenger overturned the king of the castle, and both tumbled to earth, where they righted themselves after wild leg-waving, and advanced on each other again, this time walking along a long, narrow root, trying to clash and sway each other off. Again, both fell, again, battle recommenced. Fulla pointed out other battles for other stumps. She handed me her glass. Her fingers are dry and stubby, with tight-trimmed nails. When they touched mine—in a *matter-of-fact* manner—it was electric, I tingled. I looked through the glass and suddenly, briefly, lost my sense of scale, seeing armoured monsters lurching on a rugged battlefield, glossy carapace, and wonderfully articulated, tremulously wiry limbs. I was about to say, they were *glaring* at each other, but that is pure anthropomorphism. I asked Fulla if they met each other's eye, and she said that was an interesting question, she didn't know, and took the glass back. They must emit smells, she said. I said—it had been waiting to be said, and my anthropomorphic observation drove me to saying it—that I had always thought the idea of learning about sex from the birds and the bees was simply foolishness. Dogs, and cows, I said. Fulla put her fingers over my lips to keep me quiet. The challenger was rolled over. A third male was watching from the edge of the ring (the rim of the rotten trunk). Fulla's fingers on my lips were sharp as a bee-sting. I thought of biting them, and did nothing. Surely she *knew*, I thought, what was going on—in some ways ludicrously, I could see that, but it wasn't how it felt. The king of the castle climbed back up, and made a dash at the new intruder, who backed off.

"I want you," said Fulla, "to help me with an experiment."

"Is he dead?"

"No, no, they don't hurt each other, usually. Unlike the aggressive *Anthidium*. No, it's just male territorial dancing. These creatures are getting rare. There's a belief that the biggest always wins. Unlike territorial battles in butterflies, where the one in possession always beats off the challenger. What we need to do is label the males, and remove them one by one, and record their weights, and the fights, and the winners, as we remove and return them. You can keep them quite safely in plastic boxes with airholes and damp sand—so they don't dehydrate—and I'll give you a set of coloured, numbered discs to attach to them. We did a very successful series of observations on male *Osmia rufa* bees by this method."

"Why me?"

"Well, you appear to be underoccupied. And I have to go to Turkey. And also back to Oxford. And I *want to know* about these creatures, before we extinguish them." She hesitated. "You know," she said, "the first insect I collected was one of these. I found it dead in the road, on a holiday. I put it in a box and labelled it "stag beetle." I used a Swedish word I thought I'd made up, *hjortbagge*, literally *stag* plus *beetle*. Then they told me that was wrong, the word is *ekoxe*, literally *oak-ox*, which is much less accurate, I think. Your friend Linnaeus called it *Lucanus cervus*, which does mean stag beetle. So I thought I'd been fanciful, but later I discovered that the old Swedish word was truly *hjortbagge*. I'd imagined it rightly. I collected a lot of other things as a little girl—snailshells and

245

seed-pods, and butterflies and many other beetles—and just gave them names from nowhere, for fun. I remember putting an elm-bark beetle—*Scolytus destructor* it was called then—it's been renamed *Scolytus scolytus*—in a matchbox and labelling it *The Valise Bug*. It's a rather boring beetle, though it makes wonderfully patterned interconnecting tunnels in the bark of elms—they look like great centipedes—or dragons. It looks like a neat little zipped-up leather suitcase. Of course, it isn't really boring, it spreads Dutch elm disease, it's changed the whole landscape of Europe." She stopped a moment. I said,

"Do you think *everyone* collects things when little?"

Moths brushed through my mind, multi-coloured tiny glass spheres glistened. What was I doing?

"I don't know. I used to hold parties for bugs in boxes. I never liked dolls. Dead human beings that had never lived, I always thought. With nasty sickly-sweet faces. Then I got interested in fitting the bugs together. Then into fitting the insect world into the rest of the world. Boxes in boxes. Of course, *all* the naming's arbitrary. The new genetic group-ings—the clades—are going to sweep away the Linnean fami-lies and genera and species, and reconnect everything quite differently. It's possible, for instance, that a mushroom is more nearly related to you than to a chrysanthemum or a slime-mould."

I said I would like to help her with her project. She was right that I had no function in the world at present. I said I would like to help her, but I wouldn't know how to start with-out her.

"That's OK," she said. "We've got plenty of time to set it up. Before I go."

And she lay back spreadeagled on the turf, amongst dried

rabbit-pellets and deer fewmets, amongst the secret entrances to the nests of bumble-bees and slow-worms, amongst gossamer and starry daisies and dandelion clocks and roaring golden dandelions, and her amazing hair spread like another life-form over the grasses and things flew into it and slid over it on bellies and innumerable tiny feet.

And she opened the top two buttons of her shift, so I could clearly see her freckled brown breasts in their lacy cups. They put me in mind of bird's eggs, or the shadowy entrance to foxgloves. And when she saw me looking, she put up her quick little hands and pulled my face down between them. All of me, all of me, trembled and exploded.

We rode back from Richmond decorously side by side on the top of a bus. It was as though my left side (her side) burned and was so to speak dissolving into steam, or gases. Other people may often have experienced this secret journeying with the intention of sex at the end, but I was new to it, as I was new to what Fulla had done to my skin and bone-marrow, my fingers and toes, not to mention the most obvious part, or parts, of me. I could have stroked her, or gripped her, or licked her, all that long way back, but putting it off, waiting, *keeping still,* looking uninterested, was so much more exciting . . .

She was staying in someone's flat in Fulham. I followed her scent up the dark stairs of the house (it was an attic flat). And . . .

I began this piece of writing with the moment when I decided to stop being a post-structuralist literary critic. It seems a long time ago. I seem to remember that I began with a revulsion from Empedocles' idea of the fragmented body-parts in search of each other. I think I was so taken by Ormerod Goode's revelation of Destry-Scholes's biography of Elmer Bole precisely because the over-determinism of Literary Theory, the meta-language of it, threw into brilliant relief Destry-Scholes's real achievement in describing a whole individual, a multi-faceted single man, one life from birth to death. I appeared to have failed to find Destry-Scholes himself. I have to respect him for his scrupulous *absence* from my tale, my work. It will be clear that I too have wished to be *absent*. I have resisted and evaded the idea that because of Destry-Scholes's *absence* my narrative must become an account of my own presence, *id est*, an autobiography, that most evasive and self-indulgent of forms. I have tried both to use my own history, unselfconsciously, as a temporal thread to string my story (my writing) on, *and* to avoid unnecessary dwelling on my own feelings, or my own needs, or my own—oh dear— *character.* It will be clear to almost any attentive reader, I think, that as I have gone along in this writing (we are now at page 161, ms) I have become more and more involved in the act of writing itself, more and more inclined to shift my attention from Destry-Scholes's absence to my own style, and thus, my own *presence.* I now wonder—after the last few pages I have written about the birds and the bees (and the stag beetles) and Fulla B—whether *all* writing has a tendency to flow like a river towards the writer's body and the writer's own experience? I began with what I still consider a healthy desire to *eschew the personal* (the tangential, the coincidental). Yet I am now possessed by a burning desire to describe making love to Fulla Biefeld, and, worse than that, to describe how that experience differs from the (no less intense, whatever a reader may think) experience of making love to Vera Alphage. And the intensity of the liberation into writing lyrical (banal but shocking-to-me) sentences about foxgloves and freckles, spiderwebs and hairs.

I had already—before the loss of my job, before the impulsive picnic—arranged to visit Vera Alphage on the next day. I wondered, out of a mad sense of either decorum or personal inadequacy—whether to cancel. I felt in some primitive way that Fulla's musk was all over my body, lingering in every crevice. Fulla's love-making is fierce and wholehearted, not prolonged but repetitive (I was pleased by my capacity to rise to these repeated occasions). She cries out, she laughs, you would not suppose her to be the rather grim and severe world-moralist I met in the Linnean Society strongroom. She is all liquid gold, all grip and drive. She bites nicely. I had little blue florets, I found in my shower-room, in the hollows of my collar-bone and stepping along my hip from my groin. When I saw this shadowy blue, with its rose-and-black gooseflesh, on my skin, in my naked solitude, I thought of Vera. Not, as you may imagine, because I thought Vera might detect Fulla's activities from the blossoming of my belly. How could she not, indeed, when you think about it, but I am slow to read signs, as I have said before, and also, there was a half-chance, for Vera always made love with her huge eyes closed and the long lashes damp on the dark shadowed hollow beneath them. No, I thought of Vera, because I always, always think of Vera when I see that particular blue, of bruises and shadows, of the dark where the pulse of her blue vein beats in her wrist, or the root of her elegant neck, or the inside of her white thigh. I think also of the almost-midnight blue, the night-blue, she has chosen for the background to her photographs of our invisible inner lives, made with frequencies of light our human eyes cannot see. I thought of Vera, it has to be said, as Fulla pushed her warm little face fiercely along the bones of my hip and pelvis, I thought of the *life of the bones,* under, in the invisible world of the body, Vera's world. I thought of them together. Fulla wandered the plains of my flesh, causing every hair to rise to her, and inside my nerve-strings sang Vera. (I am getting better at my lyricism, but am not sure that last sentence works. Let it stand. Who will ever read all this stuff, anyway. *And,* it's true.)

I think, up to that juncture, I had been *grateful* to Vera for allowing me to sleep with her. I did not realise, until I was faced with the straightforward ferocity of Fulla's desire, how much I had supposed that I was a small, insignificant being to whom the beautiful, secretive Vera was simply being *kind.* Fulla set me aglow—with sex, but also with a kind of pleasure in myself I'd never known. I liked my body. I liked Phineas G. Nanson. And—it has to be admitted—I wanted to show this new, strutting, gleaming Phineas G. to Vera. I wanted to bring to her—to *give* her—some of my new-learned inventiveness.

I think—from reading novels—that there is a compulsion, faced with two women, to decide that one is "the real one" and that the other is *"only"* something or other. *Only* for sex, *only* for relaxing, even *only* for friendship, as opposed to the Romantic welded dyad. Which I suddenly see, having had that thought, in terms of the hermaphrodite silver paperknife with which I laid about Erik and Christophe. A weapon for cutting paper. We have a cultural need to present it to ourselves this way. Only, I didn't. I wanted to go from Fulla to Vera (and back to Fulla) forever. I even wanted to teach Vera to look at me. Covered with the love-bites of a Swedish bee-taxonomist. It was a long way from Ormerod Goode and the Glenmorangie. I suppose he too had his life as a body with other bodies. I'd never thought about it, despite his erotic scribblings in dusty seminars. So I went to see Vera. As usual, and not as usual. When I got there, she was bent over some new arrangement of Destry-Scholes's marbles. This one entailed a central circular figure, I remember, with one very large, slightly chipped one in the centre, with yellowish clear glass round a spiralling blue core of lattice-work, with a red vein spiralling inside it. From the circle she had made long radiating tentacles, or flagellae, on some principle I couldn't discover. They bent around, at their ends, to form a swastika-like form. She did not look up when I came in. She looked somehow different. I immediately knew that she knew about my adventures. I approached, crabwise. My—that is, Destry-Scholes's—that is, Vera's—shoeboxes were on a side-table.

"I got the boxes out," she said, from inside a tent of dark silk.

I went, not to the boxes, but to her. I asked, inanely enough, what she was working on. She said, liquid, it didn't matter. Really, it didn't matter.

I saw, then, round drops of liquid splashing on to the round glass marbles, running down into the baize . . . She sniffed, discreetly, almost inaudibly. I very nearly turned on my heel to retreat. But I didn't. I put my hand on the ripple of her weeping shoulders. I stroked the dark hair. Mum. Terrified of losing her. I said, in the end, as more tears rolled on more marbles,

"Shall I just go away?"

"I'm sorry to be like this. Perhaps it's better."

"I'll go then."

"I can't expect you to get wound up in my problems. We aren't like that, I know—"

"Vera. What is it?"

"I can't go on."

"With me? I understand, of course—"

"Don't be stupid. With *my job*. I did something unforgivable."

It was nothing to do with me. I breathed oxygen, I gathered her in my arms, I called her my love, my darling (words until then unknown in the Nanson vocabulary, at least with that possessive adjective). I led her to her sofa and held her wet face against my shirt, where the tears spread and trickled. Tell me, I said, tell me. She did. I don't recall that anyone had ever trusted me with anything *like that* before. I stroked her hair, like a tamer with a frightened creature.

She had taken a series of photographs from a scan of the base of the skull, the nape of the neck, the spine, of a young man who had had an earlier operation for a rare cancer of the neck, which had entailed removing his arm and shoulder. He had, it had appeared, made a complete recovery, had learned to live one-handed and scarred, in a swashbuckling series of painted jackets, and brilliant caps on his shaven crown. And then there had been troubling symptoms. They had done the scan, to investigate. Vera had hung rows of photographs on a lightscreen, and through the plates the light had showed the filaments and sproutings of the cancer, wound round and into the vertebral column, obscuring its form, eating its edges, reaching for the bone-marrow. They were, said Vera, lovely photographs. We couldn't have got anything so delicate, so precise, even five years ago. There were a lot of them. The young man's eye ran from one to the other; the surgeon pointed out the invasive malignant cells, with a red laser, and Vera watched the young man read his death—his inevitable death—in the details of her work.

And suddenly she began to weep uncontrollably, as she saw his lips tighten, and his throat constrict, and his eyes stare. She wept and wept and fell to the ground, and had to be helped away by the surgeon, who should have been helping the dying man with the deadly knowledge. My darling, my love, I murmured into her hair. I said that perhaps the young man had been grateful, that she cared so much. She said no, he had given her a cold, faraway, *malignant* look, the young man, because she was alive, and making an unnecessary scene, and he was vanishing down a tunnel, out of touch. I wiped her tears, I kissed her, I said truthfully I had not known how she had walked so calmly in the valley of the shadow, day after day. As I wiped her face with my handkerchief and told her she was brave, I remembered Erik and Christophe and their duck-egg blue ones, and Fulla's tongue on her handkerchief on Erik's blood on my own face. Fulla had defended me, and now I felt enough of a man to console Vera. I told Vera she could not be kind to anyone if she was not kind to herself. She said she had *no life* although she was not dying, only this austere vocation, and I said, solid Phineas (truthful Phineas), yes, she did, she did have a life, she had me.

We went to bed in the dark. She said she did not want me to see her face all swollen, and as a result she did not see Fulla's love-bites. I felt with my lips and fingertips the slow tears still welling between her closed eyelids. I noticed, I thought that Vera's scent, which I thought of as silvery, combined quite differently with my own from the way Fulla's did, which I thought of as golden. How did I get to these synaesthetic metaphors? Vera (my love, my darling) is a darting silver fish, a sailing moon in an indigo sky, quicksilver melting into a thousand droplets and recombining. Fulla is gold calyx strenuously spread in gold sunlight, Fulla is golden pollen clinging to bee-fur, Fulla is the sailing fleets of dandelion clocks. Fulla is lion-pelt, cats' teeth. I do not think I have got lyricism quite right yet. The urge to commit it is overwhelming. The results not so. But it can all stay in, for the moment. We think in clichés because clichés are ideas which have so to speak proved their Darwinian *fitness* over time (I say nothing, here, of truthfulness). I could compare Fulla and Vera to tea and coffee, or Glasgow and Birmingham, but clichés are requisite here, like tap-roots into the common (in every sense) consciousness from which slightly adapted, new mutations are generated.

We lay there in the dark. She had let go her grip on my arms, her fingers were relaxed, though the tears were still brimming over. I curled myself round her limp body with careful protectiveness, stretching my spine to encompass her contracted one, my sex stirring in the cleft of her white (invisible) bottom. I had the idea of massaging the nape of her neck (I read signs badly) but desisted, after my touch induced a massive shudder. So I stroked her hair, and face, and ears, over and over, and she wept, more quietly, less convulsively. In the morning, she was still weeping. I said she shouldn't go to work, she should go to the doctor. She said the surgeon had advised that. I said, "I'll stay with you." She tried to say no, but I saw that she needed me. She accepted. I thought then, Fulla wouldn't know where to find me, and then, that I must get in touch with her whilst Vera was at the doctor's, and arrange—arrange what?—well, at least the next stage of the stag-beetle experiment.

Over the next long, empty day, Vera wept and dozed and wept. I made her little meals. And I went back to work on the card index.

My next grouping is drawn randomly from Destry-Scholes's cards—or rather, not at random, but following some thread of connectedness, some clue of my own. I begin with a quotation I tracked down to Pearson's biography, recognising his unique tone of voice with no trouble (Vol. IIIA, p. 411). It concerns *Kantsaywhere*, an eugenic Utopia written in Galton's last year of life. It is card no. 411 in the shoebox. I do not think there is any meaning in this coincidence.

Thinking over the problem of books that have had a lasting influence on mankind his thoughts turned to those ideal polities, Plato's *Republic*, More's *Utopia*,

Harington's *Oceana* and Butler's *Erewhon*. Why should he not exercise a similar influence on generations to come by writing his own *Utopia,* a story of a land where the nation was eugenically organised? A modern Gulliver should start his travels again and seek a bride in Eugenia. Only a fragment of this *Utopia,* which was termed "Kantsaywhere" has reached me, it deals with "The Eugenic College of Kantsaywhere." The book purports to be "Extracts from the Journal of the later Professor I. Donoghue [footnote 'I don't know you'!"] revised and edited in accordance with his request by Sir Francis Galton, F.R.S." On my last visit to Galton on Dec. 28–29, 1910, I was told with an air of some mystery by his niece that he was writing a "novel," that he would probably not mention it to me, but that if he did, I must persuade him not to publish it, because the love-episodes were too absurdly unreal. It is perhaps needless to say that I should have given no such advice. Galton was failing in physique but not in mind, when I talked with him less than three weeks before his death; and to recommend him to destroy what he had thrown time and energy into creating would have seemed to me criminal. If Swift had died before the issue of *Gulliver's Travels,* or Samuel Butler before the publication of *Erewhon,* their relatives might possibly have destroyed with equal justification those apparently foolish stories. I do not assert that Galton had a literary imagination comparable with that of Swift or of Butler, but I feel strongly that we small fry have no right to judge the salmon to be foolish or even mad, when he leaps six feet out of our pool up a ladder we cannot ascend, and which to us appears to lead into an arid world. We must remember that Galton had set before himself in the last years of his life a definite plan of eugenics propagandism. He wanted to appeal to men of science through his foundation of a Eugenics Laboratory; he had definitely approached separate groups like the Anthropologists in his Huxley Lecture, and the Sociologists in his lecture before their Society and in his subsequent essays; he had appealed to the academic world in his Herbert Spencer Lecture at Oxford, and to the world that reads popular quarterlies in his Eugenics Education Society. But there are strata of the community which cannot be caught by even these processes. For these he consented to be interviewed, and for the still less readable section who read novels and only look at the picture pages of newspapers, he wrote what they needed, a tale, his "Kantsaywhere." His scheme of proselytism was a comprehensive one, but I think Galton knew his public better than most men.

An Ibsen or a Meredith with far more imaginative power would, if they had taught Galton's creed, have struck above the level of those for whom Galton intended his tale . . .

Card no. 413   Letter from G's niece

I was just thinking of writing to you about "Kantsaywhere" when your letter came. When I began the work of execution, my heart misgave me so much that I thought I would begin by merely "Bowdlerizing" it and then see. So I destroyed *all* the story, all poor Miss Augusta, and the Nonnyson anecdotes, and in fact everything not to the point—but there are a good many pages that I felt myself incapable of judging. So I am returning the mutilated copy, hoping . . . that Professor Karl Pearson might see it . . . Mutilated as it is, poor "Kantsaywhere" can never be published, and it is as safe from *that* as if it were destroyed altogether, but I think what remains might interest Prof. Pearson, and possibly, though I doubt it, be useful. Besides, if *something* survived, I should not feel quite so much like a murderess!

Card no. 414   [Pearson, of course]

No doubt those who took upon themselves to pass judgement on Galton's last work were fully conscious of the responsibility they shouldered. But the fealty of a biographer is of a different kind; his duty is to give a *full* account of his subject; if there were weaknesses, they were compensated by strengths; if he is called upon to describe the actions of his subject when young, he must equally describe those of his old age.

I insert now, out of sequence, two cards which seem to me to bear a relation to the final card in the "Kantsaywhere" group. I have read what little Pearson was able to salvage of "Kantsaywhere"—a rather childishly cheerful and dogmatic work, harmless enough unless you think *all* eugenic ideas are intrinsically evil. And, having seen some of Vera's more terrible photographs, I am inclined to support research into genetic therapies. But I don't like Utopias, and I don't like Galton's sanitised world, which he himself treats, perhaps, I'm not sure, with a *milky* kind of irony.

Card no. 24   G on Energy

Energy is an attribute of the higher races, being favoured beyond all other qualities by natural selection. We are goaded into activity by the conditions and struggles of life. They afford stimuli that oppress and worry the weakly, who complain and bewail, and it may be succumb to them, but which the energetic man welcomes with a good-humoured shrug, and is the better for in the end.

The stimuli may be of any description: the only important matter is that all the faculties should be kept working to prevent their perishing by disuse. If the faculties are few, very simple stimuli will suffice. Even that of fleas will go a long way. A dog is continually scratching himself, and a bird pluming itself, whenever they are not occupied with food, hunting, fighting, or love. In those blank times there is very little for them to attend to besides their varied cutaneous irritations. It is a matter of observation that well washed and combed domestic pets grow dull; they miss the stimulus of fleas. If animals did not prosper through the agency of their insect plagues, it seems probable that their races would long since have been so modified that their bodies should have ceased to afford a pasture-ground for parasites.

Card no. 99   G on the self (selves)

I suspect that much of what we stigmatise as irresolution is due to our Self being by no means one and indivisible, and that we do not care to sacrifice the Self of the moment for a different one. There are, I believe,

259

cases in which we are wrong to reproach ourselves sternly, saying, "The last week was not spent in the way you now wish it had been," because the Self was not the same throughout. There is room for applying the greatest happiness of the greatest number, the particular Self at the moment of making retrospect being not the only one to be considered.

Card no. 101   G on selves and cells

We as yet understand nothing of the way in which our conscious selves are related to the separate lives of the billions of cells of which the body of each of us is composed. We only know that the cells form a vast nation, some members of which are always dying and others growing to supply their places and that the continual sequence of these multitudes of little lives has its outcome in the larger and conscious life of the man as a whole. Our part in the universe may possibly in some distant way be analogous to that of the cells in an organised body, and our personalities may be the transient but essential elements of an immortal and cosmic mind.

Card no. 414   The Religion of Kantsaywhere

Their creed, or rather, I should say, their superstition—for it has not yet crystallised into a dogmatic creed, is that living beings, and pre-eminently mankind, are the only executive agents of whom we have any certain knowledge. They look upon life at large, as probably a huge organisation in which every separative living thing plays an unconscious part, much as the separate cells do in a living person. Whether the following views were self-born or partly borrowed I do not know, but the people of Kantsaywhere have the strong belief that the spirits of all the beings who have ever lived are round about, and regard all their actions. They watch the doings of men with eagerness, grieving when their actions are harmful to humanity, and rejoicing when they are helpful. It is a kind of grandiose personification of what we call conscience into a variety of composite portraits. I expect that the many visionaries among them—for there are visionaries in all races—actually see with more or less distinctness the beseeching or the furious figures of these imaginary spirits, either as individuals or as composites. There seems to be some confusion between the family, the racial, and the universal clouds of spirit-watchers. They are supposed to co-exist separately and yet may merge into one or many different wholes. There is also much difference of opinion as to the power of these spirits, some think them only sympathetic, others assign the faculty to them of inspiring ideas in men, others again accredit them with occasional physical powers. Everyone here feels that they themselves will, after their life is over, join the spirit legion, and they look forward with eager hope that their descendants will then do what will be agreeable and not hateful to them. I have heard some who likened life to the narrow crest of the line of breakers of a never-resting and infinite ocean, eating slowly and everlastingly into the opposing shore of an infinite and inert continent. But that metaphor does not help me much, beyond picturing what in their view is the smallness of actual life with the much larger amount of elements of potential life.

Reading the whole of Pearson's account of all this, I noticed that Galton had given his Utopians a central interest in composite photographs, which became both family and religious icons, being used in the (cheerful) funeral services. "In Kantsaywhere they think much more of the race than of the individual . . ."

I add, as a footnote for Fulla, something else I found in Pearson, but not in Destry-Scholes's shoebox. It is from a letter to his niece, Milly, Mrs. Lethbridge, who was responsible for the semi-destruction of Kantsaywhere. He is discussing, among other things, the design of his sister Emma's tombstone, which was decorated with drawings of Galtonia—the *Hyacinthus candicus,* named for Galton himself by Professor J. Decaisne in Paris. It is a South African bulb, shooting up to five feet and more. I derive this information from Pearson's footnote to Galton's letter. The letter is dated December 17th 1904. It is on page 533 of Pearson, Vol. IIIB (I have been driven insane enough by Destry-Scholes's lack of references to find myself unable to omit this one, even for *no possible reader*). Plate LVI facing page 534 is a line drawing of Galtonia.

Dear Emma's gravestone is not even yet put up . . .
I send you a photo of the inscription which you will

Galtonia *(Hyacinthus candicus)* from tropical South Africa

like to keep, all the more for having helped in drawing up the words. The Galtonias at either side are utter failures. The artist has no excuse, for he was supplied with many drawings; but accuracy is not the strong point of artists. They think as much of shadows as of substances, and a bandbox casts as black a shadow as a block of granite. (That metaphor might be worked up!) . . . The last rose of summer—the last rat of the year! You will have to keep and pet him or her. But the large probable families of rats are appalling. I heard that all the hives full of Ligurian bees in England, for many years, were descended from a single queen bee, sent by post to England from the Riviera. Is it possible?

I add some more random cards from the shoebox. They are random, that is to say, I picked them from their places (widely separated) and rearranged them in this document. The threads of connection are my own. In that sense at least, I am becoming the biographer of Scholes Destry-Scholes, or at least *organising* the quarry of secondary materials into an ur-shape, a preliminary form.

Card no. 79   [Henrik Jaeger, *Dagbladet,* 27 Feb. 1891— my added ref. PGN.] [Review of opening of *Hedda Gabler*]
    "The applause weakened as the play progressed . . . Ibsen has treated the psychological conflicts portrayed here as Pasteur and Koch treat bacteria."
    And Georg Göthe in *Ny Svenske Tidskrift:* "No dramatic talent can make a character as obscurely complex

as Hedda Gabler really clear and dramatically consistent."

Card no. 113   [Georg Brandes to Professor C. J. Salomonsen, Dresden, 1874. PGN.] [Salomonsen a biologist. PGN.]

The man sits there producing very little, unable to draw intellectual nourishment from the world around him because he lacks the organs to do so, and is rigidly set in all kinds of prejudices and eccentricities. He has a sure eye for only one thing, namely the prejudices of his homeland, everything that is obsolete in Norway and Denmark; but the lack of any systematic education makes him desperately limited. Fancy—he seriously believes in a time when "the intelligent minority" in these countries "will be forced to enlist the aid of chemistry and medicine in poisoning the proletariat" to save themselves from being politically overwhelmed by the majority. And this universal poisoning is what he wants. The Germans, too, amongst whom he has lived for so long (without getting to know a single intelligent one and without reading more than one or two books a year—literally), the Germans too he knows very incompletely, and his acquaintance with one or two crazy Catholics has led him to throw in his sympathy with the Catholic faction, the while he calls himself a Freethinker. In short he is lost in an endless chaos of characterlessness.

Card no. 2   [From Ibsen's Balloon Letter to a Swedish Lady, despatched by Ibsen from the siege of Paris during the Franco-Prussian War of 1871. In this letter (passages *not* collected by S D-S), he tells her he can't send the letter by carrier pigeon because he has no doves, wch. are the birds of hope. "In this cramped ground, but owls and ravens build. No messengers for a lady." He has been up the Nile with a group of international fellow-passengers

> Eleven cocks from France, four Spanish
>   stallions . . .
> A kind of ram from Switzerland . . . and of course
> A herd of German wild pigs, almost tamed.

Ibsen's Swedish Lady was Fru Frederika Limnell. PGN]

> Where personality is lacking,
> Where there is neither hatred, indignation,
> Nor joy, no beat of pulse nor flush of blood,
> Glory is but a dry rattle of bones.
> Who has not seen Juno in his mind's eye
> Pale in her wrath as she surprised her lord? . . .
> But the Egyptian gods were otherwise.
> Static, they never, like the gods of Greece
> And men, sinned, groped, and raised themselves
>   from sin.
> And so this culture, from millennia old
> Lies like a bloodless mummy in a crypt.

[Galton's niece, an ancestral Queen Bee, Ibsen's Swedish Lady, pointless hooks into my own story. And

266

goddesses, too, for I have discovered that Fulla is a Scandinavian nature-goddess, handmaid to Frigg.]

Card no. 134

Although philosophers may have written to show the impossibility of our discovering what goes on in the minds of others, I maintain an opposite opinion. I do not see why the report of a person on his own mind should not be as intelligible and trustworthy as that of a traveller upon a new country, whose landscapes and inhabitants are of a different type to any which we ourselves have seen. It appears to me that inquiry into the mental constitution of other people is a most fertile field for exploration, especially as there is much in the facts adduced here, as well as elsewhere, to show that original differences in mental constitution are permanent, being little modified by the accident of education, and that they are strongly hereditary.

Destry-Scholes had as usual not bothered to annotate this, and in my mind I wrongly for some time associated it with the citations from Ibsen amongst which I have now placed it. It is in fact from a paper in *Mind* (Vol. IX, pp. 406–13, 1884) on "Free-Will, Observations and Inferences," by Galton. Destry-Scholes can never have imagined *me* when he left this amorphous dossier. I suppose the only reader he can have imagined was himself, and he must have had a *photographic* memory, quite extraordinarily well-trained, to know his way around all this. I was quite pleased with my running-down, in indexes, of the previous citation, which took time. I then found that I could have found it in Pearson—whom I increasingly respect, at least as a constructor of thorough footnotes and index.

Card no. 98   [Reported speech of HI]
Before I write one word, I must know the character through and through, I must penetrate into the last wrinkle of his soul. I always proceed from the individual; the stage setting, the dramatic ensemble, all of this comes naturally and causes me no worry, as soon as I am certain of the individual in every aspect of his humanity. But I have to have his exterior in mind also, down to the last button, how he stands and walks, how he bears himself, what his voice sounds like. Then I do not let him go until his fate is fulfilled.

Card no. 137   [Reported speech of HI]
As a rule I make 3 drafts of my plays, which differ greatly from each other—in characterisation, not in plot. When I approach the first working-out of my material, it is as though I knew my characters from a railway-journey; one has made a preliminary acquaintance, one has chatted about this and that. At the next draft I already see everything much more clearly, and I know the people roughly as one would after a month spent with them at a spa; I have discovered the fundamentals of their characters and their little peculiarities; but I may still be wrong about certain essentials. Finally, in the last draft, I have reached the limit of my knowledge; I know my characters from close and long

acquaintance—they are my intimate friends, who will no longer disappoint me; as I see them now I shall always see them.

Card no. 197

The points I have endeavoured to impress are chiefly these. First, that character ought to be measured by carefully recorded acts, representative of conduct. An ordinary generalisation is nothing more than a muddle of vague memories of mixed observations. It is an easy vice to generalise. We want lists of facts, every one of which may be separately verified, valued and revalued, and the whole accurately summed. It is the statistics of each man's conduct in small, everyday affairs, that will probably be found to give the simplest and most precise measure of his character. The other chief point that I wish to impress is, that a practice of deliberately and methodically testing the character of others and of ourselves is not wholly fanciful, but deserves consideration and experiment.

[This is from Galton's essay, "Measurement of Character." PGN]

Card no. 6   From *Peer Gynt*

BUTTON MOULDER: The Master, you see, is a thrifty
       man.
    He never rejects as worthless anything
    Which He can use again as raw material.
    Now you were meant to be a shining button

On the waistcoat of the world. But your loop
    broke.
So you must be thrown into the rubbish bin
And go from there back into the great pool.
PEER: You don't intend to melt me down with other
    dead men?
BUTTON MOULDER: That is precisely what I intend.
    We've done it, you know, with a number of people.
    At the Royal Mint they do the same with coins
    That have got so worn you can't see the face on
    them.
PEER: But this is the most sordid parsimony!
    Oh, come on, be a sport and let me go!
    A button without a loop, a worn-out shilling
    What are they to a man in your Master's position?
BUTTON MOULDER: Oh, as long as a man has some
    soul left
    He's always worth a little as scrap.

And I add, myself, because presumably Destry-Scholes
saw no need to copy out a passage so famous, Peer Gynt and
the onion.

You're no Emperor. You're just an onion.
Now then, little Peer, I'm going to peel you
And you won't escape by weeping or praying.
[*Takes an onion and peels it layer by layer.*]

The outmost layer is withered and torn;
That's the shipwrecked man on the upturned keel.
Here, mean and thin, is the passenger;

But it still tastes a little of old Peer Gynt.
And inside that is the digger of gold;
Its juice is all gone, if it ever had any.
The next one's shaped like a crown. No, thank you!
We'll throw that away and ask no questions.
Here's the student of history, short and tough;
And here is the Prophet, fresh and juicy;
Like the man in the proverb he stinks of lies
That would blind an honest man's eyes with tears.
This layer now that curls up so softly
Is the sybarite living for ease and pleasure.
The next one looks sick; it's streaked with black.
That might mean a priest; or it might mean a nigger.
[*Peels off several at once.*]
What a terrible lot of layers there are!
Surely I'll soon get down to the heart?
[*Pulls the whole onion to pieces.*]
No—there isn't one! Just a series of shells
All the way through, getting smaller and smaller!
Nature is witty!

When I had collected all these, I added a quotation from
Linnaeus's *Nemesis* about ghosts, Spöka, which in the early
days I had asked Fulla to translate. I wasn't sure it belonged
here, but I wanted something from the third Personage to
complete the arrangement. It fitted with the spirit bands of
Galton's Kantsaywhere, and, much earlier, with Destry-
Scholes's fanciful version of Linnaeus's untruthful account of
his journeyings in the far north. I had tucked Vera into her
bed, and read Fulla's neat, tiny, taxonomist's script in her little
living-room.

Card no. 100

They spoke of "spirits" in Holy Scripture, in ancient days, above all in the days of legend. You hear less about them in flourishing kingdoms, where they are mostly spoken of in the countryside. They are mostly extraordinary. I have never seen one.

Frightened children believe in ghosts, most of all when they are outside, in the dark, or in the daytime when the shutters are closed. This becomes rooted in them, and stays for the rest of their days: the fear of blackness. Above all in cemeteries, and round gibbets. Out of a thousand tales, hardly a single one is true.

The Holy Scriptures say that everyone has his angel, who, night and day, protects him from evil and comes to his aid in adversity. Does this being follow the body like its shadow?

I tried to make sense of the shoebox. I tried to make sense of Destry-Scholes's whole project, always supposing it was one project, and not three. It was not a forerunner of what we currently call group biographies. These are now fashionable because we don't believe as Karl Pearson did, in great men, and we like to see human beings as parts of large social structures whose mechanisms and inter-relations we can uncover and describe. I had the feeling that Destry-Scholes's Personages were somehow in his mind, interwoven—like the Persons of the Trinity. Why *these three,* I asked myself, trying to stand back. What were they three aspects of?

A taxonomist, a statistician, a dramatist. Students in their own ways of the connectedness of things and people. Who separated out different aspects of these things and people for study. Like three nets laid over the nature of things with different meshes and weaves.

Galton saw the separate Selves that inhabit one man as cells working together in one organism. Georg Brandes's acid descriptions of Ibsen's microscopic world described germs and bacteria, invasion and dissolution. It was Ibsen the tragedian, not Galton the eugenicist, who wanted to poison the lower classes.

All three moved from microscope to macroscope, from the minute to the vast. Their descriptions of detail overlapped and interconnected—madly, sometimes, arbitrarily, *arranged* by Destry-Scholes (and also, lately, secondarily, by me). They were like one of Galton's composite portraits, which were perhaps a clue to what Destry-Scholes had been reaching towards. Was the composite portrait the face of Destry-Scholes? Was it, seen in some mad mirror, my own?

There was also the question, beyond the shoebox, of the three fictive fragments of biography, where the biographer had quite deliberately woven his own lies and inventions into the dense texture of collected facts. Was this a wry comment on the hopeless nature of the project of biographical accuracy, or was it just a wild and whimsical kicking-over of the traces? I seemed to understand that the imaginary narrative had sprung out of the scholarly one, and that the compulsion to *invent* was in some way related to my own sense that in constructing *this* narrative I have had to insert facts about myself, and not only dry facts, but my feelings, and now my interpretations. I have somehow been *made* to write my own story, to write in very different ways. They slipped in and out of focus, on a multiplicity of scales, from the minute to the vast. They formed one of Galton's composite portraits—more blurry than the genetically homogeneous ones. Was the composite Destry-Scholes? Was it, since I had had to arrange and rearrange, Phineas G. Nanson? I had a sudden moment of appalling vision. I knew that whatever had driven Destry-Scholes to write the three fictive (lying, untruthful) biographical fragments, was whatever was (is) now driving me to form this mass of material into my own story, to write (as he did, for no reader) of my love for Fulla, my love for Vera, my fear of Maurice Bossey, my half-envy of the affections of Erik and Christophe. I saw also that all Destry-Scholes's fiction had concerned ghosts and spirits, doubles and hauntings, metamorphoses, dismemberment, death. There are a very few human truths and infinite variations on them. I was about to write that there are very few truths about the world, but the truth about *that* is that we don't know what we are not biologically fitted to know, it may be full of all sorts of shining and tearing things, geometries, chemistries, physics we have no access to and never can have. Reading and writing extend— not infinitely, but violently, but giddily—the variations we can perceive on the truths we thus discover. Children are afraid of the dark; a double walks at our side, or hangs from our flesh like a shadow; and we put a whole lifetime (which is brief indeed in the light *even of history* let alone of the time of the world) to discovering what these things mean for us— dark, and shadows.

I found that I had in a way *invented* Vera and Fulla, whilst at the same time being constantly surprised by their independent and unpredictable reality. I saw them, for instance, in their own colours. Vera in the lovely blues and shining blacks and shimmering greys of the dark, and the half-light. Fulla in the colours of sunlight and pollen, yellow dust, the gold fur of bees. I could say that I had imagined a goddess of the night, and a goddess of the daylight, and I could add that once the mind has started spinning such dangerous metaphors it embroiders and elaborates them.

But I must be very careful. For Vera is a real woman, not an angel of death. She is a real woman who spends her life studying proliferating cells, living and feeding, growing and killing. And Fulla is a rather opinionated idealist, who has a sense, yes, of the endlessly interconnected threads of the living surface of the earth, but who also, like all scientists, fights her own corner doggedly.

Where has all this got me? Destry-Scholes's Trinity is and is not Destry-Scholes (I keep saying that, I know, but he and they keep sliding in and out of focus). I am not sure I have much further to go in my researches. And I have decisions to make about my life.

I needed to see Fulla. Moreover, I had promised to become her assistant in the stag beetle project, and I needed to observe her observing the creatures in order to become precise in my own watching and recording. I judged that Vera—who seemed somewhat calmer, and was sleeping, could be left for a time. I told her quite truthfully that I was helping someone with their research. (How useful the increasing acceptability of the slightly incorrect use of the plural possessive.) I phoned Fulla from a phone box. We met in Richmond Park, in the tournament glade. We met in the morning: the beetles seemed to be most active in the late afternoon, and in the crepuscular time before the park closed. Fulla had brought plastic boxes for the segregation of large horned males, and plastic boxes of Nordic sandwiches full of delicious shrimp, spring onion and watercress. She asked, as ants carried away our crumbs, how my research was going.

What could I say? The whole thing was so mad and so tenuous, how could I describe it to a precisely concentrated taxonomist, keen on describing and saving plants and pollinators? I said I thought I would give it all up. I said I had come to the conclusion that literary scholarship was pointless, and so had embarked on biography, which was a form of history, and now thought that was pointless, too. Fulla was relaxed, in a way that suited her, and made my sensory equipment—all of it, nose, skin, eyes, ears—prickle with desire. Her pugnacious mouth was relaxed (I slid my tongue in and out, like a bee, between sips of apple-juice), her colourless lashes cast delicate shadows over thoughtful eyes. She said, you've got to have history. Even I, I need the museum I work in, I need the type specimens the old bug-hunters collected, I need all the knowledge all the dead field naturalists left, which we are still correlating. She spoke of the discovery of bowerbirds from the evidence of Victorian hat-decorations. Of bees not seen since Alfred Wallace pinned the type on a card and labelled it. We need to get all this on the Net, she said, so that researchers in rainforests can log on to a complete taxonomy, and know what they have found, and what (if anything) is known about it.

I said I had been trying to find out about Destry-Scholes.

Who had been trying to find out about a taxonomist, a statistician, and a dramatist. Who had appeared, I said, explaining a very little, to have been more interested in what they had in common than in what made them unique. Who had seen them as overlapping and interwoven, like Galton's composites. Before that, I said, he'd written about Elmer Bole, who had contained multitudes in one man, had been soldier, statesman, explorer, translator, linguist, even bee taxonomist. I know, said Fulla. His Turkish bees are in Oxford. Still only partly catalogued. He was good on solitary bees, said Fulla Biefeld. She had to confess to a predilection for solitary bees herself. Entomologists have emotions, like anyone else. She had always been both attracted and repelled by the idea of the super-organism. The bivouac of army ants, the hive of honeybees, the genetic repetition, the single will. Of course, she said, anyone going to an airport might suppose that humans are a super-organism. We are held together by threads of dependence as much as the ants. Mechanics and pilots, air traffic controllers and clerks, lift-operators and restaurant managers, police and passengers, electricians and painters and escalator-attendants and terrorist scanners—we're all part of each other. Maybe your Destry-Scholes was trying to describe that. Without the Internet, before the Internet, we were a super-organism.

"But you like solitary bees," I said.

"I like oddities and rarities," said Fulla Biefeld, her faint accent more pronounced. She put a hand in the waistband of my trousers. Her strong little fingers pummelled and wriggled. I danced—my skin danced—to her rhythm. I said, fatuously, that I was only a cuckoo bee. I toiled not, neither did I spin. I thought, super-organisms would flourish in Kantsay-where. Fulla's fingers reached my erection. I thought (profoundly, banally) that all sex is the same, and every time is different. I turned to her with a little moan. (I am back in lyrical mode. Note at which juncture.) And *at* this juncture, precisely, there was a crashing and leaping in the trees on the rim of our grassy bowl.

I thought at first it was a stag. It was horned and two-legged, its head crowned with fantastic curved and pointed peaks of platinum and shrill rose. It stood maybe seven feet high, aided by platform soles like those on which Greek tragic actors stamped the scene. It had supple leather legs, bounding and glistening, ornamented with glittering zips and buckles. It appeared to be flayed above the waist, but wore, in fact, a scarlet silk vest or shirt, clinging to wrists, pectorals, navel, ending half-way up the white neck like the line of a delicate decapitation. It appeared to have a curling tail, which was a complicated bunch of trailing leather and metal cords and thongs. It was laughing, with a huge full-lipped red mouth in a chalky skin; its nose was Grecian and its brows (like other parts of its anatomy) bulging. I thought of Dionysos, and of Hern the hunter, before I thought of mugging. Fulla went very still. The statistics for the possible victories of smaller males, amongst *Lucanus cervus* and other coleopteran males, are not wholly reliable, but wholly discouraging. He came straight at us, leaping down the slope, laughing. It was not possible to pretend to be invisible. A second figure appeared, in shadow, among the tree-trunks. This one was slight, slender, elegant in an Armani jacket and designer jeans. It was Christophe. He ran lightly after the laughing demon, caught at his dangling braids, touched his bottom. The other turned to embrace him. Fulla sat up and made a snorting noise. Christophe saw us.

He was not disconcerted. He patted the rump of the Dionysos reassuringly, and strolled towards us.

"A queer place to find you again, Phineas. I didn't know you spent *your* days off on this beat."

"We are making observations," I said.

Christophe said he hoped the local fauna was displaying itself satisfactorily. The Dionysos laughed. Mildly, considering his fearsome aspect. Christophe introduced him as Dean. My friend, Dean. He came here sometimes on his day off, he said. Fulla was looking cross. I realised that this was not because we appeared to be pursuing stag beetles in the middle of a lek of gay men, but because Christophe, when last seen, had been, according to *her* view of the matter, attacking and damaging myself. This reflection caused me to remember that matters were, in fact, the other way round. Christophe's paperknife scratches were still in evidence. I asked, in a very small voice (I meant it to be bigger, but it was a squeak) how Erik was.

Christophe said Erik was fine. He added that he had been trying to reach me, but I was not ever at home. I kept quiet. I didn't want to give anyone at all Vera's address. Christophe said that they had acted—reacted—hastily. That they hadn't at all realised what I had been going through with Maurice

Bossey. That they very much hoped I'd come back. That they were distressed I hadn't got in touch. Dean, standing legs apart against the sun, smiled benignly. Christophe said he'd like to cook dinner for me (they'd never invited me home, before). He included Fulla in the invitation. She snorted again. Christophe said, with real Gallic charm, that they did in fact genuinely want her advice on whether actively useful taxonomical holiday cooperations were possible. Dean grinned more broadly. Fulla said she had had that idea herself. She looked now more like her sharp public self, and less like my earthwoman. I said the whole of my life, the whole of my life and work, needed rethinking. But it didn't necessarily exclude a return to Puck's Girdle. And I should like to come to dinner, I said. And me, said Fulla. Thank you. Christophe touched Dean's arm. "We'll be off," he said. He turned back. "Oh, and Phineas. We owe you a holiday. You never took your holiday."

So Fulla and I dined with Erik and Christophe. I do not think they thought we were a couple. I do not know what they thought. I don't know whether Christophe saw where Fulla's fingers were when he emerged from the trees. Nor do I know—since I am listing what I do not know—what Erik made of Christophe's forays into the territory of Hern the Hunter. I was more worried about Erik's reaction to myself. He had urged my sacking, after all, not Christophe. He met us in the entrance hall of the Notting Hill house where their flat was, and crushed me in a bear-like embrace, stroking my legs and shoulders, ruffling my hair, roaring with laughter. He then, perhaps excessively, embraced Fulla too, lifting her from the ground, and welcoming her in rapid Swedish. His face was lost in the thicket of her hair.

Their flat was a surprise, after the modern beauty of Puck's Girdle. It was a mixture of exaggerated Regency and Victorian Gothic, with carved silver thrones, peacock-feathered china, thick shimmering velvet curtains, and hosts of small lamps, with jewel-coloured shades—emerald, crimson, cobalt—casting pools of delimited golden light amongst thick shadows. We ate a salad of smoked halibut and marinated mushrooms, a jugged hare with chestnuts and spiced cabbage, a lemon syllabub and feathery biscuits. I mention this food—I hate food in ordinary novels, though I would forgo none of Proust's, or Tolstoy's, or Balzac's—because I saw I was horribly hungry, having lived on my own meagre and incompetent cookery in Willesden, and, much more than the champagne and burgundy, it made me feel spoiled, and soft, and unreal. And because they had gone to some trouble, for me (and for Fulla) and this was generous, since I had cut them with their own blunt instrument, and accused them of snuff movies. Fulla ate fiercely, and with obvious pleasure.

We sat on heaped velvet cushions, and drank Turkish coffee. Erik and Christophe devoted their considerable charm to getting Fulla to talk. She told fearful tales of possible lurches in the population of pollinators (including those of the crops we depend on for our own lives). Tales of the destruction of the habitats by humans, and of benign and necessary insects, birds, bats and other creatures, by crop-spraying and road-building. Of the vanishing of migratory corridors, even where habitats existed. Of the over-dependence on the farmed honeybee, which was all too successful as a competitor for nectar and pollen, but which was not necessarily either the best or the safest pollinator for many plants. She spoke of the rapid spread of the mite *Varroa jacobsoni,* which originated in the Far East and is ravaging the hives, now, of almost the whole world. Of the dangerous Africanised bees moving northwards in the Americas. Of the need to find other (often better) pollinators, in a world where they are being extinguished swiftly and silently. Of the fact that there are only thirty-nine qualified bee taxonomists in the world, whose average age is sixty, and of whom only two, both over eighty, are training successors. Of British bumble-bees, of which there were once five species, one already extinct. Of population problems, and feeding the world, and sesbania, a leguminous crop which could both hold back desertification, because it binds soil, and feed the starving, but for the fact that no one has studied its pollinators or their abundance or deficiency, or their habits, in sufficient detail. (It is pollinated by leaf-cutter bees, *Megachile bituberculasta, Chalicodoma sp. Xylocopa sp.* These bees can be managed, as they will breed in reed stems, bamboo, blocks of wood.)

She described—in detail—a world of small deaths and vanishings, of long strings of unconsidered, unexamined, causes and effects, of baffled creatures and lumpen human decisions. She was practical and furious.

Erik and Christophe said that they knew that people went on ecological holidays.

"Further unbalancing and disturbing the disturbed Galápagos—" cried Fulla.

"It needn't be there. It could be anywhere. It could be useful. It could provide funds and helping hands—"

The money, said Fulla, goes to glamorous things like tigers and pandas, which are doomed anyway. The tourists want to see shiny fish and parrots and monkeys. Not bees. Not beetles.

They could learn, said Christophe.

Fulla said she had a project studying Mediterranean bees. Many of our plants are derived from Mediterranean plants, and we need to find viable alternatives to the honeybee. Possibly very quickly. But the EU and everyone else think bees means honeybees, and funding comes under apiculture, which is circular, and that is that.

Her eyes flashed. Her hair flared and glittered. If we sent you tourists, said Erik, could you teach them?

Could you *use* them?

Fulla said she would need several semi-trained people— parataxonomists—or the tourists would simply be trampling nuisances. But there *were* no parataxonomists.

Christophe said that it appeared that Phineas was on the way to becoming a parataxonomist.

I said, sipping my grappa, that I was a drop in the ocean.

Erik said oceans were made up of drops.

Christophe poured more grappa.

Fulla said, anyway, she was off back to Turkey herself in exactly a fortnight.

That was the first I had heard of that, but I said nothing. I said nothing, then.

We went home to Fulla's little flat and went to bed. (I had told Vera I was out and would not be back for the night. She was up and about again, wandering the house, occasionally turning the marbles.) I still said nothing. I had no idea what to do with myself. None at all.

I decided to return to see Ormerod Goode. I rang and made an appointment—from Vera's house, using Vera's phone. I had done so much work, and indeed, so much writing, but had nothing to show for any of it except this manuscript, which for obvious reasons, cannot be public property. I had had a further thought about Scholes Destry-Scholes which I should have had much earlier. I wanted at least to put that point to Ormerod Goode, before admitting defeat.

Goode sat in his brown study and offered me nothing. He asked how I was doing, and I said badly. I told him about the three brief lives, the fact that they contained obvious lies, and the existence of the shoeboxes. I made a halting attempt to describe the cards and the photographs.

"Is that all?" said Ormerod Goode, without entering into any discussion of Ibsen, Galton or Linnaeus.

I said it was. It was all. (I had not mentioned the marbles, I should say, or the trepanning instrument.)

Goode said it was not much. He added, musing, that I appeared to have little aptitude for biographical research. He attempted to mitigate this severity by saying that he was sure he himself would be just the same, which was why he had chosen place-names to study. Public property, can't move off, he said. Stay put. Interconnected. Satisfactory.

I said there was one thing he might be able to help me with. I had realised that one of the few "facts" I had about Scholes

284

Destry-Scholes was that he had perhaps drowned in the Maelstrøm. It struck me that my only informant about that had
been Ormerod Goode himself. I wondered exactly where he
had seen the information?

It hardly mattered, said Goode, considering the dearth of
other material, surely.

I said it did matter, to me personally, though I took his
point about my failure as a potential biographer.

"I got it from Jespersen in the Scandinavian Department,"
said Goode. "He showed me the cutting. He collects anything
to do with the Maelstrøm. Myths and legends, films and car-
toons, metaphors in poems, news items, any old grist to his
mill. He's mildly dotty. He told me. He said something like,
'You know that odd chap who came and talked about biography? He seems to have been sucked into my funnel-thing.'
You can't quote that, of course, that isn't *what* he said, which I
certainly don't remember with any exactitude after all these
years. I don't know how anyone ever believes hearsay wit-
nesses in courts of law, do you, Nanson? I could take you up
to see Jespersen, if you like. He lives along the top corridor in
the Roman Jakobsen building."

So we went to see Thorold Jespersen. A word I was quite
fond of, in my post-structural, post-psychoanalytic days, was
"over-determined." In terms of this story (for what else am I
writing?) Thorold Jespersen was over-determined. I suppose if
he had been young and brisk and surgical I should have been
equally satisfied to find him in the story, because of the element of shock or wonder. But there he was, in a dusty attic,
behind a dusty table loaded with precarious heaps of leather
volumes and yellowing papers, and crumbs. There should
have been spiderwebs, but there weren't. His window was a

semi-skylight, and just as filthy as the window of Gareth Butcher's room where the Critical Theory seminars had taken place. Indeed, this one had a rim of lively green slime, or moss, round its veiled dimness. He had two noticeboards on the non-mansard walls, covered (I was later allowed to survey them) with photographs and drawings and steel engravings and geographers' charts of the Maelstrøm. Jespersen sat in the gloom, in a nest of ivory hair, his long white beard wound into his papers, his long white hair merging into it, his papery-white, wrinkled face and his pale, cracked lips, revealing walrus-horn yellow teeth, peering between his locks with watery blue eyes (purging rheum, as Shakespeare said) under jutting headlands of white brows (with crumbs in them. There were crumbs everywhere. Also dropped currants, or maybe mouse droppings). The room, and the man, looked as though there should have been a smell of rotting, but there wasn't. It was all dry, and dusty. It took him a moment or two to recognise Ormerod Goode. When he did, he asked him in a high, spider-thread of a voice, if he had had any luck with his barrow.

"Barrow?"

"Louven How, Green Swang, Cock Lake Side."

"Black Cock, the Lake. They still perform a lek there. I don't know how much longer. They're threatened with extinction. Dig's going well, yes. They used to think Black Cock was the Devil, but it's only a bird."

"Pity," said Jespersen vaguely. There was a silence. Goode introduced me.

"Phineas Nanson. He's got a question about the Maelstrøm."

286

"Ah, the explorer. Come to the right place."

Not an explorer, I said. Nanson, son of Nanson. A researcher, I said, leaving it vague.

"Ah," said Jespersen. "Just as well. Dangerous, the Maelstrøm. Treacherous. Tricky. Some people think it's the same hole as Dante's Ulysses went down. The end of the world. The known world." He said, "Lots of ways to the Underworld, all on land. *Facilis descensus Averni.* In pits and mountain bellies. This is the watery one."

Goode said I wanted to know about someone who had apparently drowned in it. He said, rather firmly, that he remembered Jespersen mentioning it.

"Ah yes. I've got a file of those. Drowned and disappeared. As many suicides as Beachy Head, but mostly never recovered. A good way to disappear. Your man's name, young man?"

"Scholes Destry-Scholes," I said.

"Ah—" he said, and rose up (he was over six foot and very thin). "Let me see."

His filing system seemed more orderly than his desktop suggested.

I imagined, even at this point, that there would turn out to be nothing. His dry fingers shuffled dry pages.

"Here," he said. "Here it is. There's a photograph. Out of a newspaper. Here it is. British writer presumed drowned."

I was about to see the face of Destry-Scholes.

Jespersen creaked towards me, and handed me the newspaper cutting.

"Hope is extinguished for the British writer, Scholes Destry-Scholes, who left the fishing-port on the island of Vaerøy, in the Lofoten Islands, in a small boat a week ago. The boat was found, with no-one aboard, not far from the Moskenes Current, more famous by its fifteenth-century name, the Maelstrøm. Mr. Destry-Scholes was on a solitary fishing and walking holiday, and had expressed an interest in the famous whirlpool. Mr. Destry-Scholes achieved some success with his three-volume biography of the larger-than-life British eccentric, explorer, diplomat, scientist and writer, Sir Elmer Bole. His publishers say he was hoping to submit another work shortly, and had been researching both in Norway and in South Africa. The search for authenticity in scholarship can have its dangers. They were not sure who his current subject was. They described him as reclusive, uncommunicative and solitary."

The photograph that accompanied this text was of a dark rowboat, floating on a choppy dark water, with three gull-colonised rocks and a stocky mountain in the background. "Lots of those," said Professor Jespersen cheerfully. "Lots of that motif, the empty boat on the water. I've got nearly fifty of them. They like to get Mosken in, and the gannets. Picturesque."

The paper was the *Yorkshire Post*. I could, in theory, have gone and searched its archive. But I didn't think I would. I stared at the empty boat, and the dark newsprinted water, and thanked Jespersen, and thanked Ormerod Goode, and went home.

I have nearly reached the end of this story. Not of my life, but of that segment of the tapeworm that began in one dusty-windowed room in Prince Albert College, and ended in another, with a photograph of an empty boat. I have admitted I am writing a story, a story which in a haphazard (aleatory) way has become a first-person story, and, from being a story of a search told in the first person, has become, I have to recognise—a first-person story proper, an autobiography. I detest autobiography. Slippery, unreliable, and worse, imprecise. (I am trying to avoid the problem of the decay of belief in the idea of objectivity by slipstreaming towards the safer, ideologically unloaded idea of precision. I don't think this tactic quite works.) Autobiography, as I write, is fashionable. The "flavour of the moment." (Can I perpetrate a phrase like that? Let it stand. Try anything once.) Everyone is writing his or her "memoir." They resemble each other like Galton's photographs, or eighteenth-century portraits as perceived by Ibsen. They are rather repulsive. I was brought up as a child to believe in self-effacement, and as a student to believe in impersonality.

So I am going to stop writing this story. The problem is, I have become addicted to writing—that is, to setting down the English language, myself, in arrangements chosen by me, for—let it be admitted—pleasure. I have become addicted to forbidden words, words critical theorists can't use and writers can. Words to describe the different scents of Fulla's and Vera's skins. This is difficult but not impossible. I have just discovered that Linnaeus made a taxonomy of smells, too. *Fragrantes* (fragrant), *Hircinus* (goaty), *Ambrosiacos* (ambrosial), *Tetros* (foul), *Nauseosos* (nauseating), *Aromaticos* (aromatic) and *Alliaceos* (garlicky).

Fulla is goat and aromatic. Vera is fragrant and—not garlicky—but lily and daffodil. Cool and rooty, with vanishing flowers touched with green, in deep corollas and tubes. Fulla is the sharp spicy air of the *compositae*, almost bitter, almost harsh, but enticing. Vera's hair is ferny and Fulla's hair is—this is hard—honeysuckle is too sweet, hawthorn too almond, I am thinking *hedges*, not the precise smell—there is a touch of ragwort and fennel, mixed with dog rose. Interesting to know whether this precision—which has cost me a lot of pencil biting, staring into space, imagining absent odours with intense recollected pleasure—would communicate accurately to anyone else the erotic delights of either? A further question—would these two skins (these two women) smell different to anyone whose skin smells differently from my own? For my nose flares myself as it flares them. I am getting baroque. Back to what I was writing, which was a renunciation of writing.

In terms of writing—of the way this story has funnelled itself into a not unusual shape, run into a channel cut in the earth for it by previous stories (and all our lives are partly the same story, beginning, middle, end)—in terms of writing, this looks like a *writer's story*. PGN was a mere Critick, steps centre-stage, assumes his life, Finds his Voice, is a Writer. That was the way it would almost have had to have been in the 1920s (a good time for Writers, though not the best). But I feel a kind of nausea at this fate for my hero, myself. It doesn't seem very much of an anything. To be addicted to writing is not to want to be, to become, a Writer.

. . .

So. If I were telling the "1920s" version of Phineas G. Nanson, it would end with an "epiphany." (Another forbidden word, though still allowed in Joyce criticism.)

And there was an epiphany, there was very precisely an epiphany, so I shall write it down, for pleasure, *cliché* and all, and then *stop writing*. Or how shall I see what to do?

Fulla taught me how to set up the stag-beetle experiment. She provided plastic boxes, little coloured bee-labels, a delicate little hand-held balance to weigh my captives. She also talked enthusiastically to Erik and Christophe about setting up various projects—worldwide—between taxonomists, pollination studies, and intelligently motivated tourists and wanderers. She could have been the managing director of a global company, I thought. She had vision, and prevision, she saw to details. I went back to my job. There was a presumption that I would help Fulla with pollination tourism in due course. Vera also went back to work, pale and composed. We massed the marbles randomly in a great glass bowl I bought her for a present. We stood them where the soft light filtered through them. I have never said how much more beautiful and variegated Destry-Scholes's marbles were, with their rich colours and forms, than mass-produced modern ones. We put the lids on the shoeboxes, and the tribal lists of marbles in the suitcase. We did not discuss these moves. Her first day back at work went well. She came home to me, white and smiling. We made love. Fulla set out to spend a month in the Middle

291

East, for the Anatolian Project, leaving me in charge of the beetles.

So for a week or two I watched these strange creatures excavate the rotten tree trunks, fly noisily across the clearing, strut, display, fight and mate. It did seem to become clear that the largest—the heaviest—always won. I tried to be what I thought of as detached and scientific, and think of my population by numbers. But I ended up by giving them literary names of horned gods—Hern and Moses, Horus and Actaeon (the smallest, who always got crunched). The females I called Moira, Clotho, Lachesis and Atropos. A rather lost scuttling one I called Norn. The males jousted along twigs and promontories, jabbing and weaving with their serrated pincers, butting and rushing not unlike the stags themselves. The project was to reverse, dislodge, overturn the antagonist. The fallen combatant would return, but never more than twice. After three falls he crept away, and the triumphant beetle would mate with the waiting female, who would obligingly raise her rear. The females showed no preferences, and mated with all winners. I am, as this narrative shows, an obsessive lateral researcher, and I began to poke about in the literature of entomology for beetle-jousts. I found references in W. D. Hamilton's great essays on life in rotting wood, and fighting males in fig wasps and other insects. Hamilton remarked that in his experience of arranged tournaments between stag beetles the *second* largest came out the winner. He added that this was possibly because such arranged battles usually took place in cardboard boxes, whereas in real life the beetles liked to confront each other along twigs or edges; where sheer weight would be more useful. He also remarked that he did not share Konrad Lorenz's belief that extravagantly developed weapons on male creatures were necessarily designed only for display, or to attract females. A weapon is a weapon, according to Hamilton, who has a gloomy view of competition between creatures which appeals to my own sense of the nature of things. He said that his observations led him to think that Lorenz's belief that animals, unlike humans, did not fight to the death, was false. There was at least as much real desire to damage, in my subjective opinion, among my beetles, as there was ritualised weaving and avoidance. I got rather sorry for Hern, who was smaller than Moses and bigger than Horus and Actaeon. He went for Moses with great vigour and reck-lessness, and was ruler of the roost when I had abstracted the patriarch. The patriarch, returned to his tree-trunk, easily dis-lodged the briefly triumphant Hern. I therefore, on my own initiative, glued a small brass nut to Hern's back before releas-ing him again—he turned the scales at 1.2 grams more than Moses with this artificial gravitas. I was pleased to see that, once he was heavier, even though his horns were shorter, he was able to dislodge Moses for the ritual three times. I had proved something. I wasn't sure what. I wrote it all down, and removed the brass nut, whereupon Moses resumed his dominance.

All this activity happened towards sunset, which is also, of course, the time when the Rangers close the park. I was once or twice politely ejected from my hollow by mounted men.

On one occasion, when dusk had advanced suddenly and unexpectedly, I looked up into the trees and saw a long green flash, bright green, what I thought of as *artificial* green— between the branches. I rubbed my eyes, which were bleary with staring at beetles. More green flashes. Then a rushing and a rustling and a loud, rasping screech. There was not one parrot, but a whole flock of emerald birds, pink-billed, long-tailed, some with rose-red collars, gathering and roosting in the tree above me. I thought—I really thought—they were a hallucination. But they were dropping real guano, and their conversation was lively. I don't know why I was so moved, so deeply moved, by this manifestation of the tropics in English oaks. The English sunset caught their feathers in a way the dying light where they originated could never quite have done. I don't know what it *meant.* It could equally have been a sign that I should stay in England—since all, including bright tropical birds, was possible here—or whether, more eccentri-cally, I should take it as a good omen, that I should travel, and help Fulla with the pollinators, the swamps, the savannahs, the dry hillsides. What it said to me, oddly—in the moments before the Ranger came and moved me on, kindly enough, observing that the feral rose-ringed parakeets were on the increase and might prove to be a pest—what the vision of these very real, chattering birds said to me, was, that the senses of order and wonder, both, that I had once got from lit-erature, I now found more easily and directly in the creatures. As a boy my hair had prickled at the beauty of a Shakespeare sonnet, or a Yeats rhythm, or Donne's bright hairs and brittle bones. That was gone. But I was left with the peculiar conker-leather brown of the elytra of *Lucanus cervus L,* the pink hook

of strong beaks, horns and claws, stamens and pistils, the beat
of demonic wing-cases, and descending circles of brilliant rose
and emerald wings.

*   *   *

A farewell to Literature doesn't, all at one blow, get rid of a
new-found addiction to writing. I used to notice, scornfully
enough, in my callow days as a pre-critical reader, that bad
writers are inspired to put pen to paper by unfamiliar sur-
roundings. By holidays, by tourism, by travel. I write this in a
small notebook I brought to record the creatures in. I am
indeed on a holiday—on *the* holiday, promised by Erik and
Christophe. They told me to go anywhere in the world, and I
am here. The manuscript, that is the document, of all that
other writing, is on my machine (and backed up on disk) in
London. I have seen golden cloudberries, sea pink and sand-
wort, scurvy grass (a kind of cabbage, which grows into a
thick green mesh), marsh marigolds and a kind of giant hemlock. The air smells of seaweed and salt-water. It is balmy
because of the Gulf Stream, and cool and wild because we are
far to the north of the Arctic Circle. We have seen the great
sperm whales sounding, and grey sea-eagles circling; we have
seen puffins nesting, stockfish hung out to dry, and thousands
of gulls of all kinds wheeling, and shrieking, and plunging
and tearing at flesh, bobbing on white wave-crests and diving
into dark water from a clear sky. We have walked causeways,
mountain paths and bog-trails. We have sailed through the
Trollfjørd, where impossible crags go up and up, dark above
us. We have come south through the Lofoten Islands and are

now at Vaerøy, where the houses are built along a wide shore, sheltered by a broad mountain ridge. We have seen storms come racing over the horizons and pelt our windows; we have smelled wild winds, and basked in the sun of the Stranden beach at Heia, under a twelve-hundred-foot vertiginous vertical wall of rock. Tomorrow—which is our last day—we shall take an accompanied boat trip to the island of Mosken, and take a look—from a safe distance—at the Moskenes Current, the Maelstrøm. I suppose this is why I have been unable to resist the urge to start scribbling again (did I say that Destry-Scholes's fabrication of Linnaeus's fabrication of his visit to the Maelstrøm was a pastiche of Edgar Allan Poe?). I shall look at the current—I can imagine its heaving and racing and rushing and suck, but what I shall see will be different—and I shall know no more than I know now about the whereabouts of Destry-Scholes. We wondered if he too had paced the lovely beach at Heia. We read about the whales who had been swallowed by the whirlpool and cast up on the shores, and about the mythical *draugen,* a kind of ghost-demon who farms under the ocean, whose oats and corn are sometimes caught in the gills and stomachs of deep-sea fish.

I say our last day, but it has been one long day, for the midnight sun has never set. We found a strange, urgent kind of perpetual wakefulness had come upon us, which we allayed with love-making, in white Norwegian beds, in the open air, in coves, on mountainsides, amongst rocks on beaches. Vera, whom I think of in darkness, has become palely golden in all this space of air and hard rock and tenacious sparse vegetation. She is happy. I realise I did not believe she could be other than sad and cautious. She throws back her head and laughs into the wind, in which her dark hair streams and whips.

That is *enough writing*. That is dangerously on the edge of the unacceptably—what? Emotional, romantic? Happy? You don't write about happiness.

Tomorrow, as I said, we are going to see the Maelstrøm. And I have got to stop writing, because Vera has woken up, and is smiling, and holding out her arms.

* * *

I was flipping through this notebook, and I saw what I wrote, a year ago now, saying pompously and untruthfully that you don't write about happiness. There was also a kind of fastidious nausea about writing about exotic places, which I set down baldly, which persists. Though, come to think of it—I have only just thought of this as I take up my pen—there is a good use to which I could put all this persistent itch to write down different words and sentences in English. I could write—not autobiographical travel books—but useful guides, with bits of "real" writing in them for those necessary non-destructive ecological tourists. I could mix warnings with hints, descriptions with explanations, science with little floating flashes of literature, which still haunt me and will not be exorcised. I could combine my two splendidly dovetailed lives as tourist manager and parataxonomist, with a kind of ghost-writing, a ghost of writing.

I could write about the Turkish hillside where I am sitting. I am in charge of an experimental transept in a scattered strip of red tulips *(Tulipa agenensis, Tulipa julia, Tulipa armena)* mixed with two kinds of anemone, *coronaria* and *Ranunculus asiaticus*. We are studying the pollinators of red bowl-shaped flowers. These have no nectar, and are odourless, or at least with no scent detectable by humans. Some, many, have dark centres at the base of the bowls. We have also created models of flowers, using coloured, odourless plastic cups (red, blue, yellow, green, brown, white) mounted on sticks 15–25 cm high (the average height of the red guild flowers). We also have a spread of groups of 9 cm red petri dishes—one plain red, one containing a dead female beetle, one with a black patch, larger than the beetle. We have discovered, we think, that the red guild flowers are pollinated by *Amphicoma* beetles, which appear to be attracted by the red colour, and especially by the red-black contrast. This is interesting because beetles were previously believed to be unconcerned with colour, possibly unable to see it. Beetle-pollinated plants tend to be strongly scented with what Linnaeus would have called *nauseosos* smells—dung, fermentation, decay, ripe and overripe fruit.

We are also watching a small halictid bee, *Lasioglossum (Evylaeus) marginatum,* and a large anthophorid bee, *Synhalonia plumigera,* both of which visit the red flowers, but not exclusively.

Our plastic cups and petri dishes (containing a few drops of detergent to catch the landing beetles and prevent any emission of volatiles) are not romantic, though they are curious. But the drifts of red flowers on the sparse hillside are brilliant and lovely. *Tulipa agenensis,* also known as *oculis-solis* (the tulip of the eye of the sun), is a sumptuous crimson with velvet black stamens and pointed petals. The crimson and the black are glossy as lacquer: the flowers are stiff and delicate. *Tulipa armena, Tulipa julia,* take varying forms, sometimes pure scarlet, sometimes yellow feathered, sometimes black-bowled, sometimes not. There are geraniums and eremurus. The eighteenth-century Ottoman Sultan Ahmed, whose reign was the *lale devri*, the Tulip Era, grew millions of tulips in the mountains, and despatched hundreds of gardeners and slaves to grub up millions more. After his fall, these hillside nurseries fell into desuetude. Before we came here, Fulla and I went to Istanbul, took boats along the Bosphorus, visited Topkapi and saw the formal tulips wound into garlands in the glazed tiles of Ahmed's apartments. Fulla disliked the harem. She is happier here, in the fresh air, on the mountainside. I do not say that she does not find the tulips beautiful; I do not even say that she does not admire the artifice of the glazier and the mosaicist who also found them beautiful. I sent a series of postcards of the mosaics in St. Saviour in Chora to Vera in Willesden. I sent a glittering glass peacock, shimmering in tesserae of rich blue and emerald green, streaked with shocking pink and iridescent with gold.

Literature is threaded in my brain along with my daily language. I remember Browning from childhood.

> The wild tulip at end of its tube, blows out its great
>   red bell
> Like a thin clear bubble of blood, for the children to
>   pick and sell.

I remember Tennyson's goddesses coming down the Idalian hillside for the judgement of Paris.

> And at their feet the crocus brake like fire.

299

I discovered, after we had been working for some time, that the *Anemone coronaria* (crown anemone, poppy anemone), blood-red, dusky-centred, sooty and powdered (which we simulate with our petri dishes), is the fabled flower which first bloomed from the spilled blood of Adonis, enlivened by Aphrodite, who sprinkled ambrosia on it. Golding's Ovid goes:

> This sed, she sprinckled Nectar on the blood, which through the powre
> Thereof did swell like bubbles sheere that rise in weather cleere
> On water. And before that full an howre expired weere
> Of all one colour with the blood a flowre she there did find.

Sir Philip Sidney thought that poets made better flowers than Nature.

> Nature never set forth the earth in so rich tapestry as divers poets have done—neither with pleasant rivers, fruitful trees, sweet-smelling flowers, nor whatsoever else may make the too-much loved earth more lovely. Her world is brazen, the poets only deliver a golden.

Not so. As long as we don't destroy and diminish it irrevocably, the too-much-loved earth will always exceed our power to describe, or imagine, or understand it. It is all we have. I have to stop writing now—I can see Fulla, coming up the mountainside, quick and surefooted as a golden goat, bringing yogurt and honey. I have just time to remember that Fulla is the name of a minor Norse goddess—a hand-maid of Frigga, who kept the jewels of the Queen of Heaven, and spent her time tending woodland and forests, fruit trees and hives, cloudberries, blackberries and golden apples. Here she comes, with that amazing wing of crinkled hair, like an electric pulse, like a swarm, like an independent creature. I can see her severe little face. How beautiful upon the mountains are her sturdy feet in their Ecco sandals. That is an over-the-top sentence. And Fulla is at the top, and I must stop writing and put away this notebook.

ACKNOWLEDGEMENTS

I am very grateful to those who have patiently and intricately answered more than usually outlandish requests for information. Chris O'Toole, at the Hope Entomological Institute in Oxford, has provided me with help on bees and taxonomy, on pollination and leks. He even made suggestive and useful plotting suggestions in that regard. I have appropriated his experiment on the pollination of red-bowled flowers, and transferred it from Israel to Turkey. It was also Chris who provided me with the names of the beetle that carries Dutch elm disease and the parasitic wasp that preys on the beetle. The beetle is *Scolytus scolytus,* formally known as *Scolytus destructor.* The parasitic wasp is *Phaeogenes nanus.*

Steve Jones, Professor of Genetics at the Galton Laboratory, University College London, has also been endlessly courteous, showing me Galton's memorabilia in his laboratory, suggesting reading on Galton, and even weighing the nut he once attached to the back of a stag-beetle, in the interests of fictive accuracy.

Claudine Fabre-Vassas provided conversation and a steady supply of books by and about Linnaeus, some, of books not available in English, in French translations.

303

I am grateful also to Gina Douglas, the Librarian of the Linnean Society, who showed me Linnaeus's collections, library and manuscripts, and with whom I was briefly enclosed in the strongroom in the dark. She suggested further reading on Linnaeus which proved extremely exciting.

My Danish friend and translator, Claus Bech, provided all sorts of information, linguistic, entomological and mythic. He told me about the minor goddess Fulla, translations of "stag-beetle," and many other things.

John Saumarez-Smith, most resourceful of booksellers, suggested and found many books, including Blunt on Linnaeus. And I could not have done without the resources and unfailing courtesy of the London Library and its staff.

I am, as always, grateful to Gill Marsden for precision, energy and moral support when most needed. Also to my agent, Michael Sissons, for wisdom and enthusiasm, and to Jenny Uglow, most imaginative, most patient, and most intelligent of editors. My husband, Peter Duffy, saved me from many errors and found the right name for the Strange Customer's wine.

The mistakes are, as always, all my own.

A patchwork, echoing book like this should acknowledge its sources. A long reading-list is inappropriate, but the following books were indispensable:

Michael Meyer, *Henrik Ibsen*—a biography in three volumes, 1967, 1971 and 1971. Also Michael Meyer's translations of Ibsen's plays.

Karl Pearson, *The Life, Letters and Labours of Francis Galton,* 4 volumes, 1914–1930.

Wilfrid Blunt, *The Compleat Naturalist: A Life of Linnaeus,* 1971.

I also used Robert Ferguson's biography, *Henrik Ibsen* (1996), and *The Sayings of Henrik Ibsen,* ed. Roland Huntford (1996). D. W. Forrest's life of Galton (*Francis Galton: The Life and Work of a Victorian Genius,* 1974) was very helpful, as was the collection of essays on Linnaeus edited by Tore Frängsmyr (*Linnaeus: The Man and His Work,* 1994). I suspect the germ of the novel lies long ago in my own first reading of Foucault's remarks on Linnaeus and taxonomy in *Les mots et les choses.* Lyall Watson's fascinating *Jacobson's Organ* (1999), which is a study of the sense of smell, uses Linnaeus's taxonomy of smells. It arrived just as I was finishing my book, and I was able to add information from it.

A NOTE ABOUT THE AUTHOR

A. S. BYATT is one of Britain's leading writers. Her novels include *The Game, Possession* (winner of the Booker Prize in 1990) and the sequence *The Virgin in the Garden, Still Life* and *Babel Tower.* She has also written two novellas, published together as *Angels and Insects,* and four collections of shorter works: *Sugar and Other Stories, The Matisse Stories, The Djinn in the Nightingale's Eye* and *Elementals.* Educated at Cambridge, she was a senior lecturer in English at University College, London, before becoming a full-time writer in 1983. A distinguished critic as well as a novelist, she lives in London.

A NOTE ON THE TYPE

THE MAIN TEXT of this book was set in Adobe Garamond. Designed for the Adobe Corporation by Robert Slimbach, the fonts are based on types first cut by Claude Garamond (c. 1480–1561). Garamond was a pupil of Geoffroy Tory and is believed to have followed the Venetian models, although he introduced a number of important differences, and it is to him that we owe the letter we now know as "old style." He gave to his letters a certain elegance and feeling of movement that won their creator an immediate reputation and the patronage of Francis I of France.

The text of the "three documents" was set in a type called Baskerville. The face itself is a facsimile reproduction of types cast from the molds made for John Baskerville (1706–1775) from his designs. Baskerville's original face was one of the forerunners of the type style known to printers as "modern face"—"modern" of the period A.D. 1800.

Composed by North Market Street Graphics,
Lancaster, Pennsylvania
Printed and bound by Quebecor World,
Fairfield, Pennsylvania
Designed by Virginia Tan